DEATH AT THE BOSTON TEA PARTY

DEATH AT THE
BOSTON TEA PARTY

A John Rawlings Mystery

Deryn Lake

This first world edition published 2016
in Great Britain and the USA by
SEVERN HOUSE PUBLISHERS LTD of
19 Cedar Road, Sutton, Surrey, England, SM2 5DA.
Trade paperback edition first published
in Great Britain and the USA 2016 by
SEVERN HOUSE PUBLISHERS LTD

Copyright © 2016 by Deryn Lake.

British Library Cataloguing in Publication Data
A CIP catalogue record for this title is available from the British Library.

ISBN-13: 978-0-7278-8617-0 (cased)
ISBN-13: 978-1-84751-718-0 (trade paper)
ISBN-13: 978-1-78010-779-0 (e-book)

This is a work of fiction. Names, characters, places and incidents
are either the product of the author's imagination or are used fictitiously.
Except where actual historical events and characters are being described
for the storyline of this novel, all situations in this publication are
fictitious and any resemblance to actual persons, living or dead,
business establishments, events or locales is purely coincidental.

All Severn House titles are printed on acid-free paper.

Severn House Publishers support the Forest Stewardship Council™ [FSC™],
the leading international forest certification organisation.
All our titles that are printed on FSC certified paper carry the FSC logo.

Typeset by Palimpsest Book Production Ltd.,
Falkirk, Stirlingshire, Scotland.
Printed and bound in Great Britain by
TJ International, Padstow, Cornwall.

For my wonderful family and to Dan, Kevin, Paula and all my other great and good friends, with thanks.

ACKNOWLEDGEMENTS

Without Mark Dunton, archivist extraordinaire, who went with me to America on that memorable trip where we ate clam chowder and saw the beauty of Boston and its surroundings in all the colours of the Fall, very few of my books would have been written.

ONE

I t was the smell that first struck John Rawlings. Standing on the deck of the *Breath of the Sea*, early in the morning, before the rest of the few passengers had stirred, he inhaled deeply and knew at once that the wind had changed, that there was a depth to it that he had not noticed before, that something indefinable had added itself to the salt and spume that usually blew in his face. Puzzled, he leant forward, tightening his eyes to peer through the waves of fog that enveloped the ocean. He could see nothing but grey mist. And then, just for a second, the veil broke and he glimpsed the sight he had been desperately longing for – a vague hint of coastline.

It had been a ghastly voyage from England to the American Colonies. In mid-Atlantic the ship had run into a violent storm which had blown them about as if they were made of leaves. The captain had informed his heaving passengers that they would be delayed in their arrival at the town of Boston and then announced that they had been blown off course to boot. As if all this had not been enough to chill the hearts of sturdy Englishmen, John's nursery maid, Hannah, had been taken ill for the entire length of the journey and had spent her time moaning on her bed of pain. Thus, the care of his three children had fallen on the shoulders of the Apothecary and his former coachman, Irish Tom. Yet had it really? His eleven-year-old daughter, Rose, had taken over the management of her twin half-brothers with all the ease of a woman of style, which, her father thought, she was rapidly becoming.

A movement at the ship's rail drew John's attempts at peering through the mist back to life on board. Despite the earliness of the hour Rose was already up, her crimson hair dampened by the weather conditions, clinging round her head in a plethora of tight curls. She looked up at him.

'We're near land, aren't we?'

'Yes, how did you know?'

Rose tossed her head back, laughing. 'I just did.'

John put out his hand and tumbled her locks. 'Miss Clever Cat.'

'Miaow.'

'How are your brothers?'

'Still asleep. They look like Mrs Elizabeth.'

'She is – was – their mother, so that is hardly surprising.'

'They often stare into the sea to see if they can glimpse her.'

John sighed. 'I suppose I should not have told them that she had gone swimming with the mermaids.'

Rose looked at him with her usual strange wisdom. 'What else could you do? They were too young to comprehend death.'

John opened his mouth to reply but at that moment the ship hit something under the water and gave the most almighty judder. His daughter said in the calmest of voices, 'I think she is going to sink, Papa.'

John stared at her as the whole vessel lurched to one side and saw by the look on her face that she meant every word she said.

'We must wake the others,' he answered, but before he could make a move the deck which had been abandoned suddenly sprang into life. The doors leading to the cabins below were flung open and a dozen or so people ranging from country women with their nightcaps askew and a couple of gentlemen of elegance, George Glynde and Tracey Tremayne, poured forth.

'What's happening?' one drawled at John, as if he were the key to all knowledge.

'I believe we are sinking,' the Apothecary replied crisply.

An extremely fat woman screamed loudly and fainted at the feet of a wisp of a man who looked bewildered.

'Leave her,' John ordered. 'I'll deal with her. Trust me, I'm an apothecary.'

At that the boat lurched again and the sea poured over the deck. Pandemonium ensued as scantily clad people headed for their cabins to grab what they could. The two elegant gentlemen looked at one another.

'Damme, George, I think the ship has foundered.'

'Damme, Sir, I think so too. What say we swim for it?'

'Is there anywhere to swim to?'

'Odds fish, I saw it myself this morning through my spy glass. A coastline, clear as Lady Camden's corset. I'll wager a guinea I'm the first to land.'

'Make it two and you're on.'

They shook hands, grinning like apes, unaware that the sea must be bitterly cold. Or perhaps, John thought, they were aware and were just making as light of the situation as possible. He admired their bravado.

The fat woman groaned as he leaned over her and attempted to raise her top half from the deck.

'Wake up, Madam. This is no time to lose one's senses.'

She stared at him with very wide, harsh eyes then promptly slapped him on the nose. 'Unhand me, you young devil. How dare you molest me so? I would cry out for my husband had he not been called to Jesus this last year.'

John's lips twitched but he said, straight-faced, 'I am sorry to hear that, Madam. But I suggest you rise and get some warm clothes on. I'm afraid the ship has foundered.'

She groaned and clutched at her enormous breast. 'You are a bearer of ill tidings, Sir. I am undone.'

'No, Madam, you are quite intact, I assure you. Now do rise up. This ship is sinking and we must all swim for the shore.'

'But I can't swim. Bevis would never allow me to do such an undignified thing.'

For a moment John remembered, his mind seeing Elizabeth with her scarred, lovely face, her eyes with their depths which he had never been able to read, her triumphant and tragic death in the sea which she had adored and which had finally taken her away for ever. He looked down at the large widow woman who was attempting to rise.

'Never mind, Madam. I'll find you something to hold on to.'

Having got her on her feet and seen her lumbering towards her cabin, he sped for his. The twins were awake and Rose was busily occupied trying to dress one of them; the other had struggled into his own clothes with certain strange results. Hannah, the nursery maid, was stepping into various flannel petticoats as John hurried on to wake Tom. But the big Irishman had already felt the dying struggles of the ship and was dressed and coming to find him.

'How far's the shore, Sir?'

'About two miles away – that is, it was when I last saw it. Then the fog closed in.'

'We've struck a rock somehow. I imagine we've been blown miles from Boston.'

'Obviously. But come on, Tom, there's not a moment to lose. Will you take one of the boys on your back? I'll take the other.'

'But what about Hannah and Rose?'

'Well, my daughter can swim like a fish but I don't know about the other one.'

'The trouble is, Sir, what the devil will the sea be like?'

'It's calm. Dead flat.'

'No, you don't take my meaning. I'm thinking about the temperature, Sir.'

John gazed at his old companion, shocked. 'It's probably freezing. God help us, Tom, we'll have to find something to float on.'

'Leave that to me, Sir.'

Tom rushed up the wooden stairs to the deck while John hurried his family upward from the clammy atmosphere below the planking.

At sea level there was pandemonium. Several of the sailors had already taken to the water in a clapped-out rowing boat which looked fit to sink at any moment due to overcrowding.

The fat woman, complete with portmanteau, had either insisted or bribed her way on board and was occupying a place which could have been filled by three people of normal size. John gave her a cheerful grin – as cheerful as it could be in the circumstances – but she did not see and stared gloomily out into the dense fog which surrounded the fast-sinking vessel.

John hoisted Jasper on to his shoulders and Tom was just about to do the same with James when the ship listed a third time, the wooden doors leading to the hold burst open and pieces of furniture began to float into view. Wondering at Tom's amazing agility, the Apothecary watched, flabbergasted, while his former coachman seized a table with one hand, wrenched from its moorings by the power of the sea, and simultaneously lifted the other twin on to his back. He turned his head to look at Rose but she was already in the water and doing her best to assist Hannah, who was sinking and flailing. Shouting 'Hang on for dear life, Jasper!' John swam towards them.

The water was very cold, though not quite as icy as the Apothecary had feared. He could feel little hands digging into his neck with fright but was proud of his son for not bursting into the weeps. He pushed Rose, quite hard, in the direction of Tom and tried to save Hannah as he best he could. But she was going down deep and John, more than conscious of the little life clinging to him, could not dive after her. A burly man, a nodding acquaintance who kept himself to himself, did so but came up spluttering and shaking his head. Spitting out water, he growled at John.

'She's drowned, Sir. Floating down below, her hair all loose round her. Ain't no good looking. She's done for.'

What a moment to have another vivid memory. Had Elizabeth died like that, with her black hair spread out like a shroud? John found that he was trembling and knew that this was no time to let dark thoughts invade his brain. Mentally he shook himself like a dog coming in from a long walk and turned to the task ahead, brought back to the current situation by a shout as a figure dived into the water wearing nothing but a pair of breeches and an undone shirt. He recognized Sir Julian Wychwood, who had clearly been asleep in his cabin after a night of drinking and playing cards. He watched as the young blade dragged himself up on a floating chair, then saw his face turn the colour of milk as some unseen current tugged at his legs and he was carried, screaming for help, out to the distant sea. Powerless to assist him, John turned his agonized gaze on the poor wretch until he was lost to view.

Irish Tom had one of the table's upturned legs in his hand and was shouting at Rose to grasp another. She did so as John swam up to them and together they all kicked like frogs, clinging on to their makeshift raft. Then the mists parted almost dramatically and they saw an island appear.

'Make for that,' shouted John, because the sea around them was now alive with sound. Those who could not swim were drowning, and those who could keep afloat were clinging to bits of wreckage. With a final groan the ship split in half and plunged into the recesses of the murk below. A very pale girl with equally pale hair was struggling at John's side. With a great effort he managed to haul her hands on to their floating furniture and, though temporarily beyond speech, she gave him a look of true gratitude.

It ran through John's mind that if they could not reach the island soon they would die of cold and he paddled his legs hard, pushing through the chilly ocean as quickly as he was able. But his strength was going and even that great ox of a man, Irish Tom, was slowing down.

Jasper, clinging on to John's back, whispered, 'Is it much further, Papa?'

'No. Be a brave boy. Don't let go.'

'I can see a person standing on the shore.'

John screwed up his eyes and looked at the island – and his heart sank. What the child had seen was what appeared to be an Indian man, standing still as a statue, watching the survivors of the shipwreck struggling towards the shore. The Apothecary had been amongst the crowd of Londoners who had made a point of going to see members of the Cherokee tribe when they had been on display in 1760. But he, in keeping with many of his contemporaries, had not known what to make of these proud people who had stared above the heads of the masses with a certain disdain and dignity. He only hoped that, if they managed to outlive the cold sea, instant death did not await them on the island.

He and Irish Tom were both swimming feebly now, and poor Rose had given up kicking and was just being carried along by their wooden support. The fat woman sailed right past them, sailors rowing while she wallowed in a somewhat uncomfortable state, the boat sinking lower and lower in the water, overcome by her weight. Raising his eyes to glance at her, John saw that quite a crowd had now gathered on the far shore and that canoes had been launched, but as to the ethnic origins of the people within them he could not be certain. The distant squeals of the fat lady pierced his eardrums.

'I won't be manhandled, I so won't. Hit them with your oar, sailor.'

'Are you out yer mind? We can always fight 'em orff when we gets ashore.'

'How very dare you speak to me so? I'll have you know that my late husband was Sir Bevis Eawiss.'

This entire conversation was carried on the wind and was followed by an enormous plopping sound, as somebody who was clearly bored to sobs by the sound of the fat lady's voice had tipped her into the ocean's frigid waters.

They were floating nearer and now John could clearly make out the figures in the two canoes that were coming to either rescue or murder them. That they were Indian people there could be no doubt. Their black hair glistening about their heads, long but caught back on either side by bands, their noses straight and strong, their eyes bright and gleaming, narrowed now as they skimmed across the ocean, the rowers bending over their paddle with determination. The Apothecary was amazed to see an enormous white fellow sitting in their midst, his hair the same colour as the seeds of a sunflower, while crouching behind him was another European whose face could have been made from a post boy's leather bag.

The canoes were of the dugout type and half empty so that passengers could be taken on board. John stared in amazement as an Indian, supple as a fox, dived overboard and pulled the struggling widow out of the water and into the canoe, which denoted considerable strength. Her rescuer's only reward was an ear-splitting shriek and a cry of 'Unhand me, you blackguard, you scoundrel.'

The man merely looked down his nose and John watched as the bag man then leapt into the sea with a splash and pulled out a drowning sailor, who gasped for air as his head was pulled from the water. He felt encouraged to shout out, 'Help! Over here. I have three young children.'

A third canoe which had just been launched must have heard him, because he saw its savage prow turn towards them and the blades slash the waves like daggers. This vessel, too, contained a white man, who had a hat upon his head made entirely of fustian, with a red strap beneath his chin. He leant out a muscular arm and with a certain anxiety John watched as James was hauled from Tom's back and landed in the vessel, followed by Jasper. John saw that Rose's eyes were closed.

'Help my daughter, I beg you,' he called, and had never

been more grateful than when that powerful limb appeared once more and, without even drawing a breath, the man lifted in first Rose and then the pale young girl swimming beside her. Still trying to work out who his saviours were, John felt a wriggling beneath him and, before he could ascertain its cause, was lifted clean out of the water by a pair of dark arms covered with many beaded bracelets. He gasped as he was then grabbed by the fustian hat man and put on the floor of the canoe where he crouched, half in fear, half in gratitude, while the boat turned and headed for the shore.

It would appear, as John and his family were helped on to the rocky beach, that this tribe of Indians were not only kindly disposed towards white people but had managed to co-habit without warfare alongside the handful of settlers who had chosen this out-of-the-way place on which to build their homes. Dying to find out more and having checked that his children were safe with Tom, John walked in shaky fashion towards the man with the fustian hat who grinned at his approach, displaying a mouth full of rotting brown teeth.

'*Bonjour*,' he said. 'You have had a lucky escape, *non*.'

'You are French,' John exclaimed, staggered by the surprise of it all.

'Yes, indeed. After all, this island belongs to France.'

'I beg your pardon?'

'It is perfectly true, *mon ami*. It was discovered in 1604 by Samuel de Champlain, who named the place Isle au Haut. So, therefore, it belongs to the greatest country in the world – France.'

John chuckled. This was no time to get into an argument about the greatness, or otherwise, of one's land of birth. Instead he commented on the island. 'Isle au Haut, eh? High Island. I can see why.' He gazed at the three towering peaks which dominated the skyline. 'So how do you come to be here?'

The man laughed. 'How do you think? My brother and I were on the run in Paris – wanted for a royal murder, no less, which we planned and successfully carried out. But the authorities were after us so we hid ourselves as sailors, working aboard a ship that foundered on the very rock which brought yours down. We swam for the shore – it being summer and the waters much warmer – and when we arrived we found a tribe of Indians ready to string us up.'

'Why didn't they?'

'Because my brother – he's standing over there, by the way' – the Frenchman waved in the general direction of the man whose face resembled a post boy's bag – 'could play the fiddle like an angel. He had a good violin – *magnifique* – and do you know he swam all this way holding it high over his head. Anyway, I digress. He played it to the chief of the tribe and, *voila*, we were saved. They let us live on condition that *mon frère* gave them a nightly concert. And this we continued to do until the old man died. By that time more settlers had arrived and they decided to trade with us rather than kill us. So here we are – natives of the island.'

John smiled quizzically, not sure whether to believe him or not. But half of the story was at least true: the brothers fustian and bag lived in harmony with the Indians. He bowed and said, 'I am John Rawlings and I am an apothecary from London. May I know your name, Sir?'

'Hugo de Jongleur. My brother is Rafe.'

John bowed again and, turning to his three children, waved them forward. 'And these are my three offspring, Rose, Jasper and James.'

Despite their gruelling experiences, John's daughter dropped a curtsey and the little boys made a tiny bow. His heart swelled with pride and then, in an instant, he recalled the terrible circumstances of their arrival on the island and put his arms round all three of them.

'Sir,' he asked Hugo, 'is there anywhere in this remote spot that I could take my children to rest? They have just been subjected to a terrible ordeal.'

'As have all of the survivors,' Rafe answered drily. 'However, considering their youth, you may take them to our house for the night. Tomorrow we must make further plans. Who knows, some of those saved might wish to settle here.'

'Well, I shall not be one of them,' said a loud voice angrily, and they turned to see the fat lady approaching, very out of countenance and wobbling as she walked. Hugo de Jongleur gave a slow wink at John and then, turning to the woman, said, 'Madam, please forgive the informality of our island. Had we known you were coming we would have laid on a proper celebration.'

She rewarded him with a glacial stare. 'I'll have you know, Sir Foreigner, that my late husband was Sir Bevis Eawiss.'

Hugo clutched his throat and reeled back, as if in horror. '*Mon Dieu*, why did you not say so before, Madame? This throws a completely different light on the matter. Allow me to take you to the village at once.'

She gave him a regal smile. 'You may do so, my good man.'

But their conversation was cut short by the arrival of the two dandies, exhausted and drained of vitality, having swum to the island and, by some miracle, actually got there. Following them slowly came the pale young girl who had shared John's raft, assisted by a young buck Indian, raven hair flowing loose about his shoulders, his face set and intent. Hugo addressed him in a tongue that was completely foreign to John's ears, to which the young man answered in similar vein.

'What language is that?' the Apothecary asked, genuinely interested.

'Alnombak dialect. The Indians are part of the Penobscot Abenakis. For that is where we are, in Penobscot Bay.'

'Our ship was heading for Boston but got blown off course.'

'A long way. It will take you quite a while to get back there.'

'But it will be possible?'

'That, my dear Sir, is entirely up to you.'

And with that reply John had to be satisfied as the small procession set off, leaving the beach and heading inland to what Hugo, joined by Rafe, the post boy's bag man, called civilization.

TWO

The disgruntled comments of Lady Eawiss died away as she fought for breath on the sloping terrain. The young buck Indian, after glancing in the direction of the pale girl – who totally ignored him – left the group and hurried on, presumably to tell the others that some of the survivors were making their way towards them.

John, looking back at the beach, saw that about twenty people had got to the island from a total complement of forty, which included the crew. Irish Tom, who had stayed with them to help those too weary to walk, was busy making fires out of dried driftwood round which the poor wretches could sit. The Apothecary cupped his hands and shouted, and Tom looked up.

'Will you join us later?'

Tom nodded. 'I'll stay with these people overnight and come and find you in the morning.'

'Very good. Any sign of Julian Wychwood?'

Tom shook his head slowly.

They had entered a forest, the trees tall, throwing glinting shadows on to the mossy turf below. Through the lacework of branches the Apothecary could see a hint of blue which, as they approached more closely, revealed itself as a glittering lake. Winter sunshine reflected on it like a million shards of mercury, leaping with light. Close to the shore but still within the shelter of the forest was a village built of wigwams. John stared. His very basic knowledge of the Indian people had always led him to believe that they lived in triangular dwellings but these structures were round at the top and made of bent birch bark, covered with mats made of woven cat's tail or bulrush. A little apart from the village, and looking oddly out of place, were a few log cabins, and it was to these that Rafe, speaking for the first time, pointed.

'That's our place where you can rest your kinder for the night.'

But John had no chance to do more than murmur a word of thanks before a great crowd of Indian people surged out of their homes and stood staring in a not unfriendly manner at the newcomers. The women had their brilliant black hair in plaits or tied in loose bunches, their eyes, shining as night, looking out boldly at the strange sight that the strangers must present. Old men, with sculpted, haughty faces, a single feather adorning their grizzled heads, gazed with tired eyes, as if they had seen everything and nothing new was strange any more. Little children stared and one child broke free from his mother's restraining hand and was approaching Jasper and James with a broad grin before his mother snatched him back. But the twins were having none of that and with a sudden spurt of new-found energy rushed into the very heart of the village and began chattering in English. John ran after them as Hugo called out to the tribe in their native tongue.

It was as good an introduction as any and the Indians broke their ranks and clustered round the newcomers, talking animatedly in a language that only the two small Frenchmen could understand. The young buck Indian appeared from a wigwam and stood silently watching. John turned to the fair girl who was leaning against him, almost fainting with fatigue.

'Excuse me, I have yet to learn your name.'

'It's Jane Hawthorne, Sir.'

He could not bow because she was using him as a living prop, but the Apothecary inclined his head. 'Mine is John Rawlings and this is my daughter, Rose. My two sons have just run into the village to make friends.'

'They succeed well,' she answered, then slithered down and collapsed in a rather pathetic little heap at his feet.

John stooped to pick her up but collided with someone who had also come to the rescue. He straightened and met the piercing dark eyes of the young Indian who had raced to be at her side. Hugo said quietly, 'Do not challenge him, Sir.'

So that's the way of it, John thought, and stood up so that the young man could do the honours. It was a wise move because the fire went out of the Indian's gaze. The Apothecary bowed. 'John Rawlings,' he said, and pointed to himself.

'Blue Wolf,' replied the other in English with a French accent.

Hugo and Rafe chuckled in unison. 'We have taught him a great deal of your tongue, Monsieur. He can converse with you – if he so wishes.'

John felt in his pocket for smelling salts and pulled out nothing but a sodden handkerchief, forgetting just for the briefest second that he had been thoroughly soaked in the sea. He turned to the French brothers, who stood side by side, and wondered what the true facts were behind their escapades in their native land, but they merely smiled at him.

'Don't worry about the girl, Monsieur. She will become part of the tribe.'

'What do you mean?'

'Blue Wolf has taken a fancy to her. He will marry her and they will breed little mixed blood children.'

'But supposing she objects? Suppose she wants to stay with her own people?'

'That will be up to her, of course. But would you protest if you were in her shoes?'

John had to admit that, for an orphaned girl, if that was what Jane Hawthorne turned out to be, he could think of worse fates. But, on the other hand, there might be someone, even now lying exhausted on the beach, who could lay claim to her.

'I think I should await developments before making a judgement,' he answered. 'But for tonight, can you give her shelter?'

'Of course,' Hugo replied. He said a few words in Blue Wolf's language and the young Indian reluctantly released the recovering girl. 'And now, Sir, if you would like to join me.'

John called out to the twins, who came quite slowly from the settlement, and they proceeded along a well-trodden path to the furthest log cabin. Inside, despite its somewhat stark exterior, it was very comfortable. All three of John's children fell asleep at the supper table and were unable to appreciate the fact that Rafe had given up his bed for them. As he tucked them beneath the coverlet the Apothecary was aware that he must stay alert and be on his guard to protect them from the strange environment in which the four of them had been inextricably placed.

Like a band of desolate pilgrims, the next morning saw Tom arrive with his straggle of followers. At the sight of them Lady Eawiss had burst forth from her log cabin, thankfully at some distance from the one in which John and his family had stayed, crying loudly for help. She clutched Tom's arm as he made his way along the path, seeking out his employer.

'My man, you must help me. I did not get a wink of sleep all the long night. I was too frightened even to close my eyes.'

Tom looked at her from his considerable height. 'And what were you frightened of, Madam?'

She lowered her voice a little. 'Of God knows what evil practices these island people are capable. I leave it to your imagination.'

Tom frowned. 'I can't think what you mean, Madam.'

She heaved her redoubtable bosom. 'Don't be silly, fellow. What all women are afraid of.'

Tom looked puzzled, then his brow cleared. 'Ah, you mean of getting a spot on the end of their nose.'

Her eyebrows flew. 'If my husband Sir Bevis Eawiss were alive he would challenge you to a duel.'

'Begging your pardon, My Lady. I'm just a foolish chap from Ireland. Now if you'll forgive me, I have lodging to find for these poor people who slept rough on the beach last night.'

And he set off, leading the rest of the shipwrecked party to a place where they could rest in some comfort and decide on their next move. It was there that John caught up with them, sitting outside one of the cabins where the kindly couple living within had provided freshly baked bread and meat for the hungry victims of the shipwreck. There was also home-made beer and cider with which to swill the breakfast down.

John looked round the group and thought them fairly typical of those who wanted to start a new life in the Colonies. But of all the crowd with whom he had passed the time of day aboard ship, six people were outstanding. One, for obvious reasons, was the over-large widow, Lady Eawiss; the second was the quiet, modest Jane Hawthorne, the third and fourth were an oddly matched couple: she a great beauty of yesteryear who reminded him in the vaguest possible way of Elizabeth; he a gentlemen of rough-hewn appearance with long dark hair and wild blue eyes. The fifth and sixth were, of course, the pair of beaux who had swum to the island and actually come out alive. Now they were eating, not elegantly but like wolves. And the thought of this made John wonder about the Indian called Blue Wolf who had such an obvious liking for Miss Hawthorne. He considered how that would end if she decided to forge on to Boston.

Irish Tom was speaking. 'So I suggest, good people, that you think very carefully about whether you wish to undertake the hazardous journey to Boston or whether you would rather build a life here in these pleasant surroundings.'

A man spoke up. 'But what about the tribe who live so close by? Might they not rise up in the night and cut our throats?'

Rafe, who was sitting with his brother on the edge of the crowd, answered, 'They are a peace-loving people. Leave them to live their lives quietly – don't start any of that religious preaching at them – and they will ignore you.'

One of the two dandies who had swum ashore said, 'Well, George and I were intending to live in Boston, don't you know, so that's where we'll go. We prefer town life to all this tranquillity, don't we?'

'Damme, but yes,' drawled the other, and there was a low murmur amongst the assembled people, clearly in awe of the pair's upper-crust accents.

John stated his case. 'I have business commitments in Boston so feel duty bound to make the journey on.'

And indeed he had. In the autumn of the previous year – 1772, to be precise – he had received an unusual letter. It had been from that very town, from a certain Josiah Hallowell, asking him if one of his representatives could make the difficult journey to the Colonies to set about drawing up an agreement between them. It appeared that Josiah's niece had recently travelled to the Colonies to live, bringing with her a bottle of carbonated water prepared by J. Rawlings of Nassau Street, London. It seemed that Josiah ran the Orange Tree Tavern and wanted to sell the water to his customers, and indeed the letter had arrived at just the right time. John, still mourning the death of his magnificent father, Sir Gabriel Kent, had been looking for something to lift his spirits. At first he had not known whether to take his children with him or not, but in the end had decided that to leave them behind would be both selfish and cruel. They had accompanied him and, thank God, had survived the sinking of their ship.

The former beauty spoke up in not at all the voice that John had expected and he was immediately drawn back to the present.

Instead of enchanting, modulated tones she talked at full pitch, making sure that everyone gathered could hear her.

'I, too, must reach Boston. My husband and I will accompany you.'

She caught the Apothecary's eye – and what eyes she had. He thought of violets growing wild and felt that he could hardly look away from their vivid elegance. But Irish Tom, who had obviously become the self-appointed leader during the night's vigil, was speaking again.

'How do we get boats to the mainland? That's the problem.'

The man with hair like sunflower seeds, a braw Scotsman with a glorious Highland accent, said, 'We'll have to ask the Indians for canoes.'

At this Lady Eawiss let out a shrill scream. 'Lord have mercy on me – I would never trust myself on the high seas in one of those contraptions ever again.'

'Then, my dear Madam, you will have to swim for it,' Tom answered drily.

At this the lady fainted – or pretended to – slumping down on the person unfortunate enough to be sitting next to her. It was Jane Hawthorne, who virtually vanished beneath the folds of stained clothing and unwashed bulk. Reluctantly, John rose to his feet and went to assist. He pulled out Jane, who looked slightly nauseous, and automatically slipped his hand down the fat lady's back to loosen her stays. She immediately woke up and hit him over the head with her portmanteau, which had not left her side since she came ashore. John reeled back. At this the big Scotsman bellowed, 'Stop that,' though to whom he was speaking was not at all clear, then crashed to John's side. Jane burst into tears, mostly due to the strains of the last few days, and as if by magic Blue Wolf – who must have hearing beyond normal capabilities – leapt out of the forest and stood glaring at the entire group. Jane saw him and cast her watery eyes down-wards, weeping harder than ever. John, meanwhile, was still shaking from the shock as the Scotsman with a mighty arm hauled Lady Eawiss to her feet.

'I will not have this behaviour, Madam, ruining life in our peaceful community. How very dare you strike out when this man was only trying to help ye.'

'The villain had his hands on my nether garments,' she retorted, purple with wrath.

'The man is an apothecary, Ma'am. Had you not heard? He may look where he pleases.'

'Not on me he doesn't.'

The mighty creature drew her upwards so that his face was an inch from hers. 'You will leave and go to Boston, Madam. We will not allow you to live here amongst us.'

'If my late husband, Sir Bevis Eawiss were alive . . .'

'Well, he's not, is he, Milady. So stop blathering on about him. Now, go retake your seat and keep mum until this meeting is over.'

She sat down with a great deal of huffing. Nobody moved except for Blue Wolf, who came a fraction closer to Jane and folded his arms. John looked at him in silent admiration.

Miss Hawthorne wiped away her tears and spoke. 'I worked as a housemaid and it took me ten years to earn enough money to sail to Boston. I would very much like to get there.'

At these words Blue Wolf turned and vanished – almost literally – into the forest. John surmised that the man knew far more English than even Rafe was aware.

'So,' said Tom, 'it is about half for going and half for staying.'

And so it was. John, looking round, considered his fellow passengers to Boston. Besides himself and Tom were his three children, the two dandies, the Beauty and her younger husband, Jane, the large Lady Eawiss and a jolly ox of a man and his several children, though with a conspicuous lack of wife.

'Going to Boston to find a spouse,' the man announced cheerily to the entire company. 'Got to have someone to keep my house and kinder for me.'

'Couldn't you get anyone in England?' a voice called out.

'Not to my liking,' he answered.

John smiled, thinking him a useful chap to have on one's side in an argument.

'Well, I'm going with my employer,' said Tom, standing up. 'So all bound for Boston come with me.'

Lady Eawiss turned to Jane. 'Will you act as my lady's maid, child? Unfortunately my servant . . .' she pronounced it *savant*, '. . . was drowned. I will pay you a respectable wage. Fortunately

I packed all my money in my portmanteau which I brought with me.' She patted the bag which her chubby hand never left.

'Then we'll have to borrow off you to pay the Indians,' somebody remarked.

Hugo, who was loitering nearby, interposed. 'Money is of no use to them. You'll have to offer them something tangible.'

'And what would that be, Sir?' enquired George Glynde, one of the two dandies.

'A dead deer,' answered Rafe dryly.

'Is that a true fact?'

'I don't lie,' replied the Frenchman, frowning and looking more bag-like than ever.

'Then Tracey and I will go hunting,' George announced cheerfully.

All the men in the party agreed to go with them with varying degrees of enthusiasm. John was particularly queasy about the whole idea but knew that he must brace up for the occasion. He preferred not knowing the origin of his food, unlike most other males, but told himself that he was in pioneering country now and must drop the fairly civilized ways of London. So with a brave face on it he marched into the forest with the others, pretending that he was Robin Hood and bracing himself for the kill.

In the event it was swift and done with a single arrow fired by Matthew, the broad-shouldered raw countryman who was going to Boston in search of a wife. They carried the heavy beast home and went straight with it to the Indian village. Here, it was explained by Hugo that the party wished to borrow two large canoes with skilled oarsmen. The chief, who appeared in full ceremonial headdress, replied that they would consider the undertaking on a day when the sea was calm. And with that they had to be content.

That night John went to sleep with a sensation quite strange to him. He felt that not only was he on the brink of a terrifying journey but that many adventures lay before him – both for good and for ill – before he would be able to see his native land again.

THREE

For the rest of that month and four weeks afterwards the sea boiled and broiled and roared about the coast of the Isle au Haut. Angry breakers lashed against the rugged ocean line and the wind took up its vicious complaint and howled around the little community of inhabitants. The Indians, hardened to the ways of the weather, remained mostly in their stoutly built wigwams, only venturing forth to hunt. John Rawlings, itching to get back to his old life as an apothecary, began to study the herbs used by the tribe and was fascinated to find the medicine men compounding things like skunk cabbage for nervous disorders and horsemint for back pain. Most of the herbs were brewed into teas which the population drank without question, unlike some of John's patients in London, who were curious about what they were being given.

Then, one day in March, the weather changed and the sea calmed down. John knew that his days on the island were limited. He, his servant and the children had taken rooms with an elderly widow woman who'd lived alone since the death of her husband and was glad to have two able-bodied men around the house to do the chores that were now beyond her. At night, however, Irish Tom went about his own affairs, into which John never enquired. But his former coachman was always back by dawn and drawing the widow's water from a pump which the settlers had organized. John, fascinated by people as he had always been, preferred to spend his evenings with the brothers Hugo and Rafe rather than sit in a rocking chair and stare at the ceiling. And on his last night before the journey to Boston began he was invited to dine and share in some wine which they had brewing in their storeroom. Perhaps because he was a little drunk and perhaps because he had always been immensely curious, John asked them the question which had puzzled him ever since the day of his arrival.

'Tell me, if you would be so good, who was the subject of your assassination in France?'

Rafe laughed – a fruity sound. 'A very good question, that.'

John stared at him. 'Don't keep me in suspense. Would it have been anyone I might have read about?'

Now it was the other's turn to chuckle. 'Of course it would. The name was familiar throughout Europe. The trouble was that somebody very powerful found out and we had to run for it.'

'Well, who was the target?'

'The Pompadour.'

'I beg your pardon?'

'The Pompadour. Louis XV's *maitresse-en-titre*. Surely you've heard of her?'

'Of course I've heard of her, but I thought she died in her early forties of tuberculosis.'

The leather man and the fustian man laughed simultaneously. 'Tuberculosis, my eye. We mixed arsenic in with her *maquillage* and she died, slowly but very, very surely.'

John was astounded. So much so that he finished his glass of wine at a swallow.

'Unfortunately a canny physician tested some of her make-up and found traces of the deadly substance.'

'But why were you and Rafe suspected?'

'Because we were part of her entertainment and always in and out of her apartments. We were tumblers in our heyday – and bloody good at it we were.'

The conversation was growing more bizarre by the second and John sat with his mouth open, listening.

'Of course, the physician told the King and he started making enquiries, discreetly you understand, conducted by men with unsmiling faces who infiltrated her group of servants.'

'And?'

'We were tipped off that they were about to make an arrest so we fled for our lives. The rest you know. We became sailors and were shipwrecked close to this island.'

'But who paid you to do it? I know Madame Pompadour had many enemies at court. Was it Richelieu? Or her husband? Who?'

Hugo looked teasing. 'Guess.'

'I couldn't. I don't know enough about French affairs.'

'It was a woman. The Pompadour's husband was happy, miles away and enjoying life. The Duc de Richelieu – by the way, he was of the same family as the great cardinal, the Eminence Rouge himself – was prepared to play a waiting game. No, it was Marie Louise O'Murphy.'

John shook his head in bewilderment. 'I've not heard of her. Who was she?'

Rafe took up the story. 'By God, but she was a pretty little thing. Allowed herself to be painted naked, sprawled out on a sofa, bottom up, legs apart. Makes me grow hot just to think of it. Casanova fell in love with her when she was only thirteen years old and had a nude portrait of her painted – in a very similar pose to the one I have just described.'

'So what happened to her?'

'Well, Louis XV couldn't wait to get his breeches down when he saw the painting. Mind you, that was the only thing that was down. Everything else was raised up to great heights.'

John laughed raucously. 'And?'

'She was just fourteen when the King debauched her – she suffered a miscarriage by him and later gave birth to a daughter. And then, when she had become one of his many, many courtesans and had been in place for just two years, the stupid little creature made a great mistake. She sought to replace the Pompadour.'

'Really?'

'Overplayed her silly tiny Irish hand. You can imagine Madame's reaction to that. The adorable childish plaything was married off to Jacques de Beaufranchet pretty damn quickly.'

'But where does the poisoning come in?'

'For years she nursed a private hatred as only a thwarted child could. Do not forget that when she gave birth to the King's daughter she was only seventeen years old. And also recall she was not allowed to live at Versailles, despite that. She was put to live with the other minor mistresses in the Parc aux Cerfes, a small mansion nearby.'

'Stags Park,' translated John. 'How very apt. But what happened?'

'Well, husband number one was killed in battle a few days before the birth of her son . . .'

'How terrible for her.'

'Yes. Then she married again, an ageing widower with three

children, the Comte de Flaghac. This gave her enough money and position to put her long-felt hatred into a solid idea. And, *voila*. The baby girl, the King's adorable plaything, finally came across two brothers who were willing to listen to her terrible story and put the plan into action.'

John drew a breath but said nothing, realizing for the first time that he was actually in the home of two assassins but still, despite everything, liking them, notwithstanding their amazing role in bringing down one of the best-known women of her time. But Hugo was interrupting.

'The King and the Pompadour gave up sexual relations in 1750 because she felt she was too fragile to risk conception. She had had two nasty miscarriages in the years leading up to that time.'

'Did she have any living children?'

'None by the King but two by her husband: a boy who died in infancy and Alexandrine, who died aged ten, poor little soul. However, in spite of the lack of sex with Louis, she became his greatest friend, which must have taken some doing.'

John could not help but smile at the way Hugo put things.

'She used to entertain him in the evenings, give amusing supper parties for him, relieve him of the boredom of life at court. Funnily enough, his wife refused him her bedroom as well after she had given birth to ten children, the last one being particularly difficult.'

'Small wonder he had other mistresses.'

'But to what excess! Louis XV was ruled by his cock.'

'So I presume that both of you joined her merry parties, tumbling for the highest of society.'

'You presume correctly, *mon cher ami*. And that is the end of our story. Now we are simple homesteaders on a remote island off the coast of the Colonies – if this is part of the Colonies. Heaven alone knows. We are severely out of touch.'

'But people dwell on the mainland, surely.'

'The Indians tell us there are some settlers. You can probably do manual work on a farm in return for a ride in a wagon to help your journey. Or, perhaps, as you are an apothecary you will be able to find some herbs and cure the people of their various ailments.'

'Do you think it is going to be that rough? What about my children and their comfort?'

'Comfort is out of the question,' Rafe answered cynically. 'There are only half a dozen or so European communities there. In your shoes I would take an Indian guide with me.'

'Are you serious?'

'Never more so, my friend. You have been shipwrecked on a harsh and unforgiving stretch of coast. Without a guide I wouldn't give much for your chances. Any of you.'

John blanched. 'But I cannot subject my boys to that. Nor my beautiful Rose. And what about the rest of the survivors? How will they fare?'

Hugo put a hand on his shoulder. 'John, it would be wrong of us to give you a false impression. Existence is terribly hard. That is what persuaded us to stay here. Implore the Indians to let you have an escort.'

But in the event it was easier than the Apothecary could have imagined. The minute the matter was raised Blue Wolf was offered by the chief to escort them as far as Penobscot, where, apparently, there was a township of colonists. The party eventually bound for Boston agreed to this with the exception of Lady Eawiss, who said loudly, hugging her portmanteau to her ample stomach, 'I do not wish to go with that savage. He will murder us all in our beds and take our jewels.'

Irish Tom, self-appointed spokesman, retorted, 'There will be no beds to rest on, Madam. We will have to sleep rough at first.'

She threw herself into the lap of poor Jane Hawthorne, who had already taken on the role of maidservant.

'It's monstrous, do you hear me? I should die of exposure if I had to sleep beneath the stars. How can you say such things?'

'You have a straight choice, Madam. Either you stay here or you undertake the perilous journey with the rest of us. It's Boston or bust.'

There was a burst of laughter from the rest of the group, particularly from the wild boy, Jacob O'Farrell, the husband of the fading beauty who had revealed herself as Lady Conway and who, John guessed, had once been her groom. He could just see them riding side by side, the lady seated side saddle, the servant daring to look her directly in the eyes with his impertinent blue gaze. His thoughts were redirected to the present by the sound of Lady Conway's voice.

'Come along, my dear. A little courage, I beg you, or else the gentlemen will think us weak and vapid creatures. I personally am up for the challenge.'

With that her hand moved surreptitiously from her side and squeezed her husband's thigh. He turned his head and lowered one of his eyelids. The Apothecary thought them an exciting couple.

'Then we're off,' said Matthew, the countryman, going to Boston to find himself a wife.

'Yes,' chorused his two boys, while his daughter, little more than eight years of age, clung to her father's leg and looked at the rest of the company with a large, solemn regard.

Two days later they departed. Two long canoes, each with a couple of native oarsmen, took seven passengers each. John and Irish Tom, in company with the Apothecary's three children, were seated beside the two dandies, George Glynde and Tracey Tremayne, who exchanged idle banter. In the other canoe were Lady Conway and Jake O'Farrell, Matthew and his brood, and the hysterical Lady Eawiss and her maid, Jane. Blue Wolf sat silently, his arms folded, gazing out to sea. When they had left the island behind them he crouched behind the leading oarsman and navigated. Not once did he glance in Jane Hawthorne's direction. John thought his composure admirable.

It seemed as if they were sailing through paradise. Everywhere was dotted with small islands, rearing out of the water as mere outcroppings of rock or topped with vegetation sweeping down to the ocean's very edge. The sea itself was like a ribbon of silk, changing in the bright sunlight through every shade of blue imaginable. John feasted his eyes on glittering aquamarine, gentle cerulean where it lapped at the shorelines and deep sapphire further out to sea, all containing the sparkling liveliness of zircon jewels, leaping and lapping at the canoe's prow as it hefted steadily through the rippling water. Eventually two islands lying close together came into view and Blue Wolf whispered instructions to the Indian wielding the front paddle, then stood up.

'We land,' he called across the distance between the two

vessels, and both canoes obediently turned and made for a small cove. Somewhat surprisingly, Tracey, followed by George, leapt out and helped pull the craft on to the pebbly beach. Blue Wolf, still ignoring pretty Jane, did likewise. Glad of the opportunity to walk and to answer the calls of nature, both parties clambered ashore as best they could. Needless to say, Lady Eawiss had to be lifted down by a straining Matthew, and it was just then that John noticed something. Blue Wolf, who stood silently on the beach, seeing his passengers ashore, put out his brown hand to assist Jane Hawthorne, and she laid her own small wrist within his grasp and briefly, so briefly that it might have been an optical illusion, their fingers entwined. The Apothecary smiled to himself, wondering how it would all end.

An hour later they took to the canoes once more. Before they went Blue Wolf made an announcement, his French accent causing a ripple of amusement amongst the listeners.

'Now we go to Cape of the Winds on the mainland. There I will make a shelter for the old woman.'

Lady Eawiss let out a little scream of protest but was silenced by a black look from Lady Conway, for whom the older woman seemed to have a great deal of respect, tinged with a touch of jealousy.

They paddled onwards, all the passengers now moved to silence by the sheer majesty of the scenes they were witnessing. In the distance loomed the lines of the mainland, rocky and fearful, towering headlands sweeping down to small shingle coves. John thought that there was nothing warm or welcoming about the land they were heading to, the very aspect of the place sending a chill down his spine. Sitting in front of him as she was, Rose turned and said, 'It will be all right, Papa. Don't be confounded by what you see.'

He kissed her on the top of her head and said, 'You remind me of my father, sweetheart. He would have said, "Damme boy, looks a good country for an adventure, don't you know."'

'And what would you have answered?'

'Damme, Sir, I think you're right.'

George Glynde, overhearing, said, 'What do you think, Tracey?'

His friend replied, 'Well, we're brought to Point Non Plus,

old chap. Whether we like it or whether we don't, we've got to
make the best of it.'

'Very true, my dear fellow. Mind you, I don't relish the thought
of sleeping rough. I've a mind to crawl in with the elderly Bird
of Paradise.'

'She'd eat you alive.'

John smiled inwardly, thinking of the unlikely coupling of
Lady Eawiss and the young rake, hoping as he did so that Rose
would not understand a word. But she got the gist – that was
clear from the small giggle she gave. John pretended to look
severe and concentrated on the surroundings.

At the foot of the cliffs the sea pounded on the rocky surface
and the colour changed to a wild indigo, though further out, in
the deeps, it was the shade of jade. The canoes changed course
and paddled round the headland to where, in the shape of the
new moon, curved a sandy beach, rocky formations strewing it
with strange shapes.

Jasper exclaimed, 'I just saw Mama, swimming in the surf.'

'Where?' said James, craning his head.

'There, can't you see? Look!'

'Oh, yes, I can see her too.'

Even though the Apothecary knew that they were just dwelling
in childish fantasies, he nonetheless turned his head to follow
Jasper's pointing finger. There was nothing. It was a trick of a
juvenile imagination, and yet . . . Blue Wolf shouted instructions,
his voice reedy in the blowing wind.

'Land here. This is Cape of the Winds.'

'Mecadacut,' said their oarsman, speaking for the first time on
the journey.

'What's the feller sayin'?' asked Tracey.

'Damned if I know.'

'Probably 'tis his own lingo for the name of the place.'

'Ah,' replied the other, satisfied.

This time it was more difficult to get out on the beach as
everyone, including the children, seemed to be suffering pain
from their cramped conditions. John lifted out one twin, Irish
Tom the other. Rose hitched up her skirts, much soiled by
exposure to both the land and sea, and thrust out her small pale
leg. From the other canoe came shrieks as Matthew dropped

Lady Eawiss and was helped to hoist her once more by Jacob O'Farrell. Somebody – no prizes for guessing correctly – must have given her a small nip on the buttocks because she called out, 'Oh, unhand me, Sir,' to which neither of her helpers paid any attention whatsoever, though Jake winked a vivid eye at the countryman. He really was a naughty boy, thought John with a quiet chuckle, a regular out-and-outer, up for any bit of mischief that was going.

Beyond the beach there was a fine forest of trees, and it was in the shelter of these that Blue Wolf decided to camp. There had been no further contact between him and Jane, who was run off her feet attending to her new mistress. Yet there was a pinkness about her cheeks and a glint in the Indian's eye as he set about making a wigwam for Lady Eawiss, stretching cuttings from the trees over until he had a frame, then covering these with hides that he had brought in the canoe. Meanwhile, the fat woman was sitting on the ground, clutching her portmanteau and moaning on – though nobody was listening – about her late husband and what he would have said if he had found himself in these dismal circumstances.

Jasper nudged James. 'That lady talking to herself.'

James nodded. 'She be not well.'

Jasper looked interested. 'What's the matter with her?'

James looked sad. 'Nobody likes her. She be too cross.'

Jasper made a face like a wise old man. 'Poor thing,' he said, and they trotted off in unison to explore the beach.

John, looking at their small, retreating figures, felt fit to weep. Elizabeth had given him two fine sons, spirited but kindly, childish but brave. His spirits soared. Whatever his circumstances he knew that he would always be surrounded by love.

It grew dark early and the Indians set about collecting driftwood for a log fire, helped by the men of the party who were glad to have something to focus their minds on after the long journey. George and Tracey, delighted to be busy, set about their tasks with a great deal of banter, while the mighty Matthew pulled logs from the forest. Then they set up a spit, on to which they hauled a skinned deer. It was primitive and rather beautiful, in its strange way. The Indians began to sing a kind of chant, with which most of the party joined. Skins were laid on the ground by the fire and there people sat to eat their food with their fingers. The atmosphere was one of total simplicity, without falsehood or pretence of any kind. Even the duo of dandies fell silent, all affected by this enchanted night.

John dozed, his arms around his children. He did not sleep well, his eyes open, staring at the might of the universe with its zillion blazing stars and the stealthy moon weaving its secretive passage across the sky. Eventually, when the first streaks of light appeared in the east, he slept briefly but woke to see a sun, emboldened by the coming of spring, making its triumphant appearance.

John thought of Elizabeth, fathoms deep, who would never now see the sun again; of his beloved father, Sir Gabriel Kent, who could no longer strut his high fashion on the London scene; of his former lover, the beautiful Coralie Clive, sister of the famous actress, Kitty, who had sought to make her own name in the theatre and had ended her attempt by marrying one of the most terrible men in the world.

As the day grew lighter John rose gently to his feet, his children still fast asleep on the ground beneath him. The Indian rowers were leaving, making for the shore, only Blue Wolf remaining to guide his party towards the town of Boston. The two men looked at one another, separated by everything imaginably possible, yet in that moment feeling a bond of total unity. Then the Indian turned away, silent as always, leaving the Apothecary alone to contemplate his highly uncertain future.

FOUR

John could never afterwards recall the length of time that they had been travelling. It could have been months, it could have been a year. Day after day they trekked across the most beautiful countryside, sticking mainly to the coast and never venturing far inland. From time to time they came across groups of white settlers, all as uneasy as the Indian villagers, the people from whom the land had been taken. If it had not been for the fact that Blue Wolf was there to state that they were wanderers and merely passing through, John reckoned they would have been killed. All, that is, except for the children, who would have been abducted and taken to live in the Indian villages. But as it was, the natives of the great land lived in a state of high alarm, victim to the terrible diseases brought in by the white man against which they had no natural immunity, fearing the guns and savagery of their invaders and turning for help to the occasional missionary who was brave enough to live amongst them peacefully.

Eventually they came to a small gathering of settlers living in a desolate village called Falmouth. It was a place that had been wrecked several times by various invaders and now consisted of a scattering of inhabitants, grimly going about their daily tasks, keeping their faith in almighty protection. At the sight of the gathering Blue Wolf had slipped away into the forest, a terrain which the white man feared, thinking it only suitable for bears and beasts. John had been alarmed to see the disappearance of their guide – the only one left as the canoeists had turned back once the shipwreck survivors had safely landed. But Jane Hawthorne had announced confidently that he would return as soon as the group had left the village behind them.

The relationship between the two of them intrigued the Apothecary. The Indian man was fighting against some ancient tribal customs and his own flesh-and-blood feelings; the girl, aged sixteen as John had been informed, was on the cusp of womanhood and was clearly deeply attracted to the lithe and brown-skinned man who stood so tall and so handsome at the head of their little party. Despite the fact that Lady Eawiss depended on her for everything, Jane showed a remarkable independence of thought and also of attitude. As to the rest of their group, the Apothecary stole a covert look round them as they plodded into the small township.

Lady Eawiss had lost a great deal of weight – though still large, she was no longer enormous. She had also become sloppier in her presentation: the blonde wig which she slapped on to hide her greying hair now sat slightly askew and was in desperate need of a wigmaker to attend to it. Lady Conway, on the other hand, had long ago abandoned any false curls and now had her flowing dark locks tied back in a ribbon. She had also abandoned her long dress and wore breeches, so that in some ways she now resembled her husband, that naughty man, Jake O'Farrell.

Matthew and his little brood had all prospered – even the youngest child, born in the countryside, as they all had been. And, highly unlikely as it would seem, the two young rakes – George Glynde and Tracey Tremayne – had adapted to the rough life, though extremely high stepping and all the crack in their manner. John could never work out if they were in fact a pair of Miss Mollys or simply affected to the ultimate degree. Not that it mattered; they both did their share of manual work and made jokes while doing so.

Irish Tom, as usual, was the mighty stalwart that he had always been. Formerly a coachman and servant, John Rawlings blessed the day that Tom had been taken on by Sir Gabriel Kent, the Apothecary's late and adored father. Now he was a friend, a confidant, an equal in everything but education. As he trudged into the settlement to be met by a stern-faced man, he whispered, 'Oh, glory be to God, I do believe it's a religious fanatic.'

'I don't care what he is,' John murmured back, 'as long as he can give us some food and a bed for the night.'

Hector Lonsdale, who despite his Puritanical views was a kindly man, enquired most anxiously about the party from the Isle au Haut: whether they had been badly treated by the Indians, where they were heading, what kind of shape the rest of the group were in.

'They are bearing up reasonably well, Sir,' John answered. 'Even the small children, three of which are mine.'

Hector shook his head sadly. 'My children – all four of them – have died, one after the other. They contracted a disease and left this life burning with fever. I believe this place in which we live has cast shadows upon the ground.'

'What do you mean by that?' asked Tom.

'Come to my house and I will tell you.'

Glancing round, John saw that the other members of the party were receiving invitations to various dwellings and called his children to join him. Jasper and James looked like a pair of ragamuffins, with clothes handed down from a kindly Indian woman and their hair upon their shoulders. Sunburnt faces, freckles and cheerful grins gave them the appearance of children from another race entirely, and John saw Hector start back when he first looked at them.

'These boys are yours?'

'Yes. They are not as rough as they appear, I assure you.'

'They do not have Abenaki blood?'

'No, they are pure English.'

'That's as well then.'

Rose, too, was growing up and becoming so beautiful that John sometimes wondered whether she could really be his. Yet one look at her harebell eyes reassured him. They were so similar to his own that there could be no doubt. And the boys, too, had eyes like hyacinths, just a shade darker. It was the Rawlings blue, and the very thought of it made the Apothecary smile.

Hector's wife, a woman consumed by grief and suffering who could barely manage a smile of welcome through her compressed lips, served them a lowly meal of vegetables and water. But it was something different, for though Blue Wolf always managed to cook a repast of sorts over a fire, everyone was growing tired of stewed berries. She did not speak during the meal but Hector talked to them non-stop, clearly enjoying having a different audience.

'I promised to tell you why this settlement is considered unlucky,' he said.

'Yes?' asked the twins simultaneously.

'Well, it was originally Indian country known as Machigonne,

which means Great Neck in our tongue, but in 1623 it was granted
to one Christopher Levett by the King of England and its name
was changed to Casco Bay. People settled here but with no
particular success. Meanwhile, Captain Levett returned to England
and wrote a book about his journey.'

'Did he come back?' asked Rose.

'Yes, but strangely never to Casco Bay. He went to Massachusetts
instead.'

'So he never saw the settlers again?'

'No, and they just disappeared, somewhat mysteriously. As for
him, he died on the journey back to England, doing his business,
seated upon the jakes.'

The twins burst into a fit of uncontrollable laughter; anything
connected with the functions of nature seeming hilarious to all
pre-pubescent boys, especially them. John, too old to be amused
but nevertheless enjoying the mental picture, also laughed. As
for Tom, he slapped the wooden table with the palm of his hand
and roared an Irish roar. Hector's wife looked disapproving, her
tight lips compressing so hard that they virtually vanished. The
twins, seeing this, giggled even louder and John, simmering
down, decided that he must give a lead as head of the family.
Looking at Hector seriously, he said, 'What a terrible end,' a
remark which convulsed the room. Eventually their host laughed,
a short, barking sound, and the Apothecary found himself finally
able to relax.

'So what happened next?' he asked when everyone had quietened down.

'In 1633 two other men founded another colony, this one
devoted to hunting and fishing, but it was taken over in 1658 by
the Massachusetts Bay Company. They changed the township's
name to Falmouth.'

'Peace at last,' said Tom.

'Far from it. The entire settlement was destroyed by the
Abenakis in 1676.'

'Good gracious!' John exclaimed. 'We found them peace
loving and friendly.'

'That is because they live on an island,' answered Hector.
'You wait till a few more colonists arrive. Then there'll be a
bloodbath.'

John did not answer, thinking to himself that the land belonged to the Indian people after all.

Hector continued to speak. 'Two years later the settlement was rebuilt—'

'You wonder why they bothered,' muttered Tom under his breath.

'—and a powerful fort was erected. But it was all destroyed by a mass attack of the French and the Indians, at least five hundred men involved, all told.'

'Glory be to God,' said Tom, then realizing that it was probably the wrong thing to say in this Christian household, added, 'Please excuse me, Madam, but it makes me question if it was worth the effort, the rebuilding and all.'

Hector rolled his eyes heavenwards. 'It is the duty of mankind to rebuild. That is why God gave us hands and minds. Those who do not persevere shall not be rewarded in the eternal kingdom.'

Into John's irreverent mind popped the idea that, according to some schools of thought, as long as one was persevering it didn't matter how many lives were lost or who owned the land originally. He cleared his throat and changed the subject.

'Madam, I do thank you for feeding us.'

'It was our Christian duty so to do.'

'Perhaps you might tell us if there are any lodging houses within your community.'

Hector's wife, whose name turned out to be Chastity, looked severe. 'Mistress Corey has some rooms, I believe.'

John guessed at once that Mistress Corey was not a pillar of rectitude.

'She also has baths,' Chastity sniffed.

Rose, who had been quietly sitting, controlling her laughter by keeping her elbows on the table and her hands clenched in front of her mouth, spoke up. 'How lovely. I should like so much to have one. Does she let people use them?'

'Yes, she rents them out.'

'But I haven't any money.'

'Then she will ask you to work for her. She's quite good at that – making people do services in return.'

John and Irish Tom exchanged a glance, wondering if there

was a double entendre intended. They were certain there was
when Hector said reprovingly, 'Now, now, wife.'

Rose continued eagerly, 'Then I shall call on her and ask for
one. Does she have a bathing room?'

'Not she, no. She has had a hut built outside and inside are
two tin baths separated by a curtain.'

'Well, it is a room of sorts. How about you, Papa? Shall
we take the boys?'

'Yes, please,' said James, though Jasper pulled a face before
nodding brightly when his brother agreed.

Having decided to make recompense for their meal in the way
of menial tasks, John and Tom left the house.

'Well, I'm going to make enquiries about having a bath now.
What about you, my friend?'

'No, Sorrh, if it's all the same to you, I'll try and find an
alehouse in this God-fearing community. I prefer to bathe in the
rivers and lakes.'

'Um. And I prefer the water a bit warmer, Tom. So I'm off to
Mrs Corey's.'

'Good luck, dear soul. Will you provide her with services?'

The Apothecary gave the broadest of grins. 'Well, now that
all depends, doesn't it?'

'Oh, but you're a rogue, my man.'

They parted company, laughing.

John turned to Rose. 'Do I smell, sweetheart?'

She smiled. 'Through your nose, yes. But you actually stink,
Papa.'

'Then I must attend to that at once.'

They found several of their fellow travellers waiting outside
Mrs Corey's establishment: Lady Conway and Jake together with
Lady Eawiss and an exhausted-looking Jane Hawthorne. On
enquiring about Matthew and his brood they were told that all
country people bathed in water hewn from a well. After several
minutes of hanging about George and Tracey emerged looking
quite smart, both wearing new shirts made of coarse cambric, but
very clean for all that. It would seem that Mrs Corey ran a local
store as well. At this news Lady Eawiss, clutching her portmanteau
to her bountiful bosom, hurried inside to see what goods were up
for sale. Lady Conway laughed at Jake but followed suit.

The baths now being free, Mrs Corey appeared, a pale, smiling woman with an eye for the main chance, however it might present itself. John bowed low and requested the use of the baths for himself and his children.

'And you have the money, Sir?'

'Alas, Ma'am, I have none. I can merely offer you my services.'

She giggled and twinkled. 'That will have to be by arrangement, Sir.'

John nodded. 'I quite understand.'

He felt rather a hypocrite leading her on but was desperate to wash the days of travelling rough away from his family and himself. When push came to shove he would rather chop logs, draw water or work in her garden than enter her boudoir. But, meanwhile, he glinted his eyes at her and bowed again.

Rose took the little boys in and washed them before getting into the bath on the other side of the curtain. So it was that John helped a pale-faced Jane into the washing area, after his clean and beautiful brood had emerged and gone into the shop. The girl was so exhausted, waiting on Lady Eawiss hand and foot, that she seemed ready to drop to sleep at any second.

Pulling the curtain firmly across to preserve her modesty, John filled his hip bath from jugs of hot water and sank down with a great chunk of soap, closing his eyes and letting the warm waves wash over him. It was then that he heard something. Quiet though it was, he detected a sound coming from Jane's washing room. He sat bolt upright, wondering what it could be. There was a very faint noise, almost like whispered song, coming from behind the curtain. It occurred to him that Jane might have fallen asleep and could have sunk down under the water. Feeling like a peeping Tom, John drew the curtain back, only fractionally but enough for him to get a view of the other room.

From wherever he had hidden himself Blue Wolf had secretly emerged and knelt beside the tin bath, propping Jane's head on his shoulder. She had gone to sleep, quite deeply, and could indeed have been in danger of drowning. But it was not to this danger that Blue Wolf was giving his attention. He was washing her, every part of her, his hand lingering as he massaged her rosebud breasts, the delightful sweep of her flat stomach and even lower. And as he held her in his gentle embrace, he crooned to her some strange Indian lullaby.

The Apothecary realized that he was looking on a scene of true love: that whatever the future held for this extraordinary couple, the man, at least, loved the girl with all his heart. He must have let out the tiniest exclamation because Blue Wolf looked up and he and John stared soundlessly at each other. In those dark, lustrous eyes John felt he could read the suffering of this proud nation who, for centuries, had roamed their vast continent as hunters and now slowly, bit by bit, were having their land taken away from them by the encroachment of the pale-skinned people who wanted to live there, who were slowly and ruthlessly killing an entire race in order to achieve their ultimate goal.

They gazed at each other in silence for a minute or so and then John dropped his eyes and drew the curtain closed once more. He felt rather than heard Blue Wolf wake her up and the kiss that they gave one another, a deep kiss straight from their loving hearts, then the man left – God knows how he had crept in in the first place – and returned to the quiet depths of the forest.

The more John thought about what he had just seen, the more convinced he became that he should speak of it to no one. He had witnessed the dawning of a great love, had watched Blue Wolf's hands sweep over the girl's creamy flesh in an act of worship. He must keep the secret held by only him.

He made his way to the shop, bought a new shirt and hesitated over a pair of woollen breeches.

'Go on, Sir,' said Lady Eawiss. 'I shall lend you the money.'

It was the first decent thing the Apothecary had ever heard her say, and he looked at her rather suspiciously.

'I mean it. In return you can help me find a comfortable lodging when we reach Boston.'

'Do you intend to stay there, Milady?'

She simpered – actually simpered. 'Oh, well, that depends on how things turn out.'

'Perhaps you might remarry,' ventured John.

'Of course, nobody could replace my dear husband, Sir Bevis Eawiss. But who knows. It would be a comfort in one's old age to have a companion.'

John said, 'Talking of companions, how is Jane Hawthorne working out?'

'A dear child, of course, but not really up to snuff when it comes to being a personal maid. Somewhat sloppy in her appearance, don't you know.'

'As are we all, Madam, having walked miles and miles through hard terrain. I'll swear that I had so much dirt on me that I had turned quite a different colour.'

'Not the colour of an Indian, I hope.'

'I would not have worried too much. I think they are a fair-minded people. After all, we are trespassers on their land.'

'Nonsense, my dear Sir. This land belongs to the King of England.'

'It is all very fine for him to sit on his throne in Britain and claim lands that he has never seen, which clearly belong to someone else.'

She went red in the face and flared her nostrils, resembling one of the fat zephyrs that were engraved on the corners of a map.

'I think you speak subversively, Sir. I think you are a traitor. I shall definitely not lend you money for a new pair of breeches.'

The Apothecary bowed low. 'I would not have accepted your kindness, Milady. I intend to work for anything I purchase.'

At that moment Jane walked in, in full bloom after her bath and her meeting with Blue Wolf.

Lady Eawiss rounded on her furiously. 'There you are, my girl. You took your time. I thought you had drowned, so I did.'

Jane dropped a little curtsey and looked at the floor. 'Sorry, Milady.'

'I've a mind to box your ears.'

John was just about to intercede when at that moment Mistress Corey appeared, struggling with two enormous ewers of warm water. Both he and Jane went to help her and Lady Eawiss stumped out of the shop, mauve with anger. Fortunately her fury was deflected to the other bathing room where Lady Conway and Jake shared a bath in the room next to hers. How they could have both squeezed in made the rest of the party's collective mind blench but that night over supper, which John, Tom and the children consumed with the widow Corey, whose name they discovered was Dorcas, much conversation was directed to that question.

Dorcas Corey had offered them all accommodation for the night and put the children – all sharing one big bed – to bed herself, their father being offered a truckle in the same room. After their departure the discussion of the size of a tin bath had added a great deal of spice to the dinner-table conversation.

'I think they're a pair of rascals, so I do,' Tom had commented.

'You mean to say that they are confidence tricksters, Mister?' John had interrupted. 'Oh, come now, Thomas. Lady Conway is genuine enough. I read about her in *Tatler*. It concerned the fact that she was introduced to the house by old Lord Conway, who intended to marry her, but the hussy went off with the son instead.'

'What a saucy thing to do. But surely that is not her husband she is with.'

John's love of a good gossip, something he had been deprived of for months, rose unquelled.

'I am sure that Jake was a groom of her stable.'

'No question of it,' put in Tom, swigging back a glass of home-made beer. 'He's a boyo if ever I saw one, though a decent chap for all that.'

'But sharing a bath with Milady,' said Dorcas Corey in a shocked voice.

'People have been known to enjoy that sort of thing,' answered John, smiling at his memories.

'I think it's shocking,' answered Dorcas, but with a grin on her face.

Then the entire trio burst out laughing and John decided that living amongst this small community had a lot to be said for it after all.

FIVE

They worked for a week, repaying their hospitality. Everyone, including the beautiful Lady Conway and her so-called husband pulled their weight; even Lady Eawiss, accompanied by a great deal of sighing and complaining, did a little reluctant sewing. The two former beaux, now completely devoid of make-up and fashionable enhancement, were still speaking in the *bon ton* manner as they hewed logs together.

'Do you know this work is quite beneath my touch, Tracey.'

'But what option do we have, George? As you said we are at Point Non Plus and that's no bamboozlement.'

'I almost feel like downing tools and marrying some rich widow.'

'What? Have you taken leave of what sense is left in your poor, addled brain? We have come a long way and now we must be getting near Boston. Think of it, George. Civilization. I intend to get completely bosky as soon as I get there.'

'And what do you contemplate using for money?'

'I shall borrow some.'

'Off whom?'

'Never you mind.'

At the end of the week, Blue Wolf told them to be ready as dawn broke the next day, and announced that they would be heading for Portsmouth.

'Damn it, man, that's in blasted Hampshire,' George said loudly.

Blue Wolf looked down his chiselled nose. 'It is Abenaki land. But some settlers came and named it after a place in England, over a hundred years ago, when it was made into a town.'

'A town!' said Tracey Tremayne, his eyes dazzled.

Blue Wolf made an uninterpretable sound. 'They are at peace with my people. That is what allows them to build.'

'Are there places where one can go for a drink?' asked George.

'I think there are, yes.'

George turned to Tracey. 'My dear infant, race you there, what ho.'

In the event it turned out to be a longer hike than any of them had envisaged. One of Matthew's three hearty children went down with a fever and the Indian quickly improvised a contraption made of wood and skins in which the child could be carried. But Blue Wolf was clearly uneasy about something and that night talked briefly to John before disappearing into the stealthy forest.

'My friend, let me speak to you,' said the Apothecary as he caught sight of Blue Wolf making his way into the dense woodland.

The Indian man turned back. 'What is it?'

'Why are you leaving us?'

'You know why.'

'Is it because of Jane?'

The beautifully muscled shoulders rose and fell. 'Jane and I belong together. One day she will be mine.'

'Then why go?'

'Because of the fever of the child. We tribes of Indian people have no natural protection against your illnesses. In the past I have seen entire villages decimated by smallpox and measles, things against which we native peoples have no resistance. If the boy is carrying anything like that I must not go near him.'

'So you are going?'

'For the time being, yes.'

'How will we find our way?'

'Boston is only a few days' walk from here. You will be able to glimpse it shortly.'

'And with a sickly child and Lady Eawiss's corns?'

'Give yourselves a week. Don't push too hard.'

'So what about Jane Hawthorne? Do you intend to abandon her to her fate?'

'I have told you. Her fate lies with me. If I cannot marry her then I shall live a solitary life.'

John laughed. 'I cannot envisage that somehow. You are a man of flesh and blood for sure. So when will you return?'

'When you least expect it,' answered Blue Wolf and, crouching down, disappeared into the forest. John could have sworn that he saw an animal – an animal with a bluish tinge about its coat – lope off and disappear into the darkness.

During the night he gave what potions he could to bring the child's fever down and the next morning found that the boy was breathing more easily. He also discovered that during the hours of darkness the two male beauties had disappeared into the town, having talked Lady Eawiss into giving them a loan, and were now nowhere to be seen. Lady Conway and her ragamuffin husband had also disappeared into the fleshpot of Portsmouth, and so it was a rather pathetic straggle of people who made their way towards habitation the next morning. Irish Tom, carrying James on his shoulders, led the way, with John bearing Jasper a step behind. Then Matthew, conveying the litter between himself and Nick, his elder son. His nervous daughter clung to Jane's hand, while limping along in the rear came Lady Eawiss, clutching her portmanteau and moaning and groaning loudly, though nobody was listening to her.

'So Blue Wolf has left us?' Irish Tom said.

'Only fear of disease has sent him off.' John lowered his voice. 'He loves Jane Hawthorne to a fierce degree.'

'Do you think he'll come back for her?'

'I would lay money on it.'

'Let it be hoped that that is not the case, as you haven't got any.'

John lowered his voice even further. 'Do you know as he went off last night I could swear that I saw a blue wolf in the forest.'

The Irishman crossed himself. 'Now don't go telling me such things, Sorrh. I won't be able to get a wink of sleep.'

John laughed. 'It was only an illusion. The Indian is a real man, I assure you.'

And the Apothecary thought back to what he had seen in the bath house, a secret that he would never tell a living soul, and smiled to himself.

The town of Portsmouth was quite considerable, consisting of a street of white weather-boarded buildings with several squares and alleyways leading off it. It had a calm but lively atmosphere and John headed for a house which had a handwritten notice in the window saying 'Rooms to Let'. Having obtained accommodation for himself and his family, he set out to explore, leaving the children in the fluttering hands of Lady Eawiss, who had announced that she was exhausted and had immediately booked a room and a small cupboard-like space for Jane Hawthorne. Fortunately, Jane was also there to keep an eye on the young people.

As the Apothecary strolled along, he thought about the extraordinary paths his life had taken and the many highways he had trodden, but surely none so strange as this one. He had never, even in his most extravagant dreams, envisaged that he would be walking along the rustic street of a pioneering township in the wild and uncharted lands of Indian country, heading for Boston, a town he knew nothing about, to sell his sparkling water to a customer who would by now believe him to be dead.

A roar of voices broke into his introspection. It was the dull roar of a crowd of about twenty people. Interest piqued, the Apothecary walked in its direction. He found himself standing before a plain wooden house, much like the others except that it had a dark, crabbed appearance and a swinging sign outside that read The Castle. Without hesitation, John Rawlings stepped inside.

His eye was immediately caught by a game for four players – probably whist – which was causing a sensation thanks to the audacity of one particular player who appeared to be trumping everyone else. He sat with his legs thrust forward, his hat hiding his face, his long dark hair pulled back and tied with a crimson ribbon. Even as John looked at him he felt a thrill of recognition, yet could not place the fellow at all.

'I trump your ace,' the card player said – and John stood in silent contemplation. And then light dawned. It was an impossibility and yet his eyes and brain told him differently. He was looking at Julian Wychwood, whom he had last seen clinging to a piece of wreckage and screaming as a current had swept him out to the sea and to certain death.

'Julian?' John asked, still unsure.

The card player looked up then shot to his full height, over six feet tall. 'John? John Rawlings?'

'Yes, of all the taverns in all the towns! Dammit, man, how did you get here?'

'The Wychwood luck. But come, let me buy you a drink and then hear all your adventures. Tell me, where are you heading?'

'For Boston.'

'Well, damme, so am I. But then you knew that.'

'Some talk of retrieving your late mother's fortune if I recall a conversation on the ship – if such a thing exists.'

Wychwood raised a sleek black brow and gave one of his devilish smiles. 'Well, that is a thing we shall no doubt learn.'

'Indeed, indeed,' John answered, and was greatly relieved when Julian shouted 'I play no further' and they walked into a quiet corner and sat down to hear one another's story.

If John's tale of survival was amazing, Julian trumped him with all the grandeur of a professional card player. He had indeed been dragged out to sea by a wild and terrifying current but had been picked up by a canoe of Indians, who were out that far in the ocean for purposes of hiding a body of someone they had disposed of illegally.

'In short, they had murdered the wretched fellow,' said Julian in a casual voice.

'Were they blackguards?' John asked.

'Every last one of 'em.'

The story progressed. Julian was taken to an Indian village where he was stripped naked and tied to a pole while all the young bucks danced around him chanting. This wild behaviour stopped at midnight when a beautiful Indian girl had crept out of her wigwam, cut him loose and rushed into the forest with him on the condition that he make love to her.

'And did you?' asked John, thinking the tale tall but possible.

'Naturally. One should never refuse a lady. Gracious man, you must know that.'

'Well, it depends on the circumstances . . .'

'Circumstances rubbish! I always accede to their every whim.'

'Even when she's skin and bone, sour-faced and seventy?'

'Even then.'

The Apothecary laughed out loud, considering that Julian was growing more outrageous with every passing minute but glad indeed to have become reacquainted with this fantastic rogue. As they both drank more – a raw, kicking rum – the story continued but John lost the thread. According to Julian he had married the chief's daughter, led an Indian hunting party into the forest and tramped across the frozen lakes in snow shoes, then escaped and returned to civilization. On the way he had wrestled a bear and had his wounds treated by a magic man, and had slept with a willing widow who had given him her late husband's clothes. It was all too unbelievable but, knowing Julian, might just have a hint of truth about it.

The two men rolled home in the darkness, singing a patriotic song, and somebody opened a window above and hurled the contents of a chamber pot in their direction. After this they quietened down, crept into their various lodging houses and fell into a sleep aided greatly by alcoholic beverage.

The next morning saw the final trek to Boston begin.

SIX

The whole party was present as they glimpsed the gallows, which stood outside the gates of Boston town. The children halted, round-eyed, small hands creeping up to feel an adult's reassuring grasp. Lady Eawiss was preparing to faint but had a hissed, 'Courage, Madam, for God's sake,' from Lady Conway, who stood looking untidily beautiful, flanked by Jake, whose blue eyes held a hostile hardness for Julian Wychwood, loitering on her other side and clearly admiring the lady.

Rose Rawlings made a little sound and took the hands of her two brothers, who looked at the rotting corpses with wonderment. Matthew's three country kinder stood silently – Dickon having shaken off his fever – though the little girl, Anna, hid behind her father's great legs. Suicide graves and those of criminals stood round the place of execution, marked out by little heaps of stones. It was a dismal and depressing sight, and when the sudden silence was broken by the roar of a bull which stood in a nearby field, surveying them with a bloody eye, the party almost ran to the town gate.

This consisted of two arches, through the larger of which passed horsemen, wagons and herds of cattle. Through the other pedestrians walked. The entire area was called Boston Neck and was the only way of entering the city, the rest of it being surrounded by water. John found that they were standing in Orange Street which ran before them, though the name of the thoroughfare changed from time to time.

'It's quite a small town,' said Jake, his accent notably Irish.

'It's the biggest that I've seen since we got here,' answered Tom.

'La,' remarked Tracey, 'it's nothing compared with London.'

'I'd keep this kind of talk quiet if I were you. Remember that the people who live here are Bostonians and might not take those thoughts too kindly.'

'But the British sent troops here nearly five years ago.'

'That is precisely my point. How would you like it if London had an invading force in residence?'

The road upon which they were travelling ended at the State House, a magnificent building with a wide and elevated staircase leading to the main entrance, above which stood a balcony from which proclamations may be made. Above this again was another gracious, high-windowed floor, all culminating in a tall open square tower topped with a weather vane. As a symbol of being a British colony, a crowned lion rampant stood with a unicorn opposite at the corners of the roof.

'I call that a magnificent sight, so I do,' said Irish Tom, while everyone else, surprisingly including Lady Eawiss, let out small noises of appreciation.

They turned right and before their eyes Boston Harbour appeared, beautiful and sparkling, the road they were walking carrying on out to sea for half a mile in the longest wharf that John had ever seen. Large ships were moored there and he felt an enormous energy pulse through him, heard high, flirty whistles, the peals of bells from the streets, saw sailors scurrying about like ants and all the shouts and yells of tradespeople that told him this small city was teeming with life. Furthermore, Boston smelled. Of people, of fish, the bursting ocean, the sweet and lovely aroma of wood smoke.

Rose tugged his hand. 'I like this place, Papa.'

John ruffled her curls. 'So do I, sweetheart.'

Initial exploring done, the party found themselves lodging houses, Lady Eawiss going to the grandest, Matthew to the cheapest and John to the cleanest. They had all borrowed substantially from the old dame who was charging them five per cent interest on their various loans. Jake O'Farrell had suggested to her, quite straight-faced, that she should set up a bank and become a merchant, and had been quite surprised when she had looked thoughtful and her eyes had narrowed to gimlets.

John and his family had dined at two o'clock at The Bunch of Grapes. Jasper and James, in their tattered clothes, behaved very well. Rose had kept her eyes down, the trouble being that she was served by an attractive young waiter, aged about seventeen, clearly the helping hand of the house.

'Are you visitors to Boston, Sir?' he had asked John.

His voice was quite surprising, not quite English but with a certain flat pronunciation of vowel sounds.

'Yes, after a lot of adventures, we are.'

'Well, if you want anyone to show you round I'd be quite willing to act as your guide.' He made this remark directly to Rose who sat dumbly gazing at the tablecloth. For the very first time the Apothecary devoted his entire attention to his daughter. She must be rising thirteen and would soon be starting her courses, by which means the mysterious moon showed its influence over a woman's body. Or perhaps she already had and was having to deal with that enormous change without a mother to speak to. Or had Jane Hawthorne taken over and guided and explained to Rose what she must do and what it all meant? He suddenly felt ashamed of himself for being such a poor, uncaring father. Yet it wasn't as if he didn't love her. It was simply that his thoughts had been elsewhere, concentrating on all the external things rather than on family matters. But this sudden blushing at the small attention of a seventeen-year-old lad had plunged John Rawlings into deep thought. He was silent for a moment, then looked up.

'Thank you. Most kind. We may well take you up on your offer. But first of all you might be good enough to tell me where I can find the Orange Tree Tavern.'

'Oh, Mr Hallowell's place. Such a shame about him, Sir.'

A feeling of dread hit the pit of John's stomach. 'Why? What's happened to him?'

The boy's eager to please expression changed to one of such mournful mien that the twins giggled quietly.

'He died, Sir. About two months ago.'

John felt startled, his only contact in Boston suddenly swept away.

At last Rose looked up. 'What are you going to do, Papa?'

John glanced from his daughter to the boy, who stood, clearly anxious, awaiting further instructions.

'I'm not sure at the moment. But I'd like some directions as to how to get to the Orange Tree Tavern, if you would be so obliging.'

'Certainly, Sir. It's in the North End of Boston, a step or two from here. If you can wait until we close I can show you the way.'

John, who had taken a liking to the tawny-headed youngster, answered, 'Tonight at six of the clock would suit me well. I can take my small boys home and put them to bed, then meet you outside.'

'Will you be coming, Miss?' the boy asked Rose politely.

Rose's glance fluttered to contemplation of the tablecloth once more.

John was much amused. 'I'm sure she'd love to see more of Boston, wouldn't you, my dear?' he asked, very straight-faced.

'I will come if I am not too tired,' she replied with sudden spirit, and John was pleased at her reaction.

On the way home she urged John into a milliner and begged him to buy her a new feathered hat. He considered that it made her look older but then with a wry grin thought that this was probably the general idea. Silently raising his eyes to heaven, he paid for it with money borrowed from the grande dame, Eawiss, at the same time thanking the quirk of destiny that had brought him and his family, to say nothing of his many and varied friends, through the ordeal of the shipwreck and given him the ability to take his young daughter into a milliners to buy her a bit of frippery headwear.

At six o'clock he met the young man, who introduced himself as Tristram, standing at the pre-arranged meeting place. Rose, who had recovered some of her former composure, dropped him a little curtsey and said, 'Good evening, Master . . .?'

'Snow, Ma'am. And who do I have the pleasure of addressing?'

'Rose Rawlings. My father is John of the same surname.'

Tristram bowed, fairly elegantly, and John thought that his parents must have been reasonably well-educated people.

'Tell me, how do you come to be here?' he asked.

'My grandpapa was French and came to Boston when he was a boy of thirteen. He was apprenticed to a doctor, just running errands and general dogsbodying. But he worked hard, eventually went to Harvard and came back to serve out the rest of his time with the doctor, assisting him with minor cases. Eventually he set up on his own and was called Doctor Snow – his real name was Neige but he changed it so as to be easier for the patients. He's still alive and I live with him in the north of town.'

'And your parents?' asked John.

'They both died of smallpox. Boston had an epidemic of it when I was still in my cradle. My grandpa worked night and day to save them but even he couldn't do it. Then my grandma caught it as well but she survived. Anyway, it's just me and my grandpa now. It's quite a mannish household but for Minnie.'

'Minnie?' Rose asked.

'Our black slave. But she's more like my mama. She's big and jolly and she nursed me right from the start. I think she's the most wonderful woman. She's going to stay with us for the rest of her life.'

'And who are you apprenticed to?' John enquired.

'I'm not officially. I work for Doctor Joseph Warren. He's one of the younger doctors hereabouts. But he's a fine physician and he does a great deal of good.'

'Does he have an apothecary?' John asked, only half seriously.

'Yes, he has – why do you ask?'

'Because that was my profession when I lived in London.'

'Really? I am sure he would be most interested to meet you. Will you come and have dinner with us one day – and Miss Rose too, of course.'

'Of course,' murmured John. Louder, he said, 'We should be delighted. Perhaps you would confirm the date and time with Doctor Warren first.'

They had drawn abreast of a very impressive building as they walked along, and John stopped in his tracks to admire it.

'My word, Boston has some fine public places,' he said. 'What is this one?'

Tristram looked at the hall with pride, standing rather closer to Rose than was necessary, John thought with a slightly raised eyebrow.

'It is called the Faneuil Hall, named after Peter Faneuil, a local and very successful businessman who had it built. However, it was gutted by fire in 1761 and the repairs were paid for by public lottery.'

'Is it a theatre?' John asked, a picture of Coralie Clive flashing through his mind.

Tristram lowered his voice. 'There is a law against theatre in Boston. They say that plays generally tend to increase immorality, impiety and a contempt for religion.'

'Good God!'

Tristram grinned. 'But there are one or two people who have set up in barns and put on shows for the enjoyment of the population.'

'And they don't get caught?'

'Not very often.'

They walked on, passing a house near the Faneuil Hall, which Tristram pointed out as being that of Doctor Warren.

'That is where I work but it is all very subdued in there at the moment. Mrs Warren suffers with her health, you know, so I am afraid our dinner engagement will have to be delayed.'

'What is the trouble?'

The boy looked doubtful. 'I don't really know. She's just had a baby and she seems to be finding it hard to recover. But she has no actual illness.'

'Powdered Autumn Gentian might be helpful.'

'I can hardly suggest anything, Sir. It would not be my place.'

Rose spoke up. 'I think that is silly of you. I would not be backward if she were my employer's wife. Doctor or no doctor.'

'John said, 'Come now, Rose—'

But Tristram interrupted. 'Yes, you're right. I'll mention it tomorrow.'

They crossed the bridge running over the Mill Stream and found themselves in the North End of Boston. It was a strange mixture of elegant houses and those of the artisans, the vast majority of whose homes were built on land behind those of the grander folk. This had led to a spider's web of alleyways and twittens, some only wide enough for people to walk along in single file. When these walkways were roofed over the usage to which they were put defied belief. Sanitation was appalling, as the privies ran into the wells. Add the death tolls from fever and frequent fires and one would have thought that this was not a pleasant place to live. And yet there was a cheerfulness about the North End that came out in the people that John passed as he went along. Women with baskets over their arms bobbed him a brief curtsey and a man in a blue cloak flourished his hat. There was a truly neighbourly atmosphere.

They paraded as far as Charter Street, where John decided that they had had enough and should think about returning to their lodgings. He had drawn ahead of the two young people and, when he turned his head to speak to them, saw them laughing and being jolly together. He smiled.

'Tristram, will you escort Miss Rose back to her lodgings? I want to look for some friends of mine.'

'Certainly, Sir. Will you be able to find your way back?'

'Very easily. Please guard my daughter well. She is a precious girl and needs treating with reverence.'

He said this last with a fine show of hypocrisy, remembering his own early years and his longing for his master's female servants – or at least those of them young enough to give him a good run up to the top of the house where their bedrooms were concealed. With a somewhat sad shake of his head he entered the Orange Tree, which Tristram had pointed out to him. From within came the goodly smell of rum and the sounds of laughter.

It took less than a minute to see that several of his friends had foregathered there. Sir Julian Wychwood was seated at a table, intent on sharping cards as usual, Jake O'Farrell was telling a mighty story which had almost the entire gathering in hysterics, stout-hearted Matthew was laughing heartily and Lady Conway, the only woman in the tavern, was talking earnestly with a tallish man, beautifully dressed, whose very light blue eyes sparkled and gleamed in the light thrown by the inn's many candles. John stood silently for a moment, surveying the scene, then he walked up to Her Ladyship and swept a bow. 'Good evening, Milady.'

She turned with a start, not having noticed him come in. 'Gracious, you made me jump. How are you, Mr Rawlings? I did not expect to find you in this part of town. May I introduce you to my friend, Doctor Joseph Warren?'

It struck John as odd that she should have made a friend so quickly, so soon after their arrival, but he said nothing, bowing before the stranger, who bowed in return. He was a good-looking man, there could be no doubt of that, his face lively and enthu-siastic, allowing a rapid change of expressions, his eyes lighting up with a certain boyish charm whenever he spoke.

'Doctor Warren,' John said, 'I feel that I know you already, Sir. I have just spent the afternoon with your young employee. He was kind enough to guide my daughter and myself around the town.'

'Ah, you must mean young Tristram Snow. He had the day off today. I'm glad he made himself useful.'

'He was indeed, Sir.'

There was an undeniable warmth about Joseph Warren. In particular, the Apothecary noticed his hands, long fingered and incredibly clean, the moons on his nails white and perfect. Yet John felt that those outstanding blue eyes – laughing and relaxed at the moment – might hold a hint of fanaticism behind their mild exterior. But the man was speaking.

'I must not be out late. My wife is very frail at the moment, alas.'

John looked saddened but made no comment, feeling that to do so would be to reveal young Snow's confidence.

'How many children have you now?' Lady Conway asked.

'Four, Demelza. I fear the fourth pregnancy was too much for poor Elizabeth. She is very weakened by it and cannot seem to pull round.'

John was astounded – not by the story of Mrs Warren's post-natal struggles but by the fact that the young doctor knew Lady Conway's Christian name. In all the months they had travelled together he had never heard it mentioned, Jake calling his wife Ella, presumably as a shortening. Now he said, 'Forgive me, but have you two met before?'

Demelza's freshwater eyes met his in a cool, somewhat calculating, glance.

'Oh, yes, you see I was born in Boston. My family lived here for some while. I knew Joseph when he was a small boy.'

'Did you go to school with him?'

'Lud, no. He was a clever little devil and went to the Latin school. I was a girl so I was sent to a dame school and then, aged fourteen, put on a boat and made my way to England. So there was no finishing school for me, alas.'

'I didn't know they had finishing schools for young ladies in Boston.'

Dr Warren put in: 'They used not to, Demelza is jesting. But nowadays an Englishwoman runs one. What is her name now?'

'Madame Clive,' answered Demelza Conway.

'That's it, Clive,' said Dr Warren.

And neither looked at John, who had one hand out on the bar, supporting him while the words seemed to pound and re-echo in his brain. Eventually he spoke, his voice hoarse and strained. 'Did she do acting at all?'

Joseph Warren raised his brows. 'Theatrical performances are not allowed in Boston. They offend religious susceptibilities. But then there's a lot that happens here that is kept *sotto voce*. I believe Madame Clive holds performances for her girls. Nobody goes except the parents – and one or two others who creep in to get a bit of culture.' Joseph actually giggled. 'I was only fifteen when I saw an excerpt from *The Way of the World*. My parents took me. But I can remember laughing so much that I almost had a seizure. Not that I understood the play; it was the bravura of the whole occasion that I relished.'

'And where does Madame Clive put on these performances?'

'In a barn near her cottage.'

'Which is where?'

'Oh, quite a smart place, though small. It's not far from Hancock's great mansion on the east side.'

'Tell me, does she have a first name, by any chance?'

Joseph and Demelza both put their heads on one side, smiling. They looked like a pair of wise parrots. Eventually, he said, 'No. She must have, of course, but I'm afraid I don't know it.'

And that was that. Was it just blind hope that made the Apothecary's hands tremble as he went to pick up his glass, or was it just general fatigue? Could it be possible that the once great actress, disillusioned with life in Britain, desperate to get away from her daughter, had emigrated to the Colonies? Or was it just John's faint dream that yet again their paths might cross that planted the seed within his mind? One day soon, he thought, he would find the answer.

SEVEN

The first thing to do, John thought as he rose the next morning, was to eat a hearty breakfast, then to settle his children in with a healthy, hard-working girl who could act as a temporary nanny. After that he would go hunting for some useful employment which would bring them in some much-needed money until a ship sailing for London appeared in the docks. Having been given some useful addresses by his landlady, he left the children in the guardianship of Jane Hawthorne, who was having a quiet morning due to Lady Eawiss having a bad spell of gout which confined her to bed, and walked first to the Orange Tree Tavern.

Last night it had been impossible to speak to anyone about the fate of Josiah Hallowell, but John vividly recalled a niece being mentioned in the fateful letter sent to him in London and decided that it must be she that he attempted to find. The tavern was closed but there were sounds from the back of someone chopping wood, so calling out, 'Hello,' the Apothecary made his way to the paved area behind the building.

A terribly plain girl with scrawny hair tied into two listless plaits which hung about her thin shoulders had an axe in her hand and was hacking away at a large piece of wood which failed completely to yield to her savage swipes. She looked up as John entered the yard and wrinkled up her nose. 'Yes?'

'Miss Hallowell?'

'Yes.'

'My name is Rawlings. John Rawlings.'

She stared blankly, her eyes enlarged by a pair of spectacles, the sides of which sat uncomfortably on her ears. 'Who?'

'Rawlings. I'm an apothecary. Originally from Nassau Street, Soho, in London.'

'Well, this is a tavern. The herbalist is in North Square.'

'I've come about a letter I had from Josiah Hallowell.'

'He's dead.'

'I am aware of that, Mistress.'

'So?'

'If you'll just let me speak, I will tell you why I'm here.'

She looked him up and down and John concluded that she was quite one of the ugliest little things he had ever seen in his life. Her brown eyes, hugely enlarged by the magnifying lenses, had a horrendous squint and there was a gap through which one could have slid a ruler between her two front teeth.

'I'm not stopping you,' she answered, the longest sentence she had ever used as far as he was concerned.

John bowed. 'Madam, the letter from the late Mr Hallowell invited me to visit him in Boston to talk about the sparkling water I produce. Apparently his niece – who left England to live with him – bought some and liked it so much that she took him a sample. Do you know what I'm talking about?'

She put down the axe, wiped her sleeve across her brow and said, 'Yes.'

'Are you the niece?' he asked, relieved that he had finally established the reason for his call.

'Yes,' she answered, and the verbal flood gates opened. 'I wouldn't have come if I'd know what it would be like. I mean to say, I lived in Bristol, which was twice the size of this place. And when I get here, what do I find? I'm supposed to be maid-of-all-work. My uncle promised me that I could find a husband in Boston. But do I find one. No, no, no!' She sat down on an upturned barrel. 'I'm sick of the place. I really mean it. All the unmarried men are either oaves – is that right? No, it's oafs. Or too high up the social ladder. Talk about disappointing. I could weep.'

And this she proceeded to do, very noisily and with much blowing of the nose.

John said, 'Come, come, my dear. There's no need to take on so. You could always sell the tavern and set yourself up as a governess or some such.'

She looked up at him, snotty and miserable, and he said impulsively, 'I could always rent premises from you and turn them into an apothecary's shop.'

She brightened. 'Could we serve drinks on the side?'

'I don't know about alcohol but I could see no harm in serving restoring medicinal potions and cups of tea or coffee.'

'And glasses of cooling lemonade perhaps?'

'Why not?'

It was all so foolish, so quicksilver fast, like a decision made on the turn of a coin, but it appealed to the Apothecary enormously. There was one problem, however. He looked at the girl, now rapidly drying her eyes and readjusting her spectacles.

'Can I owe you the first week's rent? I am quite cucumberish at the moment.'

She smiled. 'Tell me no more of it. I have been cucumberish since my arrival here.' She stood up. 'But somehow I feel I can trust you. Where were you an apothecary?'

'In Shug Lane, Piccadilly, London, Ma'am. I had a letter of introduction from your late uncle with me. The reason that I do not bear it is that our good ship was blown off course and finally foundered in the sea off the rocky coastland west of Boston. The fact that I am here at all is nothing short of a miracle.'

The ugly little girl – she could not have been more than twenty years old at the most – clasped her hands together and said, 'You have come as my saviour, Sir. I knew you would. I read it in the tea leaves.'

They worked hard all that day, John hurrying round to a sign-maker to make up a painted emblem which read 'At the sign of the Orange Tree, John Rawlings, Apothecary of London, and Suzanne Hallowell, Tavern Keeper. The selling and prescribing of medicinal compounds in one room and delicious drinks and refreshments in another will take place on these premises forthwith.'

Three days later John had enrolled his boys into Dame Foster's School for Young Children but was still puzzling what would be the best education for Rose. Still, he had plunged headlong into his new business regardless of outside interests.

His stock of herbs was pitifully low and nothing was really ready, yet he had all his old training to fall back on, knew what to do in emergencies and was capable of making decisions, though admittedly he had sometimes acted on instinct alone. So with a stout heart and a nervous gut, John and Suzanne had opened their apothecary's shop-cum-tea-drinking establishment on a Saturday morning.

Outside, the twins, dressed in identical sailor suits, plied hand bells noisily, shouting, 'Orange Tree opening today, Orange Tree opening today,' at the tops of their voices. And those ladies who had wandered in to take some refreshment suddenly remembered that they had a megrim from time-to-time and made their way to the other room where the Apothecary stood, clean-shaven and smelling fresh, and sought his advice.

But John's greatest triumph had been when Dr Joseph Warren had rushed in during the afternoon, his looks marred by the swelling on his face, his voice barely recognizable as he said through gritted teeth, 'I can't stand this pain much longer. Take the bloody thing out.'

A former snug had been converted into a consulting room and John, seeing at once that the poor man of medicine was agonized by toothache, led him quickly inside, gave him a large brandy to settle Warren's nerves – taking a swift one himself, meanwhile – and put on his long apron. He dipped the steel pelican – a dental application that he had borrowed from a blacksmith of all people – and gripping the crown of the aching tooth, prised it out sideways. There was a great deal of blood and a howl of pain from the doctor, who had broken out in a muck sweat at the treatment. Tactfully, the Apothecary wiped him down before applying the towel to himself.

'God Almighty,' mumbled the doctor, 'that was appalling. Had it rotted?'

John passed him another shot of brandy then nodded before applying a lint soaked in Lady's Bedstraw, which he had found growing wild when out frantically looking for simples two days earlier.

Warren had shaken his head and mouthed, 'I thought so. But thank you.'

John smiled. 'I won't say it has been a pleasure, Doctor Warren. You have another one in there which I would like to have a look at, if you have no objection.'

The doctor gave a half-hearted smile and opened his poor injured mouth once more. Sure enough, there was a nasty abscess forming beside the eye tooth that had just been drawn. John pulled a face and Warren rolled a frantic eye.

'I'm afraid it's a bad one, Doctor Warren. Can you bear it now or do you want to come back?'

The doctor sighed, long and deep. 'Do it now but give me another brandy first. I'll settle up later.'

The Apothecary nodded and reinserted the steel pelican.

An hour later and it was all over. A somewhat tipsy Dr Warren had left the premises, declaring to the world in general that he had no patients that night and was going to see someone about getting some false teeth made. John had refused to take any money from him, cleverly extracting more value than teeth. The grateful doctor had promised to send him a load of his prescriptions together with various ladies suffering from minor ailments. He also agreed to recommend John Rawlings to anyone whose teeth were in a terminal condition.

'So who is this man who's going to make you a false set?'

'His name is Paul Revere. He's a clever chap and extremely loyal to the city of Boston,' Warren answered. 'He can do anything: clean your teeth, mend your umbrella, fix you up with spectacles . . .'

John made a mental note to pass this information on to Suzanne.

'. . . make rattles for a baby. He also happens to be the finest silversmith I know.'

'I must make his acquaintance.'

'Oh, indeed you must, believe me,' answered Dr Warren and made his way, very carefully, into the dusk.

EIGHT

The first month in which the group who had come to Boston through the wilds of Indian country, having been shipwrecked and saved, had passed peacefully enough. Matthew had placed his children in school and gone to work on the docks; Jake O'Farrell had become coachman to a kindly citizen, John Hancock, while his enigmatic wife, Demelza Conway, gave private lessons to women and girls in riding gracefully. Tracey and George, still revealing nothing of their sexuality, had opened a school of swordsmanship and dancing, none too successfully it would appear, the men of Boston being too down-to-earth for such fol-de-rolls and fancies. Lady Eawiss kept little Jane Hawthorne run off her feet but paraded herself each day in the teahouses and shops. Rumour was out that she was a rich widow, and therefore there were several ne'er-do-well gentlemen who made it their business to chat to her amicably, at which courtesy she blushed and simpered.

John's apothecary shop had opened in earnest. A large spare room at the back of the premises had been converted and now had a separate entrance. So though by day Suzanne served tea and cakes, by night, the apothecary having closed, they returned to their former glory as a tavern and meeting house. This was run most adequately by Irish Tom, whose very size proved a discouragement to those who wanted to make any trouble. Meanwhile, the Apothecary stayed around for a while in case of medicinal emergencies. All would have been well in his world had it not been for Rose, who had not yet found a suitable school. So it was that one evening in late April, John decided to walk to the establishment run by a certain Madame Clive.

It was situated on the east side of Boston, in a house with a barn behind it. All the way there, John felt that his legs had grown leaden, that his heartbeat was irregular, that he was as attractive to look at as a withered old fig. Thoughts that the owner must be the girl with whom he had fallen in love all those

years ago haunted him as he walked slowly on, past the trees
that hid the workhouse from public view, past the British Army
regiments, many of whom were camped on the Common and
whose common humanity resulted in a smell that hit the nostrils
as one approached.

In the fading light of an April dusk, John went through every
transition possible for a human to experience. All other thoughts
were banished from his mind except those of a young lover
approaching his sweetheart. Then he took himself to task so
firmly that he physically flinched from the castigation. And
then his mood swung once more and he laughed aloud and
thought of picking a bunch of wild flowers to take to the lady,
whether she be his former mistress or not. Rose came firmly
into his mind and his thoughts turned away from love, knowing
that she must finish her education as she had started and learn
about the finer things in life.

He passed the home of one of the richest families in Boston,
the Hancocks. There it stood in all its splendour, three storeys
high and made of glistening stone. From within, John could hear
the sound of voices, probably made by guests invited for cards.
The extremely educated tones of Sir Julian Wychwood rang out,
his British accent loud and clear in the stillness of the dusk. John
thought that of all the gang who had been saved, Julian was the
one who had fallen on his feet without any difficulty at all.
Brilliance at games of chance was international – the fact that
Julian won large sums of money merely regrettable.

A few steps forward brought the Apothecary to a dwelling
built close to the Hancock estate with the tell-tale sign of having
a barn in close proximity. There was no other building that he
could see nearby, so after a few moments of hesitation he seized
the knocker and gave a gentle rap. The door was opened almost
immediately by a black slave with a lighted candle. John bowed
his head.

'Good evening. Would it be possible to see Madame Clive,
please?'

The girl bobbed, her eyes enormous in the candlelight. 'No, Sir.
She gone out. She won't be back till later.'

John's tremendous anticipation came crashing down, leaving
him feeling somewhat small and sad. He toyed with the idea of

asking whether he could wait, then discarded that. Instead he said, 'May I deposit my card and call again?'

'Why, yessir. I'll tell Madame Clive that you came.' She held out a silver tray. 'If you would be kind enough, Sir, to put your name on this here.'

John searched frantically and found what he was looking for – an elegant card case that he had bought from Paul Revere very recently. He handed the girl a card. She read it out loud.

'John Rawlings, A-poth-o-cary. The Orange Tree, Princes Street, Boston. I will give it to Madame Clive as soon as she returns.'

But John did not answer, his eyes going past the girl and seeing a dimly lit portrait behind her. He stared at it, then said, 'Would you mind holding your candle up to that, please?'

Her gaze grew surprised but she obediently went up to the portrait and held the light beneath so that the reflection of the flame shone on it. John sighed deeply, seeing a face that had once been so familiar to him but which had changed in the way that all human faces change with the passing of each year. Yet in a way it had grown more beautiful, more tender but at the same time tougher, the lovely young girl's fine lines gone and in their place others – determination, courageousness, a fortitude born of pain and hardship. There was also a resolve to keep living, to enjoy what was left, to fight to the finish and shout hurrah at the end of it all.

He must have exclaimed and taken a pace forward, because the girl called out, 'Abraham, come ye here a minute.'

From the back of the house came the clump of running feet and a large negro, dressed in bright blue breeches and a white shirt, came, round-eyed, to see what was going on. John took a step back, apologising.

'I'm sorry if I startled you. I'll be going now. Please present my compliments to Madame Clive.'

Leaving his calling card, John backed his way out and hurried off. Near the King's Chapel on Treamount Street stood a tavern called the Duke of Marlborough, filled with the British militia, drinking beer and talking loudly. John, somewhat cautiously, made his way inside, determined to have a drink even though he had heard the inn spoken of as a haunt for Englishmen which would not be touched by the true Bostonians. Every night since the occupation by the British there were tavern brawls and affrays, the sullen men of Boston angry with the invaders. Females in the alleyways of the North End were jostled and raped by the occupying militia and soldiers were shoved off wharves and bridges to emerge spluttering in the water below. Some girls welcomed them secretly into their beds and the birth rate soared. In view of all this, John entered the tavern quietly and sat down in the shadows, consuming a long pint of ale.

A figure sitting opposite him said, 'Good evening to you,' in a cultured English voice. The Apothecary answered, 'Good evening,' and the other exclaimed, 'You're a Britisher, by gad.' John peered and saw that he was looking into the face of an officer in the occupying army from the twenty-ninth regiment. The other went on to introduce himself.

'Harry Dalrymple,' he said, holding out his hand. 'I'm a lieutenant, son of the big cheese himself.'

John gave a courteous little bow, wondering as he did so what the young man could be talking about. Then he realized that he must be the son of Colonel William Dalrymple, who shared with Colonel Carr the dubious honour of controlling the troops stationed in Boston. He was as highly regarded by the Bostonians as he regarded them. Not at all. John cleared his throat, not quite certain what to say next.

'I realize my papa is not considered to be more than a total ass,' Harry said in a whisper. 'But consider his position. You are requested by your government to sail to an unruly colony that is refusing to do all kinds of things and as a result you are universally hated. I mean, what's the poor feller to do?'

John leant forward and murmured his reply. 'Look, I only arrived here a month ago and I made a vow to myself that I would not get involved in Boston's internal affairs. I pity your father and I pity the Bostonians. They both think they're right – they probably both are to a certain extent – but far be it for me to criticize either side. Let me buy you a drink, Sir, and not talk politics.'

Harry Dalrymple grinned widely. 'Agreed,' he said. Then added, 'A glass of rum, if you please.'

They passed a pleasant evening, discussing the merits of their various billets. John and his family had moved in with Suzanne, who occupied her late uncle's strange but charming little house on North Square. The twins shared a small room at the back, while Rose slept in a slightly larger room which was her own entirely. Upstairs, in the hot and airless loft was John, slightly worried by the girl's presence, not because he felt in the least drawn to her but, with usual male conceit, wondered if she might be to him. The lieutenant, on the other hand, had been given a room in a house with three beautiful daughters and was very attracted to the eldest, Millicent, much to the annoyance of the other two, who called him names and were rude to him.

'It was ever thus,' said the Apothecary, feeling a trifle tipsy and enjoying the pleasant sensations that went with it.

'Yes,' agreed Harry in the same state, pleasurably melancholic.

They left the tavern together and walked a little way down the road where Harry saluted and turned off to a trim house with window boxes outside. John continued on his way to the North End and then it happened: in the mist of that April evening he saw a figure coming towards him. It was female, he recognized that, but as to her actual features it was impossible to see under the brim of her fashionable hat, obviously purchased in London. She swept straight past him and the smell of her exotic, sharp perfume was all about him, filling his nostrils with secret memories of moments that he and she had shared, of exotic dreams and exquisite realities. He turned and watched her retreat into the misty night, and though he said her name beneath his breath, he never cried it aloud until she was gone, far out of earshot. Only then did he say 'Coralie' in a voice filled with hope and a longing to see her again and take her into his arms.

NINE

I t was as if a kind of madness seized Boston in the next few months. With the changing seasons, as summer blazed its way into the heavens and the sun daily glared at them like a belligerent eye, the men of the town grew more and more inflamed. Secret meetings were held, John felt sure of that, watching the whispered furtive conversations, the strange handshakes, the manner in which people gave each other close and knowing eye contact.

Following the death of his wife, Dr Joseph Warren had shrunk into himself. He was still charming, polite and friendly, but his openness had gone. Now it was as if he guarded some strange secret that nobody was privy to. Many of his friends were fellow Masons and John wondered how many of these closet meetings hid an even more clandestine society to which only the chosen few were called. But the Apothecary, too, felt in the grip of a great secret which, even when he tried to rationalize it, made no sense to him. He would not – indeed, could not – face the thought of coming close to Coralie. The fact was that she had not responded to his card, a fact which had filled him with a despair that clawed at his guts like canker.

He had taken Sir Julian Wychwood on one side and entrusted him with the mission of going to see her at her working establishment and begging a place at her school for his English ward, a certain Miss Rose. The fact that John had handed his card to her servants was a mistake that he now bitterly regretted, though he had hardly thought that Coralie would enter the North End of Boston and come seeking him. He had hoped for a note, however. Yet what it was that now kept him deliberately away from her he could not name. In part it was fear of his having grown older, for she would remember him as a sky-blue youth, full of daring and love for life. Then he thought of her terrible husband and cruel daughter and knew that he didn't want to pity her either. Finally, and still very strongly within him, was the deep love he had known for Elizabeth – the precious, the ugly beautiful, the proud, courageous woman who had gone to swim with the mermaids. Or, to face reality, had drowned at sea.

He had not told Rose the real reason why she should not say who her father was, but she had given him one of her knowing looks. 'Don't worry, Paps. I will keep your secret.'

'What is this strange form of address you have just given me?'

'What do you mean?'

'Paps instead of Papa.'

'Oh, sorry. It's just that a lot of the children in Boston use it. I did not mean to be disrespectful.'

He raised a dark eyebrow. 'I know, my precious Rose. You are turning into quite the little Bostonian.'

She made a prim face at him. 'No doubt Madame Clive will teach us to speak very correctly.'

'No doubt she will. She was once a great actress, you know.'

His daughter gave him a demure smile and lowered her lashes. 'Yes, I have heard of her. And of her sister, Kitty.'

John gave her a suspicious look. She had been a small child when her mother, Emilia Rawlings, had died, so he felt sure she could remember little of her.

'Do you recall much of your mother?' he asked suddenly.

'No, only a presence. A kind, warm presence. The first woman I can really recollect was Mrs Elizabeth.'

John smiled. 'And she was somebody that neither of us will ever be able to forget.'

'Hardly possible with her twins growing up so fast.'

'My twins, too,' said John, then thought that he sounded peevish.

Rose patted him on the cheek. Then she made for the doorway, turned in the entrance, dropped a small curtsey and said, 'If you'll forgive me, Father, dear.'

'For what?'

But she was gone before she could answer.

TEN

For no reason that they could name, none of the survivors of the shipwreck sailed back for London, though trading ships, each carrying a few passengers, often came into port. On those days shopkeepers by the dozen crowded round to see what goods were being offloaded and deals were done on those pre-ordered from English stockists. It was like a small party being at the wharves at these particular times. Yet as the autumn came and went there was a tension in the air, a feeling of alarmed excitement about the place. There was a tangible sense of danger and yet, when John Rawlings tried to analyse why, he simply had no idea. Unless, something in his brain nagged, it was to do with those incessant meetings that the patriots of Boston seemed to slink off to as soon as darkness fell.

Yet on this November day John, who had ordered some herbs difficult to obtain in the Colonies, was relieved to see a large packet swung down on to the dockside with his name written on it in bold script. When he looked round he saw that all his fellow survivors were present. Lady Eawiss had trembled down on the arm of a desiccated beau who clearly fancied his chance as a catch for the ladies but, on this occasion, was paying full court to the ample figure who had taken his arm. Jane Hawthorne, wearing a maid's uniform, walked several steps behind them, looking quite lifeless. John guessed that the months without a glimpse of Blue Wolf and the relentless hard work and criticism had eaten away at her natural vivacity.

A small trader had set up a kiosk at the port side and there, sitting on a stool, was Jake O'Farrell, drinking American rum and loving it. His wife, stick thin but with henna-bright hair, was talking earnestly to Dr Joseph Warren, newly widowed and still wearing black. What was the connection between those two? John wondered. Then he remembered that Demelza Conway had been born in Boston and brought up in the Colonies, and had known Joseph since boyhood.

Matthew was working on the dock that day, heaving and sweating as he unloaded *The Porcupine*. Suzanne, still one of the ugliest girls that John had ever seen, had done her best with her looks and had had her left eye, currently covered by a dark patch, enlarged by a cut from Dr Warren's knife. Her long, rat's-tail locks were now swept up and, with her new spectacles catching the sun's reflections, John observed that his old friend Irish Tom was shouting out one or two remarks to her as he leant Matthew a hand. As for Matthew, he could hardly take his eyes off the girl. John smiled to himself, thinking that love struck in the oddest places.

There were a lot of negroes on the docks that day – some working, others drinking rum, others again come to fetch portable goods for their masters. Everybody owned slaves, though Abraham Adams – a true Puritan, rather like the Colonies version of Oliver Cromwell – promptly gave his slave her freedom. But the rest kept them, finding them useful for helping out with the general housework and running errands for their master. Many wore brightly coloured clothes and could be seen scurrying round the town. However, with hostile Indian prisoners it was different. These were given to various households without compunction, unlike the negroes, who seemed to pass down with families.

George Glynde and Tracey Tremayne strolled down to join the general jollity, looking like a pair of dandies with their new clothes shipped from London. On the arm of each was a well-dressed young woman – Miss Miriam Sheaffe and Miss Sukey Mandel, both pretty and obviously very taken with their beaux. John's cynical eyebrows flew about as he wondered if the boys enjoyed the best of both worlds.

Seeing all his friends gathered, he shouted out, 'Come on, we're together again. I'll buy you a rum.'

'Sir Julian's not here,' said Irish Tom cheerfully, wiping the sweat from his glinting brow.

'Probably sleeping off last night's card game,' answered John.

But talk of the devil, at that moment Julian popped his head through a pair of upstairs curtains masking a high window in a house overlooking the docks and shouted out, 'Did I hear my name?'

'You certainly did, Sir. Come on, you'll miss your breakfast.'

So there they all stood in the last burst of warm sunshine before winter gripped the town, and drank the rum with varying degrees of satisfaction. The two Boston misses pulled faces and said the liquid set their teeth on edge but the dandies who escorted them drank deep down and held out their tin cups for a refill. The working men, Irish Tom and Matthew drank thirstily, as did Jake O'Farrell, who never took his eyes from his wife's lithe body where she and the doctor conversed dark and low, standing slightly apart. She drank deeply, throwing her hair back, but the doctor refused as he was on his morning rounds. Lady Eawiss giggled, sipped and handed her cup to the gentleman who escorted her, but John made quite sure that little Jane Hawthorne got a full helping. Then, with a whoop Sir Julian appeared, dressing as he came and holding out his hand for a good draught. Just for a moment John felt intensely happy to see all the adults who had trekked through Indian country safely gathered together. And then his whole world spun as he saw a dark figure, quite alone but perfectly recognizable even at that distance, enter the dockland and look about her.

John straightened his back and stood gazing at her, hypnotized by the way she carried herself, her dark head, crowned with another hat of high fashion, held aloft amongst the crowd who had come down to the wharf that day. Her body, thinner now than it had been in the days when he had held it, oh so lovingly, in his arms, carried itself erect. In her way she had the attitude of a grande dame and yet the Apothecary could hardly believe that this was true, for he knew that Coralie Clive had suffered much in the years since they had last held one another close and whispered words of love. He turned away, letting out a deep sigh that came from him quite involuntarily.

Jane Hawthorne tugged his sleeve. 'What's the matter, Sir?'

He looked at the girl and told the truth. 'I used to know her. Years ago in London. We were at one time quite close. Since then we have both met and loved other people. Now, something – I don't know what – keeps me from speaking to her.'

Jane looked incredulous. 'But that is Madame Clive, surely. Your daughter is a pupil of hers. How have you managed to remain silent?'

'I asked Julian Wychwood to visit her in my place. He could charm a bird out of a tree, that one.'

Jane laughed and said forthrightly, 'He probably charmed Dame Clive straight into his bed.'

'I think that is a matter of mere supposition and not very kind of you, Jane.' The Apothecary's cheeks took on an angry flush. 'And tell me, how are you coping with the loss of Blue Wolf? You and he became very close, I believe?'

The girl's colour came up but she did not look away. 'How did you know about that?' she asked.

'It was perfectly obvious to those of us who had eyes.'

It was cruel but it had the desired effect. Jane burst into silent tears and thrust her hand over her mouth to avoid making too loud a noise. Instantly, in the manner so typical of him, the Apothecary was overcome with remorse. He took her into his arms, where she sobbed against his chest.

'I love the man,' she said in a broken voice. 'I don't care about race, or background, or the fact that he is a member of an Indian tribe. I would join it too if it meant I could be near him. I have given him my heart completely.'

'But will you ever see him again?' John asked, saddened by her response.

'When Lady Eawiss remarries . . .' Jane lowered her voice to a whisper, '. . . and I am absolutely sure that she will – she has so many cicisbeos swarming after her money that she is bound to say yes to one of them. Anyway, when that happens I shall run away into the forest and hope to find him.'

'It does not occur to you that you might find him here in Boston?'

'How could that be possible?'

'Hostile Indian prisoners are given away, here, in this very town. There is a charge for a negro slave but none for the Indians. It seems to me that if he knew this he might have allowed himself to be caught.'

This brought a fresh burst of weeping and people, their friends in particular, were beginning to notice. Indeed, Lady Eawiss raised her quizzer, an elaborate affair surmounted in gold, a new purchase from the shop of Paul Revere, no doubt. With a great effort Jane brought her tears under control and turned a rather watery smile on her employer.

'I had a piece of grit in my eye, Milady,' she offered by way of explanation.

Lady Eawiss fluttered on the arm of her companion, a Captain James Molyneux, all manners and moustache.

'Gad, Madam,' he exclaimed with an egregious smile. 'I think you ought to sit down, indeed I do. You've grown very pallid about the cheeks.'

'But I so wanted to join the others in a tot of rum. If you could find me somewhere to sit, dear Captain.'

'Of course, Milady. At your service.'

He investigated the top of an old barrel that was presently unoccupied and dusted it off rather feebly with flicks of his handkerchief. Lady Eawiss lowered herself on to it while the gallant captain fussed around her. John Rawlings winked a lively eye at Sir Julian, shameless creature that he was.

They all stood, enjoying the warmth on their backs and drinking a toast to their miraculous survival. John looked round the circle of friends and found his eyes irresistibly drawn to the enigmatic faces of Lady Conway and her rascal of a husband. They were looking at one another, exchanging a deep glance as always, and then her eyes moved right, staring at Dr Warren, who had come to buy medical supplies, with a faint smile. And just for a moment, so fleeting that John was never sure afterwards if he actually saw it, Jake's expression changed to that of a thwarted lover. Then the illusion was over and the naughty rogue was roaring with laughter and holding his hand out for a refill.

A gloom had come over the day. Looking round, John saw that the sombre figure of Madam Clive had left the quayside and moved on somewhere else. Picking up his packet of herbs, which was of a size that could be manhandled, he fell into step with Tracey and George, both standing out from the crowd of Bostonians in their fancy new fashions like two jewels dropped amongst field daisies. Before he could even ask them how their school was doing, they launched into conversation.

'My dear John,' Tracey began, 'remarkably it is the dancing side of our business that has garnered all the interest. You know, of course, that we have opened a school of dancing and swordsmanship.'

'Of course, there are one or two still interested in the art of swordplay but I would say that dancing has leaped into the lead,' confirmed George.

'With a very *grand jete!*'

They shrieked with laughter at their not-very-funny joke, then added, 'Do spread the word amongst your friends and patients. We are taking over the meeting room in the Faneuil Hall. A great many officers are coming and this, together with plenty of the locals, should make a dance of much friendliness.'

'May God be praised,' said George unexpectedly.

'What about women?' asked John, very practical.

'All the young ladies who dwell near the Common are coming. What about *your* young ladies, Mr Rawlings? Who will you bring?'

'Lady Eawiss, of course. She will be top of my list.' One of his eyebrows shot up and he saw that they were waiting for some sort of signal as to whether to laugh or weep. 'And the gallant gentleman who escorts her hither and yon. This will leave pretty Miss Hawthorne to attend, and young though she is, my daughter shall accompany me – which will save either or both of us getting into trouble – and Miss Suzanne Hallowell, who may still be wearing a dark patch over her eye as Doctor Warren has recently operated on it.'

'Do you mean to say he has cured her squint?'

'It would not be right of me to comment.'

'I think a lot of people will be there, particularly as we have a celebrity show number.'

John's interest was aroused. 'What is that going to be?'

'Ah, that you must discover for yourself. We are bound by silence.'

And waving farewell to John and Jane, they continued to prance through the crowd, handing out leaflets and good humour wherever they went and occasionally kissing their pretty escorts.

As soon as John got into bed that night he drifted into a fitful sleep and dreamed of Coralie Clive. He wondered, even though unconscious, why he was so afraid of meeting her again. Then, in his dream, he was sitting in a chair and talking to someone of great wisdom. He did not know that it was Sir Gabriel, his beloved father – he could not see the person because of the light

that shone around them, but he knew that it was someone who
had loved him very much.

'Love is like a river,' he heard them saying. 'The river can
flow into tributaries. Therefore it is perfectly possible to love
more than one person absolutely equally.'

'Elizabeth was the love of my life,' he heard himself argue.

'But is she truly dead?' asked the other person teasingly.

Now John was magically transported to a cliff top in Devon,
looking down at the sea, the waves rolling and roistering as far
as the eye could see. And there, way, way out, waving at him,
he felt sure of it, was a figure with dark, wet locks clinging to
her wave-soaked shoulders, the dying rays of the sun reflecting
on her naked, sea-drenched breasts.

'Elizabeth,' he called out.

But she turned and vanished into the ocean, leaving him only
with a glint of a fish's tail as she disappeared into the spume.

He woke, gasping for water and feeling wretched. He sat up
in bed and looked around him. The loft space was hot and
sticky and he was lathered in sweat. He suddenly felt terribly
homesick for London and Nassau Street and for all the people
he had known and loved there. As soon as next spring came he
would take the children and Irish Tom – if that would accord
with the Irishman's wishes – and set sail for England once
more. But now was the wrong time of year to consider such
things. Besides, as had occasionally happened in the past, John
had the strangest feeling that all was not well with the citizens
of the town. The arrival and invasion of the English troops had
irked them, even though they were English themselves. But
were they? John thought. The citizens of Boston regarded themselves as Bostonians, and the presence of the soldiers gave them
an angry feeling of being spied upon. In the so-called Boston
Massacre, a scuffle between a crowd spoiling for a fight and
the British army, who had eventually fired upon them, a total
sum of five people had been killed. But the town dwellers had
thought it very savage that even one had been put to the slaughter.
John could not put a name to it, but there was a general feeling
of unease that was slowly beginning to grasp everyone in its
whirlpool suction.

ELEVEN

The ball was both a jubilation and a calamity in one. First of all, everyone of importance, which included the younger set of educated ladies, together with all the gallant British officers and the hangers-on who enjoyed the chance of a free drink and a game of cards, came in abundance. They laughed merrily and roared with laughter when the master of ceremonies – some tired old danseur desperately trying to make his way in the Colonies – capered a step or two to show them how it was done, and they applauded vigorously as each new dance was announced.

The calamity was of a more subtle nature. The faces of the power people of Boston were missing: Dr Warren, Paul Revere and Sam Adams, that well-known rabble-rouser, his righteous persona spoiled by his disfiguring twitch, to name but a few. Their absence was notable and John Rawlings felt as if he had a stone in his stomach. Admittedly Joseph Warren was in mourning, but there was something far more sinister by their total marked nonappearance. This was a small declaration of war. Yet, looking round the room, John could see that he was alone in his anxieties. The officers clapped in time to the music, whirling the pretty young things of the town round and round until their skirts flew out and wild poppies flared in their cheeks. There was laughter and the sound of gloved hands meeting gloved hands, and the Apothecary was just beginning to feel a fraction out of things when Suzanne, wearing a black patch over her newly surgically treated eye, curtseyed before him and said, 'Did I book you for the next dance, Mr Rawlings?'

'Indeed you did, Miss Hallowell,' he answered, bowing low, and took her arm as they formed up for an energetic hornpipe.

They were both gasping by the time the music ended and this, indeed, was the cue for the musicians to take their rest. During the break little chairs were brought from the back of the hall and curtains were drawn closed on the small stage at the end of the

room. So this, John guessed, was to be the entertainment that
the two lads had been talking about. Struck by a premonition
that it was going to involve Coralie, John saw Suzanne to a chair
and then receded to the shadows at the back, where he stood
trying to look inconspicuous.

The master of ceremonies mounted the stage via a small ladder
and said in a somewhat enfeebled voice that he now craved
silence for a former artiste of the London stage who would be
reciting a few words. There was some half-hearted clapping and
then all the candles were doused. In the sudden, shocking darkness John drew a breath as the curtains swished back and his
former lover, clad in deepest crimson, spoke in a thrilling voice.
It was a sound rich with all the beauty that the theatre had rounded
in it over the years, yet, deep within its timbres, there lay the
whole human experience of laughter and pain, of death and birth.
John felt a tear trickle down his nose as he stood in the shadows
and listened.

> 'Full fathom five thy father lies;
> Of his bones are coral made;
> Those are pearls that were his eyes;
> Nothing of him that doth fade,
> But doth suffer a sea-change
> Into something rich and strange.
> Sea-nymphs hourly ring his knell:
> Hark! Now I hear them,
> Ding, dong bell.

Coralie repeated the last line several times and then finally
sang it in a deep, unearthly tone. There was total silence when
she finished and then those handsome officers and flibberty-gibbet
young ladies all burst into a wave of applause that seemed to
bounce off the very walls. John brought his hands together but
felt so deeply moved that he could clap little, weeping quietly
as he was. Why was he such a sentimental old fool? he asked
himself. He had no answer for it was indeed the truth. The more
of life's vicissitudes he survived, the easier he found it to cry at
the beauty that living had to offer.

Coralie, who had risen and walked to the front of the stage, looked round the silent audience and then said, 'A song for all those who have experienced the pangs of being in love.' She glanced around the room and John, snuffling discreetly into his handkerchief, could have sworn that her gaze was fixed firmly on him as she began.

> 'O Mistress mine, where are you roaming?
> O stay and hear! Thy true-love's coming,
> That can sing both high and low;
> Trip no further, pretty sweeting,
> Journeys end in lovers' meeting,
> Every wise man's son doth know.
> What is love? 'Tis not hereafter;
> Present, mirth hath present laughter:
> What's to come is still unsure:
> In delay there lies no plenty,
> Then come kiss me, sweet-and-twenty:
> Youth's a stuff will not endure,
> Not endure.'

The very words could have been meant for him. What she was saying was that she knew he was there, in the town where she lived, so why waste any more time in pretence? Why not come and see her, at least? As the applause rang out, long and deep, John made for the stage. But the curtains had swirled shut and he had to push past members of the audience as he looked for a back way in. He could not find one. Eventually he got hold of the master of ceremonies who told him, much flustered, that Madame Clive had already left the hall. Dashing into the street, John glimpsed the back of a coach vanishing in the distance and knew at once that it belonged to Coralie's neighbour, the elegant John Hancock. He looked around him with a determination borne completely of frustration. He saw a horse tied to a hitching post and approached it. It was asleep but opened one ferocious eye as he drew near.

'There, there,' John said soothingly, 'I'll return you to the post, I promise. I'm a friend of your master's.'

The horse gave a mighty snort and John quailed. His lifelong experience of maddish horses had made him nervous of the species, but he was compelled by despair. He got his foot in the stirrup and, with the reins in one hand, attempted a lithe leap into the saddle. This was not to be. The horse was off at considerable speed before he had even got his other leg across.

'Oh, help!' shouted John as he tried desperately to sit down while Boston flew past him at an alarming speed.

Eventually he got some sort of control – if one could apply that word to getting both feet in the stirrups and pulling at the horse's mouth until it reduced speed somewhat. Fortunately the creature headed in the direction of the Common and John guessed that its owner was one of the officers stationed there. He was just wondering how to pull the animal to a halt when the problem was solved for him. A quartet of riders came towards him, trotting quite fast. The beast John was riding came to an immediate halt and John flew off, over its head and into a nearby hedge, landing none too comfortably on his arse. The four horsemen laughed softly as the Apothecary's angry face appeared out of the shrubbery. One of the group, a tall, elegant soldier who looked as if he had been born in the saddle, leaned forward and asked, 'Are you all right, my friend?' in a broad Scots accent.

'Never better,' John replied acidly.

The four soldiers laughed again. 'Yon horse is a bit of a devil.'

'You know him then?'

'It's a she actually – wee Mhairi. She belongs to the regiment.'

The Apothecary shook his head. 'Talk about your sins will find you out.'

But the quartet were no longer listening and, having raised their whips to their caps in salute, they rode on their way.

John picked the grass from his jacket as best he could but realizing as he did so that he could say farewell to this, one of his favourite suits in cherry satin and tight black breeches. No amount of cleaning would ever remove the grass stains. He turned to the horse, which was regarding him with a baleful eye.

'Well, goodbye Marie, or whatever your name is. I hope your owner finds you. No need to give him my apologies. I got my comeuppance in full.'

And with that, John set out with a limping gait towards Coralie's house.

TWELVE

The same black servant answered the door and stood, huge eyes rolling nervously, while she listened to what the Apothecary had to say. Finally she spoke. 'Madame Clive has gone to bed, Sir.'

'Oh, dammit all,' John said loudly. 'I thought she wanted to see me. I really did.'

He took his hat off – battered and ridiculous after his fall – and threw it on the floor in a gesture of impatience he hadn't used since childhood. He had never felt more frustrated in his life. He wanted to talk to Coralie – she whom he had been avoiding for months – and discuss their old situation and whether there was any point in resuming their relationship. As if to tease him, at that moment there came the sound of a low laugh and his gaze lifted to the balustrade that ran round the first floor above. She was there, standing in the shadows, the crimson dress gone and a negligee of white flung over her shoulders.

'Coralie,' he called out. 'Was that last poem meant for me?'

She laughed again. 'Of course it was, you sad creature.'

He stood, poised, on the bottom step. 'Sad? Why?'

'You have been in Boston all this time yet never came anywhere near me.'

He hesitated. 'I had my reasons.'

'May I know them?'

He ascended a stair. 'Of course.'

Coralie looked down to the hall where the black girl was still waiting. 'That will be all, Binnie. You can show the gentleman up.' And with that she turned and walked away, only the point of her candle giving him a clue as to where she had headed.

John mounted the stairs as fast as was possible after the aches of his recent throw, but all was now dark. 'Coralie?' he whispered.

Right beside him, she chuckled and he nearly jumped out of his hide. He put out a hand and encountered a breast, as warm and round and cuddly as it had always been. That was enough. Months of locked-up passion, of wanting, of being too caught up with memories of Elizabeth to make a move in any direction, broke down at last. John kissed Coralie as if it was the first and last kiss he would ever give. Only it wasn't, of course. As he followed her into her bedroom and as they looked at each other by candlelight, it was as if they gazed on one another for the first time. The passing of the years did not show to them. They did not notice the grey hairs amongst the others, the extra lines around their eyes. All they could see was their old passion and in this way, with John once again inside her warm, receiving body, they became lovers. In the darkness of night he held her in his arms as both remembered the past.

He would have left at first light but she woke and asked him why he was getting dressed. 'Because, sweetness, I have my children to attend to.'

She laughed. 'But you forget that one of them boards with me. As for the twins, I will send my servant on horseback to escort them to school.'

'And what about their breakfast?'

'The slave, my Abraham – without whom I could not live – shall carry a note listing their requirements. And surely your housemate can open the shop without you.'

'Yes, she can. But she runs the teahouse and has other tasks, if you follow my meaning.'

'I don't exactly, but you can explain over breakfast.'

They talked while they ate but mainly they looked at one another. Coralie thought back to their first meeting, all those years ago in the Vaux Hall Pleasure Gardens, and a smile twitched at her full and beautiful mouth. She had saved John's life on that occasion, running after a murderer in her high fashionable heels. How old had he been then? Nineteen, twenty? But even now, in his early forties, there was much about him that was still the same. The lovely curly cinnamon hair tied back and not bewigged had streaks of grey but the bold blue eyes still sparkled with curiosity and, Coralie believed, would never grow old – too full of interest in the world, and mischief, to allow their owner to fade. John's body was more mature and tougher – all the months of walking after the shipwreck had served him well. And there was one part of it that was just as she remembered it: a giver of delight and pleasure to the opposite sex. Feeling rather old to be doing so, Coralie blushed at the thought. Fortunately, John was, as she remembered clearly, stowing away a large and hearty breakfast, and did not notice.

He looked up at her and smiled. 'You haven't changed, you know.'

'I was just thinking the same about you.'

'Nonsense, you were attacking a ham.'

'D'you know, I believe we have had this conversation before,' Coralie said wryly.

'We have. Many, many times.'

'Oh, dear, I'm not beginning to bore you already.'

John shook his head and winked as she gave him a ravishing grin.

'You will never bore me, John. Still the same old you. Crooked smile, eyebrows flying, moving about like a hare.'

'Lord, sounds like a dog.'

Coralie laughed aloud, joyfully, with great mirth, then her expression changed. 'You know that my daughter died?'

'No, I didn't. I'm so sorry. Tell me of it.'

'She took to drink, severely so. Of course, being female she could never inherit my husband's title or estates. But she resented that and was more full of spleen than ever.'

John put out a hand and laid it on Coralie's arm, shifting his chair so that he was almost sitting beside her. She looked down at all the bright china on the table as she spoke.

'To cut a long and bitter story short, she married at seventeen. A wastrel of a boy, a drunken whoremonger, who lost a fortune at cards and saw her as a way out of his dissolute life.'

'What happened?'

Coralie looked up and John saw that tears had formed in her green eyes.

'Nobody knows. They must have challenged one another to a race – or something like that anyway. They took two horses and galloped over the South Downs, going hell for leather, and that was how they were found the next day. Both lying dead, the horses standing under a nearby tree. They had bled profusely from wounds that nobody knew how they had got. I think they stabbed one another in a rage of love and hate.'

John shook his head in semi-disbelief. 'You must have suffered terribly.'

Coralie smiled sadly. 'I had done my suffering years before, when my daughter spat at me and called me a whore. That was when I left the house in which she was living. The last time I ever saw her alive she was sitting on her husband's knee, running her hands over his body and biting him on the neck with her little white teeth.'

'Stop,' said John. 'Speak of it no more. Let it just be said that you had the courage to sail to Boston and start a new life here.'

'Yes. My sister Kitty left the stage and retired to a villa in Twickenham given to her by Horace Walpole, who greatly admired her. She wanted me to live with her but I decided against it. So I chose the New World instead.'

'And is she still alive?'

'Very much so. We keep up a lively correspondence. Well, as lively as possible with the time it takes for letters to arrive.'

John looked wise. 'I remember her very vividly. Almost as vividly as her sibling.'

Coralie pulled a face. 'What was the sibling called?'

John smiled broadly. 'I really can't recollect.'

THIRTEEN

'**W**ell, where did you get to?' asked Suzanne, looking slightly cross but amused at the same time.

'Do not ask, my dear,' the Apothecary replied. 'Let us just say that I have been in heaven. But with a straight face I do apologise for being so late. Has the place been packed with ladies of greenish pallor demanding to see an herbalist?'

'At least a dozen hurled abuse at me and asked where you were. One accused you of being a bed faggot.'

The Apothecary, who was in the finest humour, gave Suzanne a wicked look and tapped the side of his nose.

'You may tease me all you will. Nothing will induce me to be angry. I shall go to my consultation room and await the swarm of complaints.'

And having said this he delivered Suzanne a playful smack and headed away. But within half an hour of arrival, during which he was alone, luxuriating in the smell of drying herbs, there was a knock at the door and Demelza Conway entered.

Seeing her like this, in the piercing light thrown by the shop window – for John had converted the Orange Tree's storeroom into a very workable apothecary's premises from which he could quite easily dispense his skills and physicks – he noticed the lines concentrated round her eyes and lips and guessed her age to be about fifty. She was as smart as ever but had a strange air about her, almost as if she had greater things on her mind and her illness, whatever it was, was a nuisance more than anything else. He bowed low, acting like the true professional.

'Can I assist you in some way, Madam?'

She came directly to the point. 'I have reached that stage in my life when my courses are most irregular. I have not had the reds for some twelve weeks.'

John looked sympathetic.

'But, on the other hand, I may have been foolish enough to

have conceived a child, a situation that is completely abhorrent to
me. Can you give me something to bring on a flux?'

This was indeed a very direct question and one which made
the Apothecary pause before answering. Eventually he said,
'There are several things that provoke the menses. But why do
you come to me and not your friend Joseph Warren?'

She laughed outright. 'He is a good man, a God-fearing man.
He does not believe in the destruction of life.'

'As I do?'

For the first time, she appeared flustered. 'I did not say that.
I did not mean that. But I ask you, John, as a fellow human
being: give me something to bring on my courses.'

'You do not know definitely that you are with child?'

She laughed without humour. 'It's Jake, the wild creature. He
cannot leave me alone. You would think we were newlywed. I
fear that I may well be pregnant.'

John's thoughts, roaming to Coralie, decided there really was
no age at which men and women felt too old for love and all its
splendid highways and byways. He nodded slowly.

'Come back tomorrow, Lady Conway. I will prepare for you
a decoction of the root of Masterwort. That will bring on your
courses.'

'You are certain?'

'As certain as I can be of anything.'

'Then I bid you good day.'

She went out, leaving John to stare at his empty shop and
think of all the strange things that had been requested of him
since he had first become a Yeoman of the Society of Apothecaries.

In the next few weeks he had several calls upon his professional
help but none quite so bluntly put or as unexpected as the request
of Lady Conway. He had prepared the decoction for her, she had
paid him and taken it away, and from that day forward had never
by look or word mentioned the subject again.

The rest of his friends he saw quite regularly. Those pretty
fellows, Tracey and George, were so delighted with the result of
their dance that they organized two more, both of which John
attended, escorting Madame Clive, which gave rise to a great
deal of local gossip. Rose, who was looking very beautiful these

days, announced that she was delighted to be taught by such a famous actress and pretended to be much shocked that her teacher was an old friend of her father's. The twins devoured their lessons with skill and were soon reading and writing ahead of their classmates. Sir Julian Wychwood appeared to be much interested in a Miss Dolly Hampden, a plain-looking girl but very well connected. Lady Eawiss accepted the proposal of one of her cisibeos and announced that she would be married in the spring of 1774. As for Matthew and his three children, they fell in with a spritely widow and mother of two, Sarah, who Matthew married before anyone could blink an eye, and set up home together in the widow's house in the North End.

But it was not all dancing and courtship. There was a feeling in the town: just put a squib and light it in the streets and the whole lot would come tumbling down about one's ears. There were patriots everywhere, but included amongst those who genuinely thought that it was time that the Colonies sought freedom from British domination was another element. The pure at heart had unwittingly drawn to them the bully boys, spoiling for a fight, brutal and ugly and ready to side with anyone who would satisfy their lust for violence. It was a marriage of thoughtful and clever men who only wanted the English to stop their ridiculous treatment, and of thugs who lusted for social revolution.

John, much to his consternation, saw notices going up in the streets demanding that all Sons of Liberty should attend a mass meeting to protest at the imminent arrival of tea ships from Britain. The British government had, in their blundering way, passed the Tea Act of 1773. Tea, which up to this point had been imported by the Boston merchants and sold far more cheaply than in England, was in future to be supplied by the East India Company to a monopoly of merchants who would then impose the tax which would be paid direct to London. The citizens of Boston were incensed. Could this just be the start? Would the British government in future tax clothing and shoes, even Madeira wine? What was the future for Boston shopkeepers when the British government chose 'consignees' to handle the goods alone? If they had done this for tea, what next?

In late November the first of the tea ships, the *Dartmouth* arrived. There was a furious public meeting which John avoided, though he may as well not have bothered to do so. His only customer of the day was a small boy who had been hit over the head by another and wanted his wound dressed, and to have a good sniffle at John's knee. There was a feeling of unrest that was almost tangible and that evening, when Irish Tom arrived to convert the tea shop back to an inn, he swore that there were gangs of men out on the streets looking for trouble.

'I think there's going to be some mighty blow-up, John.'

'I'm uneasy as hell. I've thought of getting a slave to protect the children.'

'What do you mean exactly?'

'Someone who will walk them to school and back. General care, you know. The twins are very precious to me.'

'And what about Miss Rose? Do you think Madame Clive's school is safe from the mob?'

'I don't know, Tom. Is anywhere safe? There are a lot of rough souls in Boston alongside all the good and God-fearing.'

'You could be talking about anywhere, Sir. I don't think there is a town in the entire world that doesn't have its share of riff-raff.'

'You're right, of course. But that doesn't ease my current problem. I must work to provide for my family but can't be everywhere guarding them at the same time.'

'Go to the slave market tomorrow, Sir. I'll come with you if you like.'

'Nonsense, Tom. I'm a grown man and can take care of myself.'

Despite everything, John put a newly bought pistol under his coat as he sauntered down to a place near the Faneuil Hall where sales of kidnapped black people were held. Rumour had reached his ears that the *Dartmouth* had been ordered to tie up at Griffin's Wharf, not to unload, and had spent the night under armed guard. He was right in his deep feeling that the mobs were out.

As always, the sight of the slave market, of so many miserable human beings huddled together, frightened out of their wits, depressed him enormously. Their ship had moored at a wharf near the Faneuil Hall and the occupants had been marched to a nearby square where their sale had begun. Though the practice of selling slaves was regarded as rather degrading by the lofty

Puritans of Boston, the owning of them was not. John, as a man of his day, agreed with the latter sentiment.

The Apothecary ran his eyes over the cringing people in a combination of disgust at their treatment and pity for the poor souls. And then his gaze widened. There was someone he knew amongst the crowd. Standing tall and looking down the length of his finely chiselled nose was Blue Wolf, arms folded across his chest, grouped with a handful of other captured Indians. He was staring at the ground steadfastly, as if he were too good to be part of this wretched auction of human suffering. But some sixth sense must have told him that someone he knew was amongst the onlookers, for suddenly his dark eyes flashed upwards and he and John stared directly at one another. Their extraordinary friendship rekindled in an instant and John knew, as surely as if he had been told, that Blue Wolf had allowed himself to be captured just to come near to his beloved Jane Hawthorne. In the only signal he dared give, John removed his hat and raised one of his expressive eyebrows. Blue Wolf responded with a tiny movement of his head, rapidly looking down then straight back up.

The requests for him were unusually fierce even though he was given away free. Several people entered the fray, particularly, John noted, several widowed and single ladies, but John threw caution to the winds and a generous tip to the slave master and eventually acquired Blue Wolf, who was handed to him on a chain.

'I wouldn't recommend you remove that, Mister. This fella's one big hulk of a brave.'

'I'll take my chance,' John answered pleasantly.

They hurried back through the less-crowded streets and stinking alleyways until they finally reached John's home. Here the Apothecary removed the fetters, then poured two glasses of rum and gave one to Blue Wolf. The man picked up the glass, sniffed its contents but did not drink it.

'Can't you drink?' John asked curiously.

Blue Wolf shook his head. 'It will drive me crazy.'

'I'm sorry. I didn't realize. But tell me, my friend, did you come here for Jane Hawthorne?'

Something resembling humour lit the Indian's eyes. 'Why else would I allow myself to be captured? I am the Blue Wolf. The forests are my natural home. I could escape those soldiers in a second.' Suddenly his face changed and another man peeped out from behind his uncompromising features. 'But I made the mistake of all men. I fell in love with a white woman.'

'I admire you for subjecting yourself to the ordeal. But let us discuss more practical matters. While you work for me I want you to adopt the dress of the other men in Boston. Dressed as the brave that you are, you will stand out in a crowd. I would rather that you blended in with it.'

Blue Wolf, whose command of English had improved enormously though it was still pronounced with a French accent, said, 'I know you require me to help you so what is it that you need of me?'

John did not give the answer he had practised. Instead, out of his mouth came the following sentence: 'We are living in difficult times, Blue Wolf. I want you to look after my children. Fight for them as if they were your own if it becomes necessary. My daughter is fairly safe at a boarding school out near the Common so I doubt she is going to get into much trouble. But my sons – you know the twins – live here with me. My friend, can I leave them in your charge? They are at school learning to read and write.'

A strange light had come into the Indian's eyes and he said, 'Then I will go to school with them. I, too, wish to learn to write and read.'

'But the children and the teacher will be terrified. An Indian marching into their lessons might well empty the classroom.'

'I will tell them I come to learn. In peace.' Blue Wolf had risen to his feet and John thought at that moment he was one of the tallest of his race that he had ever seen. 'I will serve you well, Mr Rawlings, fear nothing of that. I will guard the twins with my life but you will forgive me if I am free when they do not require me.'

'In your spare time you can go wherever you want. But I warn you, my friend, Boston is in a state of seething unrest and there are many who don't like the fact that Indian braves are being given away at the slave market.'

'Why?'

'Because they would rather see you dead.'

*   *   *

Two more ships, the *Beaver* and the *Eleanor*, came in and were moored with the *Dartmouth* at Griffin's Wharf. On board they had three hundred and forty-two chests of tea, valued at eighteen thousand pounds. Meanwhile, the meetings of the masses, the thinkers and the tradesmen had been moved to the Old South Meeting House, the Faneuil Hall being too small to admit their great and growing number. They were not town meetings – they had grown too wild and undisciplined for that. These were the massed discontents with the way things were, and they called themselves The Body.

The sixteenth of December came, the sky above grey with foreboding and raindrops speckling the roads. John and Suzanne, listening to the sound of the crowd packing the streets outside the meeting house, unable to get in, decided to close the Orange Tree. Irish Tom swung in through their doors at lunchtime, his face very anxious.

'You're doing the right thing, Sir. I've a feeling that tonight is going to get as rough as blades.'

Then, to the surprise of John, the mighty man put his arm round little Suzanne, swung her off her feet and said, 'Don't worry, me darling. Irish Tom will protect you.' That was a very public display of affection and John was rather astonished, wondering whether, despite the age gap, the pair might make a regular couple.

Early in the afternoon he mounted the old nag he had bought, as comfortable and as happy just to jog along as its owner, and rode to Coralie's house. She was teaching but he had a long conversation with Abraham, her black slave, who promised to lock up well at night and protect the females within. Not sure, John left some money with him and asked him to call for reinforcements if necessary. This done, he left Coralie a love note and trotted home.

By the time he got back the December sun was setting and the streets were in a ferment of unrest. So packed, indeed, that John had to dismount and lead Ruby by her bridle. He asked a passing stranger what exactly was happening.

'It's about the tea ships, Mister. They've sent to Governor Hutchinson for permission to turn 'em back to England with their cargoes. We're not going to touch 'em with this tea tax and all.'

John tried to take a few steps in the direction of his home but the crowd would not shift. His horse started to panic and he whispered in her ear, 'Go on, Ruby, make your way back, there's a good girl.' She started to push her way out and eventually made some sort of path for herself. John tried to follow but the press of people closed in. And then it happened. There was a roar from the Old South, followed by war whoops, just as if a pack of Indians was in there. The crowd within burst upon the streets exactly as if they had been shot from a gun. Above the hubbub one voice could be heard, loud and clear. It was John Hancock and he was calling out, 'Let every man do what is right in his own eyes!'

John felt himself being propelled forward by the mob, his feet literally not touching the ground. He was certain at that moment that if he were to drop down he would be trodden to death. And he knew, deep in his heart, that this was the start of a revolution, a revolution that would light the spark that would set the Colonies free of the yoke of England for ever.

FOURTEEN

Eventually the crowd thinned but not in a friendly way. Groups of people whom John recognized as journeymen, apprentices and some people he had never seen before slid off into the Green Dragon and various other hidey-holes. At last a way opened up to take him clear to the Orange Tree. Here the Apothecary found several of his friends, all agog to know the latest. Tracey and George were there, very excited and wondering if they could do anything to help the British cause. Matthew was present with his strange little wife and various children with whom Jasper and James were happy to play. Sir Julian Wychwood, absolutely abrim with pleasure, came in and shouted, 'I feel just like going out and fighting someone.'

'If I were you,' John answered, 'I would keep your eyes down and your sword sheathed.'

Julian took this the wrong way and laughed incessantly.

'And you can do that constantly as far as I'm concerned. We don't want you running into any more trouble. You're worse to look after than a baby.'

'Oh, John, I think you're getting old. You sound like an ancient crabby maid, the way you go on. Besides, I am a child with most interesting information. Would you like to hear it?'

'Yes, please,' said James, who had come back from school early. He'd run up and sat at Julian's feet, his eyes agog. He was, John decided, one of the most beautiful little boys alive. His hair was as dark as Elizabeth's but curly like his father's, his skin was fresh and clean and with a collection of beautifully placed freckles. As for Jasper, who came and sat with his brother, he was his replica, except that his complexion was more swarthy. But as they laughed and surreptitiously punched one another, it was virtually impossible to tell one from the other.

When Julian finally had everybody's attention, he said, 'They are going to attack the ships tonight. They intend to unload them and dump the tea in the harbour. They are going to disguise themselves as Indians.'

There was a sarcastic snort from Blue Wolf, who had stood quietly in the background during Julian's announcement. Other than that there was silence.

Then John broke out with 'This I have got to see,' followed by Tom saying, 'I'll be with you, Master.'

Tracey, George and Julian all leapt in the air and shouted 'Yes' simultaneously. 'I'd like to come,' said Suzanne, whose eye was almost healed from Dr Warren's operation and was looking on the point of being attractive.

There was a great altercation about who would care for the children but Matthew's wife promised to take them to her place, which was guarded by her hulking brother who did not go out in large crowds. So, that settled, Blue Wolf saw them home and promised to join the party later.

The group of men set forth, filled with a strange elation mixed with a sense of dread. It was in the air because the crowd, formerly so noisy and shouting slogans, making war whoops, had grown silent and tense. As they neared Griffin's Wharf they had to push their way through the solid mass of people which John reckoned stood at several thousand. You could almost feel their barely controlled excitement.

'Look,' said Tom, pointing a gnarled finger, 'it's the Indians.'

John gazed where he was pointing and barely controlled a laugh. He had never seen such poor disguises in his life. Tattered and tatty old clothes were supposed to pass for Indian gear, while the conspirators had smeared their faces with grease and soot or lampblack. To make matters worse, the Indians were speaking in grunts and pidgin English like 'me know you'.

But there was one Indian who caught the Apothecary's eye. Slimmer than the rest and garbed in buckskin trousers and a beaded shirt, he was the only one who even remotely looked the part. He had one red war mark painted right across his cheek-bones, concealing his nose as well. A hat was drawn down close about his features so that it was impossible to recognize who it was. However, there were several men there whom John knew at once: Paul Revere, Sam Adams and the badly disguised Dr Warren.

They watched in silence as the invaders boarded the three ships lying at anchor, demanding lights and keys from the mate of each. The sailors made no resistance but handed over the keys while the cabin boys were sent for lights. The tea chests were then hauled up on deck and the contents emptied into the water below, making a great whooshing sound, but other than that there was a terrible quiet. The men worked in silence, fierce and concentrated. John strained forward, listening for a cry or scream, but there was nothing except the sound of tea being emptied into the ocean. And then came a plop, as if something had been dropped from the rigging.

'Did you hear anything?' he asked Tracey Tremayne – or was it George Glynde?

'What do you mean?'

'An extra sound, like something falling into the water?'

'I certainly heard a noise but I just thought it was tea.'

'Yes, you're probably right. Well, I'm getting tired and I'd like a drink before I retire. I've a feeling that this tea dumping may well last till dawn and I've work to do tomorrow.'

They pushed their way through the crowd, but while the others chatted John was silent, thinking of that strange sound as something fell out of the rigging and into the sea below. He also wondered about the identity of the man disguised as an Indian who had looked so amazingly realistic, thinking that it was one of the cleverer disguises of the night.

They reached the Orange Tree, Irish Tom carrying in Suzanne, who was exhausted with all the excitement of the day. But as George took the key from him and turned it in the lock, he suddenly turned to the others and put his finger to his lips.

'There's somebody in here,' he whispered. 'There's some bastard stealing our toddy, damn his eyes.'

Rather like bad actors in a poor melodrama, they crouched down as one and proceeded silently to follow George, who was opening the door which, inevitably, squeaked and groaned in the process. There was someone standing at the bar – or rather leaning on it in a drunken posture.

'Gadzooks,' shouted Tracey, unsheathing his sword, 'I'll run you through or plant a facer on you. You're as rough as a kicked dog, damn you.'

Meanwhile, John had lit a candle tree and now swung it in the face of the reprobate who had stolen into the premises and was putting drink down his gullet as if he hadn't a care in the world. Grabbing the man's tail of hair, John peered closely into his face.

'God's life, it's Jake O'Farrell!' he shouted.

In that strange, dancing light the handsome features looked terrible. Jake was a greenish pallor and his blue eyes, normally so twinkling and expressive, were rolling round in his head as if they belonged to someone entirely different. His jaw was slack and a trace of vomit ran down his chin.

'Take him outside, Tom,' commanded John in stentorian tones. 'He's vomiting an ocean and we don't want it in here.'

'Out with you, you bag of sleazy scum,' ordered the big Irishman, and there was an unsightly scuffle followed by the noise of a rapid exit which, in turn, heralded the most disgusting sounds coming from the street.

'Lordy,' said George, dabbing at his front, 'I do hope none of that dropped on me.'

'Or me,' said Tracey.

Outside there was a mighty roar as Sir Julian Wychwood, who had been following behind, shouted, 'Don't you spew at me, you filthy bucket pisser. I'll land you a bunch of fives.'

There was the noise of a fist connecting with flesh and then the sound of a body slumping to the ground. John, meanwhile, had filled a pail abrim with water and, rushing out, threw it over the prostrate figure lying outside, dousing away the vomit and managing to splash Sir Julian into the bargain. The scene ended with the Apothecary and Wychwood dragging Jake O'Farrell inside and carrying him up the spindly staircase where they threw him on to a bed and left him to sleep it off, the pail remaining beside him for good measure.

Coming down the stairs, Julian flapped his fingers. 'I hope I haven't damaged my hand. I landed a real belter on him. I cannot abide a man who can't hold his liquor.'

'He's quite a decent chap when he's sober.'

'Yes. I wonder what got into him tonight. I presume he was watching our badly disguised friends unloading the tea.'

'And where was his wife? She doesn't let him wander far from her side on most occasions. Was she watching as well?'

'I have no idea,' answered Julian, 'and frankly I couldn't care less. They are not a couple who have ever appealed to me greatly.'

John smiled in the dawning. 'Come now, Sir. Be charitable.'

'Charity, my dear fellow, is for the weak-livered.'

And so saying, they marched downstairs and into the Orange Tree, and had a cup of coffee fortified by brandy.

FIFTEEN

I t was the decision of all the men not to go to bed that night and so they set off to their homes and their various employ- ments at an early hour. Little Suzanne was put to bed by Irish Tom, who lingered a while in her house, making John wonder if his former servant had at last found a true love, a fact which gave him enormous pleasure to consider. However, there was work to be done and a tea room and an apothecary's shop to be sweetened and cleaned before he could open for custom. Suzanne woke up, yawning and small-eyed with sleep, and at that signal John walked the short distance to his premises and closed the door.

No sooner had he whipped the covers off the counters and checked that all was well with the decoctions and concoctions he had left overnight when there came a thunderous knocking at his door. 'Help, Apothecary,' a voice was shouting outside. He threw it open to see two English officers in full uniform.

'Are you the herbalist?' one asked in a rough voice.

'Yes. I used to practice in Shug Lane, Piccadilly.'

'Well, I'll be blowed,' remarked the other. 'My father went to you once for a cure for a megrim for my poor mother.'

'What can I do to help you?'

'Come immediately. There's a body been hauled up by the Long Wharf. Dead as a drowned cat but we want you to have a look at it.'

'Wouldn't one of the doctors be better?'

'They're all out on calls – or more likely not stirring. Same with the other apothecaries. I think you're the only man in Boston that's awake after last night's little do.'

John snatched his hat and cloak and grabbed a bag of travel- ling medicaments. As he ran the comparatively short distance he wondered who it was, and for some reason felt himself grow cold with an inexplicable fear. He had had these feelings before and knew that they always augured ill.

The body was being guarded by two soldiers and was halfway up the Long Wharf, which lived up to its name and stretched far out into the ocean. As John approached he had a sense of recognition. Still visible despite the ravages of the sea, it was lying huddled up, dripping wet, and John saw the big fishing net in which it had been hauled out of the water. He felt a moment of total tenderness towards the small, sad remains before professionalism took over as he knelt down beside the corpse. He looked up at the soldiers. 'Has the body been touched?'

'Yes and no. A fisherman spotted it and we helped him pull it up. That's all.'

John removed the slouch hat from the head and gasped with shock. A straggle of long, dyed hair streaked with grey greeted him, and he had the horror of seeing a face so familiar. Dressed as a boy she might be but the dead sea-changed features that he was looking into were those of Demelza Conway. He drew in his breath sharply and one of the soldiers said, 'Do you recognize him?'

'Yes, I do. It's a woman – Lady Conway. She comes from England.'

The poor face had been changed by the amount of time she had spent in the water and the eyes, over which John tried to close the lids, were strange and glassy, as if attacked by some sea creature. As he turned her over the Apothecary could see that there was bruising on her back, but whether this had been caused by knocking against an object in the water or whether there had been a struggle before she fell in, it was impossible to tell.

Around him he was aware that the soldiers had come to the salute and were raising their bayonets before their faces. He looked up and saw that a young officer was approaching. He recognized him – it was Lieutenant Harry Dalrymple with whom he had spent a pleasant evening in The Duke of Marlborough. He got to his feet. 'Good morning, Lieutenant.'

'Good morning, Apothecary.' Dalrymple glanced down at the sodden body lying at his feet. 'What's all this? Another accident?'

John hesitated, calling up in his mind the scene of the previous night. There had been several thousand people surveying the smashing of the tea chests and the subsequent

throwing of the tea into the ocean, and he had watched the
proceedings with a group of his friends. But who had actually
been present? Irish Tom had been standing a few yards away
from him, lifting Suzanne so that she could get a better view.
But what of the others? He had spoken to Tracey – or was it
George? – without turning his head. The two men had such
similar voices, light and fashionable, using all the slang expressions current in London, so it could have been either. Matthew
had also been present but had slipped away early to go back
to his new wife and their various children. Sir Julian Wychwood
had not been standing in the little group but had followed them
to the Orange Tree hard on their heels. Blue Wolf had not
joined them at all. As for the husband of the newly drowned
woman, the impish Jake O'Farrell, could he have got into the
Orange Tree before the rest of them and then put on the act
of his life?

John's silence must have impinged on Dalrymple's consciousness. 'Good heavens! Do you suspect foul play?' he asked.

The Apothecary looked at him frankly. 'I don't know. All I
can tell you is the strangest thing about this is that an
Englishwoman – who married a title, no less – was involved in
last night's affair. That is, *if* she was.'

Harry Dalrymple pulled his earlobe. 'And why should she end
up in the sea?'

John spread his hands wide. 'I have no answers.'

The lieutenant thought for a moment, then said, 'I'm going
to have this body looked at by our top army doctor. There is
something odd about the whole business.'

'Lady Conway was born in America and knows Doctor Warren,
I can tell you that much.'

Dalrymple frowned. 'Do you think she was a sympathizer?'

'I have no idea.'

The lieutenant shook his head, puzzled, then shouted to his
men, 'Cover the corpse with a cloth and get a cart. I want her
taken to the army mortuary.'

'Yes, Sir.'

One of the soldiers removed his jacket to hide the sad white
face of the late Lady Conway while the other rushed about to
do his bidding. John stared out to sea, rapt in thought.

Harry Dalrymple came and stood beside him. 'Tell me your ideas.'

John said, 'She might have been a spy.'

'But for which side?'

'I have no inkling.'

'Look,' said Harry, 'although I don't know you I have the feeling that you are a trustworthy man. Will you act as my unofficial eyes? In my position I can do a little snooping around but not a great deal. I would be so obliged to you, my dear Sir, if you would find out all you can about the mysterious lady.'

John smiled. Was it his fate, wherever he was in the world, to be the unofficial snooper for a shadowy puppet master? Presumably, yes. He turned to Harry. 'I'll do what I can but I won't betray my friends.'

'Not even if they killed her?'

John smiled wryly. 'That remains to be seen.'

He had not followed directly behind Lady Conway's death cart, instead strolling along the Long Wharf to its very end, half a mile out to sea. There he had climbed down some rickety steps and hired a rowing boat which had taken him over the waves to the town dock, where he had alighted. Turning left he cut across King Street, Water Street and Milk Street, then down Hutchinson's Street, finally emerging in Belcher's Lane which stood immediately opposite Griffin's Wharf, the scene of last night's frantic activity. This morning the crowd had dispersed and all was relatively quiet. The three tea ships still rode forlornly at anchor, the tea chests, crunched open, littering their decks and a trail of tea floating on the ocean as far as the eye could see. It was a fairly dismal scene and one which John observed neutrally. But something was stirring in his blood. The vigour with which the previous night's action had been undertaken by the citizens of Boston could only endorse a feeling he had had earlier: the Sons of Liberty were a powerful organization who would gladly lead a revolt, the upshot of which was anybody's guess.

He was picturing it, his thoughts a universe away, when a hand plucked at his elbow. John jumped with fright and looked round to meet the piercing gaze of Blue Wolf. He was rather angry.

'Where have you been? You didn't come home last night.'

Then, realizing that this sounded peevish, he relented. 'Blue Wolf, I wanted you to act like my servant. I even dressed you as such.'

A flicker of a smile crossed the dark, intense face. 'I called on Lady Eawiss.'

'Did you? Why? To glimpse Jane Hawthorne, I suppose.'

'Jane had gone out. I bowed low – as I have seen Rafe and Hugo de Jongleur do. Then I left.'

'And you came here, didn't you? Don't deny it, Blue Wolf. I saw you aboard the *Eleanor* last night, I swear I did.'

The Indian tipped his broad brimmed hat forward. 'Yes, John Rawlings, I did creep on to one of the ships. I wanted to see what they were doing. It was easy enough. They were all disguised to look like my people.' He gave one of his contemptuous snorts. 'Huh.'

'Did you recognize anyone there?'

'Several people, including Doctor Warren. I thought he had a great deal of nerve, as a professional man.'

John could not help but smile, thinking how brilliantly Blue Wolf had mastered the English language, which he spoke like a Frenchman, echoing his teachers of long ago.

'Did you see anyone else you knew?'

Blue Wolf frowned. 'Who do you mean?'

'Like Lady Conway?'

'Yes, she was climbing up the rigging of the ship. Do not question me why because I do not know.'

'Great God! Was she alone or was she being followed?'

'I could not tell you. I was too far away.'

Knowing that Blue Wolf had the vision of a hawk, John frowned. 'So what did you do next?'

'I spotted Jane in the crowd. Furthermore, that little dark man Revere was giving me some piercing looks, so I hurried off the ship and joined her.'

'What happened then?'

'We watched till dawn. Do you know, when first light came up one could see a trail of tea going back as far as the eye could see. I believe it stretched as far as Dorchester.'

'Good heavens. And then?'

'I took my Silver Fox back to the fat old lady's apartment.'

'Silver Fox, is that what you call her?'

'Yes. I have made her a member of our tribe.'

'How have you done this?'

Blue Wolf gave a beautiful smile. 'In the usual way, Mr Rawlings. We did not need a ceremony to become husband and wife.'

It was said so earnestly that it would have been cruel to laugh or, worse, be hypocritical. John was only too conversant with the great surges and urges of love to know that denying them was extremely difficult, if not impossible. And to a true child of America, born and bred in the thundering endless landscapes, it would have been an impossibility.

He smiled. 'Good luck to you, provided she is willing to go with you.'

'Jane is not as meek as she looks.'

And that was the only comment Blue Wolf would make before nodding his head briefly and disappearing again, as fleet of foot as ever.

SIXTEEN

With thoughts of love now planted in his mind, John headed for the livery stables, Ruby having made her way elsewhere and not returned last night. There he hired a horse by the name of Hussar, and having been assured of its gentle and kindly disposition, rode it off in the direction of the Common and Coralie's house. On the way he passed a familiar sight. The cart in which Demelza Conway's body reposed was being pulled by one solitary soldier into a building standing by the workhouse, which John suddenly realized was the mortuary. Once, presumably, it had housed the bodies of the penniless people who dwelt there, but now it also had a use for the militia who were camped so close by. And remembering Harry Dalrymple's words, John made the mental connection and knew that this was where Demelza was being taken. He suddenly thought of Jacob O'Farrell and wondered whether news of his wife's death had been communicated to him – or whether, perhaps, for a more sinister reason, he was already aware.

Coralie rushed in from the stable behind her house, her face downcast. 'Oh, John, Abraham has just told me the news. Lady Conway died in some sort of accident last night.'

He kissed her swiftly, then said, 'Why are you so upset? I thought you hardly knew the woman.'

'Then you are wrong. She and Jake live in the stable block owned by Mr Hancock, and I wave to her on a daily basis. Besides, long ago, almost in another life, she and I acted together.'

'What?'

'I said that she was once an actress.'

A door, beyond which were vast and endless possibilities, opened in John's mind. 'God's life. There's some havey-cavey business here.'

'What do you mean?'

'Lady Conway's entire past takes on a different hue. I never knew she was on the stage.'

'Well, she called herself a player but she was not up to snuff. And she wasn't Lady Conway then. She called herself Moll Bowling.'

'Tare an' Hounds!' exclaimed the Apothecary. 'Why didn't you tell me this before?'

'Why should I? The subject never came up.'

John gathered himself together. 'Listen, lovely girl, perhaps this is the wrong time of day to quiz you. You undoubtedly have a room full of eager young misses—'

'Of which your daughter is one.'

'Indeed she is. As I was saying, they'll be dying to be taught how to play the harp and conduct themselves in company, so perhaps I should return this evening, when it is dark and lonely and you are wishing that you had someone to snuggle up against . . .'

'You hope,' said Coralie, sparkling, and losing twenty years as a result.

'I know,' John answered smugly, and regretted it instantly.

'Please go,' she said in a voice like a sliver of freezing glass. 'Do you think I have looked after myself all these years to be reduced to thinking of you when I go to bed? Shame on you, Sir.'

For once the Apothecary was entirely at a loss. 'Oh, my dear, I meant nothing by that foolish remark. I was talking about myself – at least, I think I was.'

Coralie smiled; she could not help it. John, the man she had known since she was a youthful girl, looked so sad at that moment, like a little boy who's been caught with his hand in the jam jar.

'John Rawlings, why have you become so pompous? I swear that fatherhood has brought out the worst in you. You must simply learn to be less serious if you wish to remain young at heart.'

'And that I do.'

'I nearly lost the gift once. Years of being in wretched company wore away at me like a dark cloud. But it came back. And do you know how?'

He shook his head.

'By remembering all the fun I used to have. Recalling how much I'd laughed with Kitty, my witty, wonderful sister. What joy I had had from hearing the audience roar with applause. The infinite pleasure of knowing you and, moreover, the amount of sheer romping that we indulged in.'

John nodded. 'They were wonderful days. I suppose it's just the hardness of life now that makes me solemn.'

'You, solemn! Don't try that old sally on me. You're as sedate as a wagon full of grinning apes. Now, do you want to hear the history of poor Moll Bowling or not?'

'Of course I do.'

'Well, apparently she was given to Mr Garrick by Samuel Foote. You know the man?'

'Quite well, in fact.'

'It seems she played a breeches part in some production of Sam's and was quite hopeless so he exchanged her for a basket of worn and smelly costumes that David no longer wanted.'

John was astounded and thought Coralie was teasing him, but said nothing.

'Anyway, I'll say this much for her – she had a wonderful ear for accents. She copied the fine talk of the *beau monde* and improved herself so much that Garrick gave her secondary roles. Old Lord Conway came regularly to the theatre and took quite a fancy to her.'

'Don't tell me, she upped and married him.'

'Not immediately. You see, she was expecting a child—'

'Who was the father?'

'Nobody knew. She disappeared to the country for a month or three and came back slim and ready to resume her career.'

'And the baby?'

'Put out to a baby farmer, I don't doubt. Or else dumped outside Thomas Coram's.'

Some years back retired sea captain Thomas Coram had started the Foundling Hospital for abandoned children after seeing all the dying babies and starving youngsters littering the streets of London, but it had become so inundated with requests from wretched mothers – many of them prostitutes – that he had been forced to operate a waiting list. Thus bundled infants were left outside his gates at night, which the good-hearted man felt obliged to take in.

'Do you know what sex it was?'

Coralie screwed up her nose. 'I don't think she officially

announced it – in fact, I'm sure she didn't – but word got round that it was a girl.'

'But it lived, presumably.'

'Presumably. Anyway, a month after that she went off with Lord Conway – who was aged ninety if he was a day – and rumour had it that she married his son instead, which caused the old fellow to have a heart attack and keel over.'

'Is this all true?'

Coralie pealed with laughter, tears pouring down her cheeks. 'Yes.'

'It's like the plot of a ghastly novel. Do you swear to the facts?'

'Indeed I do,' answered Coralie, and placed her hand on her heart.

They both burst out guffawing but, when they had collected themselves some several minutes later, John asked, 'So where does Jacob O'Farrell enter the story?'

Coralie shook her head. 'I do not know and I am only guessing. But I would imagine that he was her groom, she took a fancy to him and they eloped.'

'So they are not married?'

'I'm afraid, my dear John, that we can only conjecture.'

'Well, I intend to ask him.'

'Beware his fists. He looks the sort of fellow who could turn ugly in a fight.'

'I'll heed your words of advice, Madam.'

But strangely, when John finally tracked him down at the Orange Tree, Jake was drained of all vitality and seemed as far from engaging in a bout of fisticuffs as a new-born infant. He sat, whiter than a shroud, at a table. John looked at his eyes, which had degenerated into slits caused by the puffiness on either side, and gathered that the news of Lady Conway's death had reached his ears. In fact, so far gone was Jake O'Farrell in a mixture of sadness and being extremely hungover that he did not even hear the Apothecary come in. However, at that moment Suzanne entered the room bearing a large cup of thick black coffee.

'Drink this,' she said in a commanding voice. 'It may restore you.'

Jake shook his head as if every movement hurt him. John, watching, wondered if it could possibly be an act. Suzanne gave the Apothecary a secretive look.

'Have you heard?' she whispered. He nodded his head. 'What an awful thing. Apparently she drowned herself.'

'There's a bit more to it than that,' he murmured.

But Jake must have overheard him because he said thickly, 'What's that you say?'

The Apothecary paused, wondering just how much he should tell him. Then he made a decision. 'How much do you know about your wife's death, Jake?'

'Only that she was found drowned at the Long Wharf. But how did it happen? Did she kill herself because I had gone carousing?'

'The answer is that I do not think this was a suicide, Jake. I suspect foul play.'

Jake rose slowly, like a corpse arising from its grave. 'If so I'll kill the bastard who did it. I'll tear his throat out with my bare hands.'

'But how will you know who it was?'

'I'll find him. I'll track him down if it takes me to the end of my days.'

It was the ramblings of a man still half drunk.

John humoured him. 'Yes, I'm sure you will. But first you must get some sleep. I'll fetch you a sedative.'

To his astonishment, Jake drank down the vial of physick which John handed to him without argument.

'To bed with you,' said Suzanne firmly and, half-carrying the man between them, they took the wretched widower to the same room in which he had spent the night.

SEVENTEEN

Having informed Suzanne that the Apothecary's shop would be manned by his apprentice that day, for John had persuaded young Tristram to join him permanently – his employment with Dr Warren merely one of running errands, a neat arrangement which the doctor himself had approved – John set out on foot to cross the town. He was making his way to the mortuary, hoping to take another look at the body of the woman born Moll Bowling who had risen to greater heights.

The Apothecary walked quickly, raising his hat to various people along the way and feeling very much a part of the city. Yet for all that he missed London, the coffeehouses and the stinks, the playhouses and the gossip. And he missed word of his old friend John Fielding, his advice, his wit, his sharpness of intellect. But, as if to compensate him for all that he had left, he had found Coralie again, which was compensation indeed.

On entering the mortuary, where the bodies of soldiers lay stretched out and peaceful, each wrapped in a sheet awaiting burial, John was overcome with a certain lurching of his stomach. But he steeled himself against this and made his way to where he could see a doctor at work on a corpse.

The man looked up and smiled. 'Are you Mr Rawlings, by any chance?'

'Yes. I am here on behalf of Lieutenant Dalrymple.'

'He told me you might call. Do you want to take a look at Lady Conway? I have moved her into another room. It did not appear seemly to leave her surrounded by all these men.'

John smiled to himself. It would appear that even in death the niceties had to be preserved.

'That would be very kind.'

'Follow me.'

She lay on a bare slab, her body still uncovered, a few corpses of other women close by.

John turned in some surprise to the doctor. 'Who are these?'

'Camp followers. Soldiers' wives and sweethearts. One or two died in childbirth, the rest from other natural causes. But generally they are a tough lot. In fact, they are quite indispensable for doing menial tasks around the encampment.'

'A hard life for a woman.'

'Better than dwelling in Old Pye Street, London.'

John smiled crookedly. The doctor was referring to one of the worst rookeries in the capital. Lacking any form of sanitation, people pissed anywhere and dropped their excrement into the streams, which led to them being covered and gave rise to the foulest stench pervading the entire area.

'You're right, of course. At least the air here is clean.'

'Relatively so, yes. But you came to look at Lady Conway, I thought.'

'Yes. What do you make of her death?'

'There are one or two odd things about the corpse. Look at the hands. Notice the way her fingers are cut deep, all of them. It was as if she was clinging on to something. And why was she dressed as a young man? Some sort of Sappho or what?'

Despite the solemnity of his surroundings, to say nothing of the faint but persistent smell of death, John smiled. 'She was actually born in Boston but went to live in England at an early age. After that I know nothing until she turned up at the Theatre Royal, Drury Lane, and was given to David Garrick in exchange for some cast-off wardrobe items. She led a very scandalous life but nothing Sapphic, as far as I know.'

'Great heavens!' exclaimed the doctor. 'That's enough to be going on with. But the poor soul ended up drowned. And how did she get those damaged hands?'

'She was seen climbing up the rigging on one of the tea ships.'

'You are being serious, I trust.'

'Completely. A reliable eyewitness saw her.'

'But why did she do that, for the love of God?'

'I can only conjecture that she was being pursued and thought it a reasonable means of escaping.'

'Or perhaps somebody followed her and gave her a push.'

The Apothecary fingered his chin. 'I shouldn't think a push was possible but if you are right – and we can only guess at it – someone could have grabbed her heels.'

'And thrown her off balance so that she landed in the sea. Damme, so this could be a case of murder.'

'Exactly.'

'But why?' asked the doctor. 'What had the wretched woman ever done?'

'That,' said the Apothecary, 'is what I intend to find out.'

Leaving the mortuary behind him, John Rawlings strolled down the road towards the great mansion owned by the Hancock family and loitered behind the line of trees that protected it. The coach house, an imposing affair, stood on the far left, while slightly behind the great house was a smaller dwelling where the servants resided. John walked to the right, following the line of fencing, and eventually found a place where the wooden paling had been damaged and was leaning slightly away from its accompanying stakes. He crouched down and pushed it, and it gave way sufficiently for him – with a great deal of breathing in – to squeeze himself through. He emerged on the other side, red in the face but on the Hancock property.

Nonchalance, he decided, brushing himself down. Look as though you belong. He leaned through the hole, retrieved his hat, ran his fingers through his hair, which was tied back with a bow, and crammed the hat back on his head. Then he strolled away, humming a cheery tune.

There were not many people about. Passing a gardener, John gave him a merry, 'Good day to you,' and received the answer, 'And to you, Sir.' Pleased with this, the Apothecary walked round the back of the great house and made his way to the servants' quarters. At this time of day it was deserted. John adopted his good citizen face and entered. A very old slave, snoozing in the morning sun, spoke.

'Good morning, Sir. Can I help you?'

John looked contrite. 'So sorry to disturb you. I am an apothecary and have been asked to call on the coachman, who is feeling very under the weather at the moment.' No lies there! 'Could you tell me where I might find him?'

The elderly negro servant smiled and rose slowly from his chair. 'Well, Master, they do live in the coach house to be near the horses and all. I haven't seen Jakey this morning so guess he might be takin' his ease. Come to that, I ain't seen the lady neither.'

John raised his hat. 'How kind of you. Many thanks.' So news of the drowning hadn't reached the Hancock residence yet. He had to act fast before it did. He nodded and smiled. 'I'll make my way to see them directly.' The old man still hovered above his chair and John added, 'Just you sit down and rest. You looked as if you were enjoying it.'

'Mr Hancock, he'm be a good master, Sir. He don't throw me out just because I'm too old to work no more.'

John's heart constricted. He knew the fate of many black slaves, literally shown the door when their age became too great to allow them to labour further. He smiled at the old fellow and, wishing him a good day, made his way to the tall and imposing building that was the coach house.

The great coach that John Hancock's uncle Thomas had ordered from London, slightly battered now by age and wear but for all that magnificent, rested quietly in the large hall that the Apothecary now entered. It was covered with a home cloth to keep it spotless but John lifted the protective sheet to have a look. It reminded him vividly of London, and yet again he felt that ache in his heart which he always had when he thought of his home town. To the left of the room in which the conveyance was housed were some loose boxes, from which came the familiar stamp and whinny of horses, to say nothing of the distinctive smell of horseflesh. To the right was a wooden staircase. With a great deal of caution, John mounted it.

Above, built under the roof and with a fine display of windows which had the most magnificent views over Boston Common on the left-hand side and Beacon Hill on the right, lay two spacious rooms. The first, a living area, was furnished simply but with good taste. The second, which John approached with caution, ever fearful that Jake might have made a swift recovery and could possibly be within, was thankfully empty. The Apothecary tiptoed inside and shut the door behind him.

A large bed, the sheets still rumpled, stood inside, together with a clothes press, a chair on which lay some of Lady Conway's garments, and a wooden dressing table with a mirror above. So there had sat the late Moll Bowling, applying her powder and paint before the challenge of the day. John approached the small stool that stood in front of it and sat down. There was a sound from the stables below and the Apothecary, with nowhere to hide, stood behind the door and listened. It was a groom talking to the horses.

'Come on d'ere, Starlight. How are you, my liddle sweetie? I'll give you some oats if you is a good gal.'

Somehow it was rather touching to listen to and John felt himself relax. Not really knowing what he was looking for, the Apothecary began a hasty but thorough search. Moll Conway's clothes gave nothing away, discarded in a hurry as she changed into man's clothing for that last fateful venture she had undertaken when the rebels of Boston attacked the English tea ships. Sniffing the pillows, John detected a faint whiff of perfume from her side, while the other pillow revealed the unmistakeable odour of Jake, sweat and booze and general manliness. But it was at the dressing table, hidden in a little box behind the mirror, covered by a shawl which had been draped over it, that the Apothecary found the letter. It had been posted in London and had clearly arrived by one of the many ships that docked in the various harbours. Scanning it, he read:

At the office we were glad to have news of your arrival safely in the town of Boston. Continue with all haste upon your mission. We await, dear Madam, your next communication.

It was signed with the initial *N*.

John stared at it, wondering what it could possibly mean. What mission could Lady Conway have undertaken and who could possibly have sent it? And then he thought back to when he had met the Bishop of Bath and Wells, the most unlikely decipherer of cryptic codes, who had been employed by the Secret Office and whose extra-curricular activities were shrouded in mystery. Was it possible that Lady Conway was working for them? Putting the letter into his pocket, the Apothecary took one last look round and decided that the bedroom had nothing further to tell him. He quietly went out and left the door as he had found it, ajar.

A quick glance at the living quarters told him that there was nothing further of any relevance to be discovered and he silently made his way downstairs to where the magnificent coach, under its protective shroud, stood in all its majestic beauty. But just as he was making his way out into the grounds, the groom entered and stared at him. John inclined his head, wreathed in smiles. 'It seems that I have had a wasted journey. Mr O'Farrell is not in.'

'Oh, no, Sah, he done gone missin' in Boston. I think he might get de sack if he don't come back.'

John risked all. 'But surely his wife will know where he is.'

The groom shook his head emphatically. 'No, Sah. She gone missin' as well.'

As he had earlier thought, news of the tragedy had somehow not reached the magnificent pile built by the late departed Thomas Hancock. This, he imagined, was because the mansion lay at some distance from the town, resplendent in its own gardens and parkland. But he knew it wouldn't be long before somebody came running to tell them the tidings. He must make his exit soon.

John assumed a puzzled expression and said, 'My goodness me. Well, no doubt you'll see one or other of them shortly.' Feeling somewhat ashamed of his blatant lying, he made his way hurriedly out of the place by conventional means, the gatekeeper giving him a magnificent salute.

He would have dashed back to Boston but for a strange sight which caught his eye as he reached the lane which ran towards Beacon Hill. This too was fenced off, but presumably somebody had come up the hill from the far side and now appeared to be standing near the top, having somehow scaled the precipitate climb, and remained stock still with a pair of divining rods in his hands. John gasped aloud. If his eyes were not deceiving him the figure looked amazingly similar to Sir Julian Wychwood, the last person on earth that John would have associated with divination. He stood agape, watching the diviner walk forwards slowly until the rods suddenly dipped down. At this, Julian dropped on his knees and started scrabbling at the earth below. John cupped his hands around his mouth and bellowed 'Julian', at which the other turned his head and gazed at the Apothecary's distant figure. He waved his arm and gave an unreadable panto-mime to which John nodded enthusiastically before giving it up as hopeless and continuing on his way.

His walk back to town would have taken him back directly

to the area he knew well but instead he decided to have a look around and acquaint himself with the more distant part of the North End. Accordingly he turned right in Treamount Street and, walking quite hard, eventually found himself at a place new to him, the place where the Charles River had been dammed to form Mill Cove. It was a fairly deserted spot, not many houses having been built nearby, and had a slightly eerie atmosphere. John presumed that the powering of the mill wheel came from the tide, because this was where the Charles River flowed into the sea and fell under its influence. The mill itself stood at the top of Mill Creek, the manmade brook which virtually cut the north end of Boston off from the rest of the town. No wonder, John thought, that this place of poor sanitation and tightly packed houses held so many rebellious citizens in its grip.

Looking round him, the Apothecary stared solemnly at the sheet of water – as large in size as the whole of the Common – and felt himself go cold. He realized that he had eaten nothing since a very light breakfast – not at all his usual fare – and decided that the cove was not his favourite place. Thinking deeply and concentrating his mind on Julian Wychwood, that seducer of women and charmer of men, he pondered the problem of what on earth the fellow could have been up to on the bleakness of Beacon Hill.

EIGHTEEN

D
usk was falling by the time he walked beside the steep wooden escarpments down which water cascaded to join Mill Creek by means of a tunnel under the road, the stream eventually pouring back into the sea. Furthermore, the Apothecary felt freezing cold and realized that it was only a few days to Christmas. Rose would soon be returning home from school for the celebration of the festival.

Inside the Orange Tree Irish Tom loomed large behind the bar while little Suzanne ran round like a gnat, serving customers, clearing tables and grinning at everybody as if they were more than welcome. Big Matthew was in there and, wonder of wonders, Lady Eawiss attempting to look the height of respectability, drinking a cup of milky tea and smiling at her current *cicisbeo*, who was different since John's last viewing and now appeared to be a very tall, very bland, very young English officer who was, presumably, willing to sleep with anything provided it had money.

'Of course, I've always admired a military man,' she was saying in a loud and terribly affected English voice. 'My late husband, you know, Sir Bevis Eawiss, was a colonel, of course.'

'Really?' replied the other with a desperate show of interest.

'Oh, yes. I was a mere child bride at the time.' This remark was made very deep and loud. John and Irish Tom exchanged a wide-eyed look. 'But then my poor spouse was called to Jesus and I have been alone ever since.'

'For a long time?' asked her gormless escort.

'Oh, three or four years at the most,' she whispered plummily.

'Gracious,' replied the youthful officer, and stared fixedly into his glass of cognac.

The door opened and in walked Sir Julian Wychwood, plucking his hat from his head and standing for a moment in order to gain the maximum amount of attention. Lady Eawiss fluttered where she sat and Sir Julian, noticing this, dashed over and raised one of her fat, over-ringed hands to his lips.

'Ah, my dear Madam, how are you, pray? 'Tis an age since I've seen you. Tell me, how is that delightful little thing you employ as a maid?'

Lady Eawiss simpered alarmingly. 'Well, of course, I know I gave her employment when the poor wee soul was utterly stranded, but now I regard her as more of a daughter. She calls me Mama, don't you know.'

The Apothecary raised an eyebrow at Tom, who choked back a laugh, while the young lieutenant raised his eyes to Sir Julian's elegant frame and looked exquisitely miserable.

'How touching,' Julian chattered on. 'How one loves to hear a tale so full of enchantment.'

He turned and pulled a face at the other customers and there was a subdued laugh. 'I am always full of *pensees de assassiner* when I think of my dam.'

Lady Eawiss made a moue as the rest of the customers, many of whom were descended directly from the French, fell about in a loud roar of mirth. The young lieutenant drew out his watch and said, 'Heavens, I must report for duty,' bowed, clicked his heels and disappeared rapidly. Blue Wolf came through the door as the youth departed and looked around solemnly, finally fixing his eyes on John.

'I have to report that your sons are in bed and asleep. I also have to report that they had a very large supper which I prepared for them.'

John stepped forward. 'Thank you, Blue Wolf. I knew you had it in you.'

But his conversation with his newly appointed servant ended abruptly. Lieutenant Dalrymple entered the drinking house with an extremely earnest expression on his face.

'Excuse me a moment, if you would,' said the Apothecary to the Indian. 'There is someone I really must talk to.' Motioning the army man into an alcove usually reserved for courting couples, he said, 'I have something of interest to show you,' and produced from his pocket the extraordinary letter he had found in Lady Conway's dressing table.

The lieutenant scanned it, then read it again slowly. 'What the devil does this mean?'

'Your answer is as good as mine. I have no idea. But my feeling is that the deceased woman was a spy.'

Dalrymple looked frankly astonished. 'But for whom? On which side? And why?'

'As you know, she was born in Boston, knew Doctor Warren when he was at school, then was shipped to England. But after this her life took some strange twists and turns. Yet, supposing that, from an early age she had become indoctrinated with the thought of freedom and liberty for the Colonists. Would this not make her determined to return and fight for the cause? Particularly if she had joined some organization in London which actively supports her ideas. It's all perfectly possible.'

The lieutenant swallowed a cognac with a great gulp. 'By God, it makes you think, though. How can we find out?'

'I would go and see Doctor Warren if I were you. He won't tell you anything because he strongly believes in the movement. But you could read between the lines.'

'I'd rather you did it. You sound as if you've had more practice than I have.'

The Apothecary gave a wry little smile and said, 'Really?'

'Meanwhile, I could place the husband under arrest and question him sharply.'

John shook his head. 'I don't think that would do any good at all. He's more likely to button his lip and prefer to be beaten up. I think the best way to is to befriend him and ask him questions gently.'

Dalrymnple sighed. 'It sounds as if I should concentrate my attentions entirely on this woman. But I am sworn to keep up my army duties.'

John smiled at him. 'Surely you have an intelligence officer within your ranks.'

'We have several but their methods tend to be somewhat brutal. Could you undertake the task, Mr Rawlings?'

John nodded, somewhat reluctantly. 'I can but try. But I can't promise anything, mind.'

Dalrymple rose, bowing militarily, and at that moment Sir Julian Wychwood, suave as ever though his face was more flushed

than usual, sidled into the alcove. His eyes took in the scene and
he bowed languidly in Dalrymple's direction.

'A fellow Britisher, I see. How dee do, Sir.'

Dalrymple clicked his heels, bowed and said, 'A pleasure
to make your acquaintance, Sir. But I am afraid I must be off.
Army life, don't you know.'

'Quite, quite,' Julian answered vaguely and watched while
the lieutenant departed, then turned to John with a sudden energy.
'My dear fellow, I think I have discovered where my mother's
fortune lies.'

'Is that what you were doing on Beacon Hill strutting about
like a water diviner?'

'Exactly.' Julian went slightly redder. 'Of course, you know
all that transpired in England.'

John nodded. He had indeed met Lady Tyninghame, Julian's
mother, an incredibly beautiful and ageless woman, in Bristol
what seemed like a century ago but in fact had been the year in
which he had sailed for the Colonies. He also knew her whole
tragic story.

'But before we parted company . . .' Wychwood continued,
looking for the first time in his life positively ill at ease, '. . . I
got hold of a clue. Look.' And he thrust a worn piece of paper
under the Apothecary's nose.

It could have been drawn by a child but looking at it closely
one could see that it was a primitive sketch of Boston with one
or two recognizable features, including Beacon Hill, by which
was marked a large X. It could have referred to anything but Sir
Julian, forgetting for once his pose as a man of fashion, was
hopping about with excitement.

'Don't you see it, John? I mean, it is clear as daylight. That's
where she buried all her loot.'

'But I didn't think she had any.'

'Oh, pshaw. She positively dripped with cash. Why you only
had to look at my beloved Mama to see she had stowed away a
fortune in diamonds or some such. And now I've found them.'

'Have you? Well, congratulations.'

Julian looked down his nose. 'Well, I didn't actually have time.
Two beastly old men were puffing up the hill on t'other side and
I had to abandon my search. But the divining rods leapt in my

hands as I walked over the spot. I know it's buried beneath, John. I feel it in my very bones.'

'So when do you plan to unearth whatever may be there?'

'Tomorrow morning, at first light. I'll approach the hill from the far side so I don't have to traverse the Hancock estate. I shall take my divining rods with me, together with a stout spade, and by nightfall I shall be in possession of what is rightfully mine.'

'D'ye know, I've a mind to come with you. It will take my mind off other problems.'

'What other problems?'

'Nothing really. The death of Lady Conway still bothers me somewhat.'

John was making light of the situation, though deep within his heart he felt that the murderer was not unknown to him. It was just a question of fitting a face into the whirling pattern in his brain.

'As it does all of us,' Julian uttered in an extremely solemn voice.

But no more of their private conversation was possible because at that moment a head appeared round the entrance – a head belonging to Jacob O'Farrell, looking dejected but entirely in control of himself.

'I want to apologise for my behaviour on that terrible night, gentlemen. Will you ever forgive me?'

'There's nothing to forgive, my dear chap,' Julian answered, smiling a lazy smile. 'After such a ghastly event nobody could blame you for your behaviour.'

But, John thought, he had not yet heard of his wife's death when he turned up drunk as a wheelbarrow and was sick all over the place.

'When did you learn of Demelza's death, Jake?' he asked quietly.

Was it his imagination or did the look on Jacob's face alter fractionally? But the man answered calmly enough.

'T'was Suzanne who told me next morning when I had sobered up. I screamed and shouted but she left me alone to do my worst. Eventually I recovered my dignity.'

'I offer you my deepest sympathies,' said the Apothecary, watching Jake's reaction intently. There was nothing; not a flicker. The man was either a very good actor or was completely genuine.

Julian was drawling something. 'Terribly hard on you, old feller. Still, we must face things the best way we can. Will you allow me to buy you a drink?'

'Thank you but no. I must make my way back home. I fear that Mr Hancock will think I have run away or else. Good night, gentlemen.' Jacob made a small bow and was gone.

John and Julian stared at one another.

'He's taking it pretty well, don't you think?' said Julian.

'Indeed, indeed,' answered John, and said nothing further.

The sun rose like a prince, scaling the heavens in majesty. First came the pale pink threads of dawn, then these were lit by shades of blood, and finally the wondrous fireball could be glimpsed soaring above the horizon in all his great magnificence.

John Rawlings and Sir Julian Wychwood, clambering up the steep sides of Beacon Hill, paused, breathing faster, and looked around them. For once Julian's languidness escaped him and he said with genuine fervour, 'My God, John, but I am glad to be alive on such a day.'

And the Apothecary smiled, knowing the true character that lurked behind the foppish fellow, and answered, 'So am I, my friend.'

They were toiling up the northern slope of Beacon Hill to escape attention but John, who had never before climbed the dastardly heights, motioned towards a large hump on the western side of the hill.

'What's that?'

Julian grinned. 'It is where my mother's treasure is buried. But do you know that man Revere?'

'The short, dark fellow who comes into the Orange Tree? Quite a friendly sort?'

'Yes. He made Doctor Warren's false teeth for him. He refers to the hump as Mount Whoredom.'

'I can't imagine ladies in that profession struggling up this hill to ply their trade.'

'Nor the customers either.'

But Julian interrupted this train of thought with a shrill shriek as the divining rods which he had drawn from his pocket twitched violently.

'Come, let us hurry. We must dig from the back or we will be visible to the people in the big house.'

They set to with a spade and a small shovel, which was as much as they could carry with them. By now the sumptuous sunrise was in full glory and they had to crouch below the brow of the hill to avoid being spotted from the Hancock home. That their distant figures would have been visible to the dwellings that lay to the north they completely ignored. Julian dug with a will and after about half an hour gave a cry of triumph as his spade hit something.

''Zounds, John. I knew it was here. She was a cunning old vixen to hide something so far away. Do you think she knew that one day I would find it?'

'No.'

Julian looked slightly startled. 'Don't you believe my mother had one redeeming feature?'

'No, not one.'

The other shrugged. 'Ah, well. You're probably right, of course.'

John spread his coat upon the ground and sat down to admire the view, which from his high vantage point was spectacular. Boston was reduced in size to a miniature, a child's toy, a sweet reproduction. He looked from where the sun glistened and gleamed on the church spires to where it turned the Mill Cove into a blue sparkle and then to the sails of the ferry boat to Charlestown, shining white as daisy flowers in the glory of that early day. He was at that moment utterly filled with the elation of being alive and well.

Julian, meanwhile, was digging for all he was worth until he shouted, 'I've uncovered it, John. It's a large tin box.' Together, heaving, they pulled it out of its dark pit and attempted to open the lid. It had rusted but John, using his shovel, managed to ease the top a little.

'Damme, my boy, this is a corky moment. Shake the hand of a man about to be wealthy,' Julian exclaimed.

John's eyebrows raised darkly and he laughed. 'I hope so, Julian. Indeed I do.'

Fingernails splintering, Wychwood tore at the lid and then exclaimed in horror, 'God's wounds, it's a skeleton.'

Instantly the Apothecary peered into the box's depths. There was indeed a set of bones arrayed within but as John gazed at it he realized that it was the remains of a dog, curled over but nevertheless a canine. He put his hand inside and pulled out a leather collar with a name on it – Rover. There was also an ancient piece of paper folded into four. Carefully, John unfolded it. It read, *Here lies my faithful friend, Rover. Alas, he and I will rove no more. R.I.P.*

John did not know how to restrain himself. It was sad but laughable. Yet the expression on Julian's face was tragic. He had genuinely expected to find a fortune but instead had found nothing but the skeletal remains of a hound. He sat down upon the grass and tears ran down his handsome cheeks. At that moment Sir Julian Wychwood was as far removed from being a dandy man as was mortally possible.

'Come on, old friend. You didn't really think your mother would leave you anything, did you?'

'Yes, I thought that for once in her miserable life she had done the decent thing.'

'Well, I'm afraid that she left you nothing but poor old Rover. That is, if he was ever hers.'

Julian looked up, still weeping. 'Wretched dog and wretched me.'

'Oh, do stop. See the funny side.'

'It's difficult.'

'Let's rebury the poor creature. His owner, whoever he was or is, would prefer that we did so.'

'You're right – as bloody usual.'

John Rawlings solemnly replaced the box in its rightful setting. Then he said deeply, 'Farewell, Rover, your barking days are over but now you romp in fields of clover.'

Julian looked aghast. 'Was that supposed to rhyme?'

'I thought it was rather good.'

'Oh, John Rawlings,' Julian answered, a slow, sad smile starting to steal over his reluctant features. 'Come on, let's call on the Hancocks and see what they are up to. There's quite a pretty girl . . .'

The rest of his conversation was lost as they made their way down the hill and back to civilization.

NINETEEN

Tristram had done well, surprisingly so for a boy new to apprenticeship. And then John remembered that the young man had been assistant to Dr Warren's students and had obviously gained some knowledge while in their company. Nevertheless, the Apothecary was pleased when he walked into his shop after leaving Sir Julian, half laughing, half crying, making his way into a tavern. The place was spotlessly clean and, just for a moment, John stood in the doorway and let his mind wander back to all the apprentices who had served him in his shop in Shug Lane, Piccadilly, and all the happy memories he had shared with them. He indulged in a moment of pure home-sickness then, telling himself that there were more pressing problems to be addressed, straightened his back and went in.

Tristram was serving a customer who turned round, whey-faced, as he heard footsteps behind him. It was Tracey Tremayne, looking sick to die.

'My dear fellow, whatever is the matter?'

Tracey grabbed at the counter before he slumped into a chair that John had placed discreetly for the use of customers who were feeling weak at the knees.

'Oh, my dear John, I have a vast attack of the looseness – and so does poor George. The fact is that we started to celebrate Christmas a little early and we must have eaten something that was poisoned, for now we can neither of us leave the pan for long.'

The Apothecary put on his sympathetic face. 'Oh, you poor souls. Let me make you a decoction of Dog's Grass, the seed of which should bring about relief within the hour. Meanwhile, would you care to visit a closet?'

'Yes, I think I would.'

And Tracey disappeared, with much groaning, towards an outhouse used by the customers of the Orange Tree and all the people who worked nearby. It was horribly smelly but it was a part of life and had to be endured. John, meanwhile, took a plant down from those hanging on the shop's ceiling, bruised the roots of the herb, added the seeds and boiled the whole lot in wine. The mixture was cooling down when Tracey staggered back in, looking pale as parchment. The Apothecary motioned him back to the chair and gave him a glass of the dispensed physick to drink. Tracey sipped it.

'A pleasant enough taste. Thank you.'

'I have prepared a large bottle for George and another for you. If you have any further trouble do not hesitate to come back.'

'Thank you from the heart of my bottom,' said Tracey, and giggled hysterically at his own joke.

Tristram hid a smile but John, playing the part of serious apothecary, merely raised an eyebrow.

The dancing master finished his drink and gave the Apothecary two shillings. 'And where will you be spending Christmas?' he asked.

'With Madame Clive, I hope.'

'A very beautiful woman. How is her school?'

'Very well, I believe. My daughter, Rose, attends there.'

'Really,' said Tracey, 'I had no idea. Will she be coming home soon?'

'The day after tomorrow. Tonight they will be producing an end-of-term play in the barn behind the house in which Coralie lives.'

'The one thing I cannot abide about Boston is this Puritanical attitude they have towards the theatre. What is the matter with these people?'

As Tracey said those words a thrill of fear, conjured up by heaven knows what, ran through John's body like an icy splinter. He knew these feelings of old and had by now recognized them as a portent of disaster.

'What's the matter, Sir?' asked Tristram. 'You've gone quite white.'

John passed it off with a wave of his hand. ''Tis nothing. A moment of sympathy with our friend here.'

Tracey bowed carefully. 'Thank you again,' he said, then dashed out.

After he had gone the Apothecary sat in the recently vacated chair. 'I know it is early in the day, Tristram, but would you get me a nip of brandy from the Orange Tree? I feel I need it.'

'Of course – at once, Sir.'

Left alone, John sat silently, trying to understand his thought process. It had not been the mention of the theatre that had given him that instant frisson of fear but rather the mention of the people of Boston. He thought back to the ravaging of the three tea ships and how the mob had suddenly seemed like one angry unit. Was it probable that they were going to rise up and protest against British rule? Yet the people he knew as individuals were all so friendly and easy-going. He thought back to the night he had extracted Dr Warren's teeth. What a charming man, and yet he had been one of the thinly disguised people who had been involved in the attack. And then John considered that there had been a murderer in their midst. Possibly, no, more likely probably, a British agent whose sole purpose had been to end the work of Demelza Conway, also known as Moll Bowling. But who was it? What shadow-like person walked along the streets of Boston with a smile and a friendly nod for everyone he passed?

Tristram came back bearing a large glass of brandy which John swallowed in three gulps. Somewhat revived, he stood up, put on his long apron and then put his thoughts behind him, and prepared to face the rest of the day.

Despite the ban on theatrical performances quite a few people made their way to the barn where Coralie's pupils were due to perform their Christmas presentation. There was a cheerful atmosphere amongst the parents and friends winding their way along Beacon Street. Lady Eawiss, fat and fluttering, was accompanied by a uniformed figure who John could not identify. Following one pace behind, walking demurely, was pretty Jane Hawthorne, yet there was something different about her. Her entire carriage had a confidence that John had never noticed before, but he knew the reason beyond doubt. In some sort of secret ceremony performed by a tribe elder that Blue Wolf had located, the couple had been married. Looking at Jane long and hard from beneath the brim of his hat, John thought her more poised and calm, more serene, and he cast his mind back to the bath house and how he had glimpsed Blue Wolf touching her body as if it were a rare jewel, and knew that the couple had undoubtedly consummated their love.

Christmas was not celebrated at all by the more Puritanical members of society; however, there was another section of the population who did. These were supporters of the British crown, who went to the Episcopalian churches, decorated with sweet-smelling boughs of green brought in from the woods. These same citizens sent their daughters to Madame Clive's School for Young Ladies and laughed and joked with each other as they jostled for seats on the wooden benches which had been set in three rows in the barn, the back two raised up by planking so that everyone could get a good view. John sat in the front with Jasper and James, the long, lean figure of Blue Wolf on their other side. In the back row he observed Tracey and George, presumably cured of their looseness by John's physick. Further down sat Lady Eawiss and her entourage, while almost directly behind was Sir Julian Wychwood with a brilliantly garbed young lady on his arm. Matthew and his wife, and Irish Tom and Suzanne, arrived late and had to squeeze on the end of the back row. Then, even later, young Tristram came in, red in the face and panting audibly, with a half-hearted request to Lady Eawiss to move up a bit. Eventually all were seated and the performance began.

It was the usual rendition of girls playing solos on the pianoforte or singing in loud, clear voices, some definitely off key, alas, but the end was absolutely marvellous. Coralie and Rose acted in a two-hander playlet written by Madame Clive. It was the story of a teacher obsessed by the idea of having a doppelgänger, terrified that she will meet it one day and so bring about her own death. Rose played the part of the pupil who sees her schoolmistress dying of fright before a full-length mirror. It was a taut and fearful tale and the audience sat very still for a moment or two before bursting into sustained applause at the end. John, watching intently, thought that his daughter would have a definite future upon the stage as she played the role with great intensity and a depth of feeling that surprised him. He felt enormously proud of her and, glancing at young Tristram, saw that the boy had gone red as a rowan berry.

The makeshift curtains were pulled across and the audience fell to talking amongst themselves.

'My dear, I swear your child is a beauty of the first order, 'pon my life. How old is she now?'

'Coming up for fourteen.'

It was George Glynde who had spoken but he was almost immediately shouted down by Tracey Tremayne. ''Pon rep, but she'll make a delicious armful for some young blood who'll be dangling after her.'

John smiled a trifle wryly. 'Don't tell me. I believe she already has a young admirer.' And he cast a surreptitious look in the direction of Tristram who was standing on the edge of the crowd, turning his rather small hat in his hands, still very rosy about the cheeks.

Matthew walked up to them and said, 'I'm glad I left my children at home with Sarah's mother. I think they'd have been scared out of their wits by that play. But little Rose was wonderful in it, John.'

The Apothecary took him by the elbow. 'If I may talk to you on another matter.'

'Yes, of course.'

'You have heard the news about Lady Conway, no doubt.'

'Yes, it's the talk of the North End.'

'Tell me, Matthew, did you see anything odd that night? Anything at all?'

'I saw Blue Wolf go aboard one of the ships, though which it was I couldn't truthfully say.'

'What was his purpose, do you know?'

'I have no idea, John. As far as I could see he just stood silently, gazing round in a way that only people of his race do.'

'Do you think he was looking for someone?'

'Could have been.'

So was it possible that the young Indian was involved in some way? Clearly he was – but in what manner? For John could not accept the idea that the man who had saved their lives by guiding them across the unforgiving landscape to Boston, who had hunted for them, fallen in love with the delightful Jane Hawthorne and done so much to keep the party safe and protected could possibly have murdered one of their number.

He turned back to Matthew. 'What happened then?'

'I don't know. The person next to me said something and I turned to answer. When I looked back, Blue Wolf had gone.'

'Did you notice anything else?'

'Only that the men in disguise were raping the tea chests. They seemed so violent about it. I think there's trouble coming to this country.'

'Will you stay?'

'Oh, yes. I've made my future here. I am quite content in my little house with my big family. I'll remain, come what may.'

One thing he could be sure of, John thought, was that Matthew was in no way involved with the death of Moll Demelza Bowling Conway. He made up his mind there and then that he would go and visit Jake O'Farrell that very night and somehow get the truth out of the wretched fellow.

He left the school play shortly after and walked through a night seething with intrigue and unrest in the bitter winter darkness. The atmosphere was almost palpable; the icy wind blowing in his ears seemed to contain whispering voices and there was a sniff of danger in the very coldness. With his heart pounding John made his way carrying one small lantern until he saw the lights from the tents of the soldiers camped on the Common glimmering in the distance. The white palings of the fence which surrounded the Hancock family's mighty swatch of land suddenly loomed in the darkness and John was glad to walk beside it until he reached the whole magnificent edifice. This time he did not attempt to squeeze through the fence but instead marched up to the gates and rang the bell. A young black fellow, alert but for all that yawning widely, came out of the small hut in which he sat while on duty.

'Yassir?'

'Would it be possible to see the coachman Jake? I know that this is no hour to call but I have some physick for him. He has lost his wife in tragic circumstances and is in a terrible state.'

'I ain't seen him, Sah. But I thinks he went to call on Mr Hancock and then wuz sent straight to bed. That wuz a terrible business, that wuz. And she wuz such a nice lady.'

John's face became very earnest. 'Of course, I didn't know her as well as you do. Can you tell me anything of her?'

'Wahl, Sir. She teaches riding to young gals from the school next door. And she also teaches it to other ladies of the town. Sitting side saddle an' all.'

'She doesn't have any men pupils then?'

'No, Sah. Except one day a fellow turns up – tall and dark and a stranger as far as I could tell 'cos I had to let him through these main gates, whereas Lady Conway, she always uses the little wicket gate at the side to admit her pupils.'

'Go on.'

'Well, he spoke with a strange accent, not like the natives of Boston talk.'

'What do you mean – was he English?'

'I think so, Sah. He says, "I believe the lady of the house teaches riding, don't cher know. Be good enough to direct me to her."'

All this was said with great effort and a great deal of screwing up of the young negro's features.

'That sounds English enough to me. Did you see them meet?'

'Oh, yes, Sah. She seemed mighty startled to clap eyes on him and would have galloped away but he grabs her bridle and raises his whip to her.'

'Good gracious. Did she say anything?'

'Yus. She says, "You bird of ill omen. Why have you followed me here?" And he says, "You know demned well why I have." Then they goes out of my hearing. So that's all I can tell you, Sah.'

John fished in his pocket for a coin and pressed it into the eager young fellow's hand.

'Thank you indeed. You have been more than helpful. Now I must get this physick to Jake, who is in a far worse state than either of us.'

The coach house was decidedly sinister at night. Lanterns were hung at various points on the wall, throwing flickering shadows over everything, the most monstrous of which was the coach itself, hung in its protecting shroud. The horses moved in their loose boxes, the thud of their hooves and the sudden high whinny the only sound in the deserted building. John had been in some nerve-racking situations in his time but this one ranked highly. Cautiously, he took a lantern off the wall and started to mount the shadowy staircase that led to the apartment above. Every stair creaked under his weight, the sound ringing out in his imagination like the boom of a canon. And then he heard a faint noise above him, as if a mouse somewhere had scuttled away. The next thing he knew there was a crashing fist in his face and a pair of furious eyes glaring at him as a voice with a notably English accent said, 'Oh no you don't, you damnable little snoop.' And then all was darkness as he rolled down the staircase and into oblivion.

He came to lying in a bale of hay. Someone was putting a wet cloth on his forehead and there was an overpowering smell of horses everywhere. John opened his eyes with caution and found that he was just outside a loose box, the resident of which was looking at him with a wild, suspicious glare. Looking in the other direction John saw Jacob O'Farrell kneeling on the cobbles and swishing a piece of material about in a bucket.

'Jake,' croaked John, at which the other swung round, showing eyelids puffed up with weeping but definitely not the owner of the demonic eyes that had sent him flying backwards.

'John,' came the reply. 'How the hell did you get here? And in this terrible state?'

'I was on my way to see you, my dear fellow, when someone knocked me down the stairs with a hell of a thump.'

'Was it a case of mistaken identity, do you think? Was it me they were after?'

John nursed his jaw. 'No, I don't believe so. Look, Jake, be straight with me, please. Did you have anything to do with Demelza's death?'

'No. I swear by all the saints and on my mother's life that I did not.'

'Would you like to tell me the whole story of your relationship with her?'

'It would be a relief to confide in someone. But first, let me get you back upstairs.'

They slowly ascended the creaking staircase and Jake, having seated John in an armchair, himself opposite, began to talk.

'As you have probably guessed by now, we were never married.

I was just a humble boy from the backstreets of Dublin and I
went to England to try to find work. I'd always had a way with
horses – used to murmur to them, you know. Anyway, to cut to
the heart of it, I was employed by old Lord Conway as head
groom. He had a mistress living in the house at the time, a
very lovely creature with a well-turned ankle. He had a heart
attack – literally blue in the face and not a breath in him –
when she upped and married his son, a nasty bit of work with
dark looks and a darker heart.'

'Was her name Moll Bowling?'

Jake turned a haunted face on him. 'It might have been once.
But to me she was always Demelza.'

'Sorry. I made a mistake. I thought . . .'

But Jake was speaking again. 'She soon regretted that. He
used to beat her, black and blue. Many's the time I would like
to have landed a fist in his face but she persuaded me otherwise. Anyway, I had the last laugh. Or did I?' Jake's voice
broke and he gave an audible sob. 'He is after me, John. When
I got back here from my drunken night I found the place
ransacked. Somebody was looking for something. Her husband
must have followed us to Boston and arrived first because of
the shipwreck.'

'Him – or somebody else,' the Apothecary answered
thoughtfully.

'But who?' Jake answered in all innocence, and John realized
with a shock that Demelza's lover had known nothing about
her being a spy, that the man had been totally unaware of his
sweetheart's secret life. But somebody, probably known to them
all, had known of it and had not only made contact but had,
presumably, sent her to her death as well.

John rose to his feet, swaying slightly, but Jake was instantly
at his side.

'You're not fit to stand, man. Come with me. I'll get a horse
from the stable and take you home.'

They rode off into a night lit by stars and the lights from the
camp on the Common, John clinging on to Jake's back as tightly
as he could. Jake, showing that he really did have some secret
way with horses, encouraged the beast, striving under the weight
of two men to enter the festering streets of the North End and

clip its way through until they reached the house that John was sharing with Suzanne.

'What about your twins?' Jake asked.

'I have taken Blue Wolf on as my servant. He will care for them. Will you come in for a minute and see them?'

TWENTY

They walked into a sleeping house, John taking a look in the bedroom to check that his sons were there. They slept like two dark-haired angels, incredibly resembling their mother at that moment, yet John could see his chin and the setting of his eyes in them.

Blue Wolf was awake, sitting by the fire, his black hair hanging round his face, shutting off his expression. He looked up as the two men entered the parlour. John wondered, just for a minute, how long he had been there. If, perhaps, he had handed the twins over to a motherly neighbour and gone stalking through the streets on his own. Then he felt ashamed of himself. He was beginning to suspect everyone of deceit. And was he himself not deceiving Jake by omitting all the truth about the late Demelza?

It was time to tell the facts and John said, 'Jake, I haven't told you everything about Demelza. There is more.'

Jake gave a gruff laugh. 'If you mean about her early life, I know it. She came from humble origins, as did I. She made her way on to the stage and her real name was indeed Moll Bowling, though how you found out I'll never comprehend. She admitted all that to me.'

'Did she tell you that she was a spy?'

Jake stared blankly. 'What? How in God's name do you know that?'

'Because of this.' And John produced the letter he had found from inside an inner pocket. Jake sat down heavily and read it through, once fast, then more slowly, digesting its contents.

'Where did you find this?'

John looked shamefaced. 'From your rooms above the coach house. Believe me, Jake, it was not me who left your home in disarray. When you told me that your place had been roughly searched that was not by me. That was somebody else looking for something or other. I would not lie to you about this. That man, whoever he is, was coming again for another look but met me on the stairs and decided that the coast wasn't clear.'

Jake's face had drained of colour as he said hoarsely, 'But who was she spying for?'

'I think the Americans. You know that she was born in Boston?'

Jake nodded.

'I believe that her family must have reckoned the Colonists should be free and the idea never left her.'

'Are you saying to me that somebody from the British side is working out here?'

'Yes.'

'And that they killed her?'

'Of that we can't be certain.'

Blue Wolf stood up at this point and said, 'I am sorry for your loss, Jake, but you must consider that your wife has gone to join her ancestors.' He turned to John. 'Now I will leave you.'

Jake smiled. 'What is it you do all night, wandering the streets of Boston?'

The Indian gave him a sorrowful look. 'I go into the forests and become my own person once more. Goodbye, John, and thank you.'

And with those enigmatic words he went out of the room, leaving the two men to stare at one another, wondering exactly what he meant.

TWENTY-ONE

E arly the next morning John was awoken by a gentle but persistent knocking on his front door. The twins, who were up, still in their nightshirts, opened it to admit Jane Hawthorne, scrubbed and neat as ever, trim as a clipped hedge and smiling a little uncertainly. John, who had pulled a robe over his night attire, came down the stairs, yawning.

'Good morning, Mr Rawlings. I apologise for calling at this early hour but I wondered if you could use an extra nanny for your boys.'

'My dear girl, have you had the sack? What of Lady Eawiss?'

'She is shortly to marry Major Roebuck and will no longer need my services. In short, she has found another slavey to obey her every whim.'

'Well, I can't say that I am sorry. But come in, come in. We can't chat on the doorstep.'

He ushered her inside and into a chair, then brewed some coffee while she talked to him through the open door to the small kitchen.

'Tell me more of Major Roebuck.'

'He is a martyr to gout and presently has a foot swathed in bandages which he has to rest on a stool. As he is an army doctor it is a bit of a pitiable condition. But he had heard of Milady's fortune and had a rank sufficiently high for her to consider marriage. So she has found a black girl who will obviously work for her for nothing. And I have been given my marching orders.'

'But you know that Blue Wolf works for me.'

'He has left you, alas. Did he not say farewell to you last night?'

John came back into the small parlour, a cup of coffee in each hand. 'He said farewell but I merely thought he was going out.'

Jane smiled – a rather sly little smile. 'I am afraid not. He has gone back to join his tribe. His father is unwell.'

'Is it true that you married him in some native ceremony?'

'Oh, yes,' she answered matter-of-factly. 'My name is now Silver Fox and one day he will send for me and I will go and live with him and become his squaw.'

'And you will like that?'

'Yes, for the first time in my life I have been given love. So what could I do but return it?'

'You could have said no.'

'I did not wish to,' Jane answered, and dropped her gaze from John's enquiring eyes.

'Did you ever find any relatives here in Boston?' he asked, changing the subject.

'Yes, but now they are dead. I should say unfortunately but they did not turn out as I expected. So, my friend, I come to throw myself on your mercy.'

'Of course, Jane, it would be a pleasure for you to come and work here even if it is only till you hear the call of the wild.'

At this Jasper and James, who had clearly been listening, hiding themselves on the stairs, burst in and howled like wolves – or their interpretation of them anyway.

John stood up. 'Well, that seems to have settled something or other. Now, Jane, if you could supervise my two rascals getting to school for their last day, I must go and fetch Rose. The school breaks for Christmas this morning.'

She gave him a little curtsey and said, 'It will be a pleasure, Sir. A great deal better than Lady Eawiss shouting for a clean chamber pot to be brought at once.'

He nodded. 'I can well imagine. But I really must go and dress.'

He had only visited the tailor twice since he had been in Boston and had ordered several outfits to be made for him, one of which was a top coat in a shade of damask rose and matching breeches. The coat had been entwined with golden embroidery and this morning John, rather daringly, put it on, hoping to cut a fine figure in front of the other parents. Hurrying to the Orange Tree, he gave rapid instructions to young Tristram and then set out with a brisk pace towards the Common. His head was aching slightly but he took deep breaths and went towards Coralie's establishment determined to overcome any minor discomfort. On arrival some time later, he went straight to the barn at the back where the pupils were assembling, waiting for their guardians to collect them. Coralie, looking very becoming in a violet ensemble, stood in their midst, kissing each child goodbye.

She turned to John. 'My dear, how nice to see you. What a pleasant surprise.'

He stared at her blankly. 'I've come to fetch Rose. Is she not here?'

'No, she left last night with Miss Sopwith, a friend of yours.'

John frowned. 'But Rose did not come home. Besides, I don't know anyone of that name.'

'How extraordinary. The woman came at about eight o'clock last night and Rose seemed to recognize her or else I would not have let her go. But she brought with her a letter authorizing her to take charge of your daughter while you were indisposed.'

'Do you have it still?'

'Yes, in my house. I'll get it immediately.'

Coralie must have run, sensing John's rising panic, and a few minutes later thrust the document into his hand. He read:

> *Dear Madame Clive,*
>
> *It would oblige me if Rose could be sent home tonight. I regret that I am unwell and will be unable to fulfil the duty tomorrow. Miss Sopwith is an old friend and can be trusted completely with my daughter's safety.*
>
> *I am, Madam, your obedient servant,*
> *John Rawlings*

He turned on her a stricken face. 'But how could you, Coralie? Did the letter not reek of a forgery?'

She had blanched white as a snowdrop and regarded him with tears just visible in her eyes. 'I thought it formally worded but not overly so.'

'But the signature,' John answered, his voice shaking, 'did you not question that? Good God woman, it is nothing like mine.'

She erupted then, tears and fear combining. 'Oh, heaven have mercy, what have I done? Oh, I would rather be dead than do anything to hurt Rose. I love the girl as if she were my own child.'

John turned his head away but already his agile mind was beginning to sort the facts. This was obviously the work of an enemy – but who? Then he thought of the face that had peered at him out of the shadows in the coach house the previous evening and knew at once that he was a pawn in an altogether bigger game and that his daughter was the means by which they could get to him. He could immediately rule out Jake and Blue Wolf. Then, even as he thought this, he knew that whoever it was had the mysterious Miss Sopwith working with them and so the blame could have fallen on any one of the people who had survived the shipwreck and walked with him through the back-woods of the Colonies in order to arrive at Boston.

He turned back to face Coralie and put his hands on the tops of her arms. 'Don't cry, sweetheart. Just tell me everything that happened and what the woman looked like.'

She raised her lovely, sorrowful face to his. 'If only I didn't feel so guilty. I could die with the shame.'

Feeling immensely irritated, John somehow controlled himself. 'Oh, come on, Coralie, do. Crying is not going to help matters. Describe the woman.'

'Well, she was short and quite dark of features but her hood was up and she kept her face well hidden from me. I remember her eyes, though. They were a deep brown, the colour of melted chocolate.'

'Anything else? How did she speak?'

'With a Bostonian accent. But, of course, that could have been adopted for the purpose of deception.'

'Your description of her eyes does not match anyone of my acquaintance.'

'Nor mine. But please believe me, John, I would never have allowed Rose out of my sight if it had not been a good trick.'

He sighed. 'I do believe you. But I beg you in future to be more wary. I will return home now to see if there are any clues as to her whereabouts.'

'Take me with you.'

'No,' he said firmly. 'You have your other pupils to look after. Your place is with them.'

She looked so sad that the Apothecary relented a little. 'Be of stout heart, sweetheart. I shall keep you informed, never fear.'

And with that he walked away, feeling that he would lose his composure if he stayed another minute.

He ran home, his beautiful coat stained with sweat and grime from the streets, and arrived panting and dishevelled some twenty minutes later. He burst through the door like a volcano, startling Jane Hawthorne, who was on her knees polishing the legs of a chair. She looked up at him.

'Whatever is the matter?'

'Rose has been kidnapped.'

She looked genuinely shocked. 'By whom? Whoever would do such a terrible thing?'

'I don't know, Jane. But some unknown woman took her from the school last night.'

'Sit down,' she said sensibly. 'You're as pale as a phantom. I'll get you a drop of brandy.'

John sank into a chair and tried to breathe deeply, to calm himself and to work out what should be his course of action. But as Jane returned with the glass there was a loud knock on the door which made them both jump with fright. John leapt to his feet and went to answer it, only to see a grubby boy standing there with a piece of paper in his blackened fingernails.

'Excuse me, Mister, but are you Mr Rawlings?'

'Yes.'

'This note was given to me by a gentleman along with a shilling. He said to put it in your hand personally.'

'Thank you. Here's another shilling for you.'

The lad handed over the note, took the shilling, bit it and scarpered.

'What does it say?' asked Jane, coming to stand beside the Apothecary.

John's fingers trembled as he broke the seal. Jane, reading under his arm, gave an exclamation of horror. *If you want to see your daughter alive then come to the Mill Cove at midnight as it strikes. I'll be waiting for you.* It was unsigned.

'Oh, dear God, John. Will you go?'

'Nothing will keep me away.'

Yet for all his fine words the Apothecary knew what it meant to feel the clutch of icy fear.

TWENTY-TWO

I t was raw. Snowflakes were clustered in the darkness overhead but had not yet broken out and the sky was the colour of tar, not a star visible on this blackest of black nights. Scurrying forms bearing lanterns hurried past John Rawlings as he stepped out of his house and looked about him. There was no light at all anywhere and then, even as he thought this, an upstairs casement opened and someone threw out the contents of a chamber pot. This was not unusual, but still John stood aside as the stinking contents descended with a gurgle and plopped into the gutter. A laugh rang out from behind the shutters of a house wherein four officers of the British army were billeted, all up late and playing cards, unable to see beyond the confines of their cosy dwelling. John's hand automatically felt for the pair of pistols which he had shoved into the pockets of his great coat. He knew that he was departing on one of the most dangerous meetings of his entire existence, and that he must now use every ounce of his intelligence and in-born cunning if he was to escape with his life and rescue his daughter from the grasp of an international spy who would not hesitate to kill her and anyone who crossed him. Could it be N himself? John thought. But no, surely . . . Or could N possibly be a she? Whoever it was dwelled in London; it was from there that the letter had been sent. But was it possible that N had sailed to Boston to see his spy, Demelza, face-to-face? And, perhaps, if she was not doing her duty to his satisfaction, had murdered her? With his thoughts whirling, John entered the tunnel under Hanover Street, wherein Mill Creek ran down to the harbour, taking away excess water from the Mill Cove.

There was no light in there but the beam from his lantern picked up the figure of a girl thrust against the wall, a soldier with his trousers unflapped lunging into her for all he was worth. It was clearly no rape for she was emitting sounds of mounting pleasure while the young lieutenant was shouting with gratifica-tion. John had no wish to disturb them and crept past, trying to

keep his lantern glow low. He gained the street on the other side
as the couple reached the climax and gave a simultaneous cry
of delight. The Apothecary envied them the freedom of their
youth and momentarily would have changed places with the
young man rather than be on this desperate mission to save his
daughter's life.

Having emerged from the tunnel he turned to his left and
made his way up a deserted track to where the water mill stood,
its white building vivid against the blackness of the water
behind it. It was a tidal mill, part of the Charles River having
been cut off by the building of a wall in which had been
constructed a sluice. When the tide came in it entered the Mill
Cove through a one-way gate which closed automatically when
the tide began to fall. Many such mills were being created by
the settlers around the rocky coastland which John and his
fellow passengers had traipsed in the company of Blue Wolf.
Now the very look of the place sent the Apothecary into a
paroxysm of fear.

Nothing in the note given to him by the urchin had indicated
at which point of the Mill Creek he should be at midnight,
yet the Mill House seemed the most likely spot. Somewhere
from the town came the striking of a clock and as it did so a
dark, heavily cloaked and masked figure stepped out of the
shadows. Nobody spoke and the silence seemed to last for
eternity. John finally asked a question in a voice that had
turned into a croak. 'What do you want from me?'

He shuddered as he felt the muzzle of a pistol against his
neck. 'That you stop meddling in things that do not concern
you,' said another voice, this one behind him.

So two of them had come out to deal with him, John thought.
He spoke again. 'What things have you in mind?'

The press of the muzzle grew harder. This time the shadowy
figure answered, his companion's breathing so loud in John's ear
that he could time his own intake of breath with it.

'You are investigating matters that do not concern you, my
friend. And you have grown rather close to knowing the truth.
My advice would be to stop now.'

'And if I don't?'

'It's quite simple. We kill your child.'

'Do you mean that I am to stop my enquiries into the death of Moll Bowling?'

They knew exactly who he was talking about because neither of them questioned the fact of her actual name.

'That's right,' said the first speaker in a thick Bostonian accent. 'We guess that you're working on someone's behalf. Now, who is it?'

John considered briefly mentioning Lieutenant Dalrymple rather than her husband, but decided against it.

'I am just a naturally curious soul and am investigating on behalf of poor Jake, who is too sunk in despair and misery to enquire himself.'

'How much do you know already?' asked the man who stood in the shadows, speaking in a light colonial accent, quite pleasant in comparison with the other's Bostonian growl.

'Nothing much,' John answered. 'I know from the lady herself that she was born in Boston but left at an early age. I also know she went on the stage in London and later married the young Lord Conway. That is about the sum total of it.'

The pistol at his neck relaxed very slightly. 'And that is all?'

'All,' answered John in his most solemn voice.

'Give me your word that you will no longer poke your nose into business that has nothing to do with you?'

'You have it and gladly,' the Apothecary answered, knowing, even as he said it, that only part of his promise was true. The pressure from the pistol regained sudden strength.

'Wait a minute,' said the Boston voice. 'You don't get off so lightly. What were you doing creeping into the coach house at Hancock's place? Were you searching for something?'

'Was it you I met on the stairs?' John asked.

There was a noticeable silence, then a whispered discussion. John strained his ears but could make none of it out. Eventually the first man answered gruffly and the man in the shadows responded with a higher laugh than John would have associated with a ruffian.

'I'd knock you down the stairs whenever you try to poke your nose into other people's business.'

'And so would I, you miserable little blood,' the shadow man added.

'I was seeking Jake,' John said clearly. 'Nobody knew where he was.'

A bell was ringing softly in his brain but at the moment he could not think where it came from so had to ignore it.

'What shall we do with him?' asked the Boston man. 'Shall I shoot him?'

'No,' replied the other, 'just lay him flat and we'll be gone. Let it be hoped he has learned his lesson.'

The Apothecary half turned – but too late. A stick came crashing down on to his head and all was pitch-black darkness once more.

This time he woke slowly and in great pain. A plain-faced woman of some fifty years was washing the blood off him, assisted by another, equally devoid of looks but younger. She was applying cold cloths to his forehead. As soon as John had taken them in he looked beyond them to high, stark white walls and to hear the loud noise of a wheel creaking as it turned relentlessly.

'What's that sound?' he mumbled.

The two women stared at one another. 'Oh, the Lord be thanked,' said the older one. 'He's going to live.'

The younger redoubled her efforts with the cold cloths. 'Jesus is merciful,' she replied.

'Do you think he has anything to do with the girl we found this morning?'

'More than likely.'

John made an effort to sit up. 'You've found her? My daughter?'

'Yes, a young girl with fiery hair. She was tied up by the grain sacks.'

John redoubled his attempts to straighten. 'Was she hurt?'

'No, bless her. Just hungry. The miller and I gave her a good breakfast.'

Despite everything John smiled, his mouth twisting up crookedly, more so than usual because of the pain in his head. 'I thank you sincerely. She is my daughter.'

Later, after the miller had raised him in his arms and carried him to the mill cottage which stood nearby, the Apothecary fully recovered his senses, but Dr Warren had nonetheless been sent for. With a most delicate touch he put two stitches in the wound, after which Rose was finally reunited with her father.

'Oh, Papa, did you know I was kidnapped? It was really rather thrilling,' she said with a bit of a grin. 'I felt a little scared when I realized what had happened but the two men treated me quite well – that was until they tied me up and left me alone in the Mill House, which is extremely frightening after dark.'

'And you spent the night there by yourself?' John asked, treating the matter in the same businesslike way that she had.

'I wasn't really alone because the two men were around for a while. I could hear them talking softly to one another.'

'Have you any idea who they were? Did you recognize their voices in any way?'

'No, they talked too quietly for that. But they were quite pleasantly spoken.'

'Tell me about Miss Sopwith. Did you know her?'

'No. I thought she had been sent by you, Papa. But she was not known to those two men either. It was dark by the time we left Madame Clive's and I walked what seemed like miles with her until I saw a sheet of water and realized that we were at the Mill Creek. I became a tiny bit nervous when she started to look round as if she were expecting somebody. But then the two of them appeared out of the blackness and told her, quite menacingly, to be on her way or they would shoot her, and to say nothing about them to anyone or they would seek her out. She promised and went off in the direction of the North End. Then we went into the Water Mill house and they tied me up.'

'My poor sweetheart. You were very courageous.'

'Well, I didn't let them see that I was afraid because I knew you would come to rescue me.'

'How did you know?'

'Because I could picture it quite distinctly,' Rose said, and refused to answer any more questions.

Eventually, after Dr Warren had returned and given his patient leave to go home, John hobbled back to the North End helped by Tristram and the miller's son. And there in his house, awaiting him, looking somewhat gaunt but putting a gallant face on events, was Coralie Clive.

'Well, now, I have come to invite you all to stay with me over Christmas. I hope you will accept my invitation,' she said, looking at John with a great deal of anxiety but saying nothing further.

'We should be delighted to do so,' he answered. He turned to the children. 'I know Rose would enjoy that but what about you, Jasper and James?'

They stood together, regarding Coralie with a deep and mean-ingful stare, their eyes blue as bluebells, then James did the most disconcerting thing. He winked at his father, his small eyelid quite definitely fluttering down, before he said, 'That would be a pleasure, Madame Clive.'

On Christmas Day they walked to the Old South church, and as they passed the portals of Hancock's mansion the gates swung open and a coach and horses pulled out. Jake was not driving the equipage, yet it was very unlikely that he would be given a day off, even at Christmas. Was he keeping the festivities in the servants' hall with the rest of the Hancock employees? But why, when the coach was needed to convey the family to church? In fact, the driver had been someone entirely different: an older man with grizzled hair and a weather-beaten face. Wondering if Jake was in trouble again, John decided to visit him as soon as possible.

The organ of the Old South was thundering out and the congre-gation was singing some unknown carol. The Apothecary joined in as best he could but his mind was a million miles away, going over and over all the facts as he knew them.

First had been his discovery that Demelza Conway was working for a secret organization, probably American, and had set out for Boston to aid them. The fact that she was an old friend of Dr Warren more or less proved this. But someone had found out about it and had silenced her for ever by pushing her out of the rigging and into the sea below. Exactly why she was climbing up in the first place was a mystery yet to be unrav-elled. Blue Wolf probably knew the answer but he had disappeared back to his tribe.

Secondly, it was possible that any one of his set of cronies could have been responsible for the murder, including Demelza's own husband. Because in that vast crowd, foregathered to watch the destroying of the tea chests, anyone could have slipped away, done the deed and made their way back within the space of about fifteen minutes. John thought he could remember speaking to them all, but had he, in actual fact?

Dimly, in the back of his consciousness, he realized that the rest of the congregation had sat down and he was the only man standing, so to speak. Someone tugged at his coat and he dropped into the pew, but his thoughts were still racing.

What had been the identity of his assailant on the wooden staircase? It could not have been Jake because he was below, so who was it? He knew for certain that it was neither of the kidnappers, though they had not denied it. But there had been that stunned silence after he had asked them the direct question, followed by their low-voiced consultation. So a fourth man was involved. But who was he? As to the kidnappers themselves, John thought he knew the answer, surprising though it was. And yet it was not really, not when one thought about it closely. But there was still one woman who could no doubt tell him more – the elusive Miss Sopwith who lived somewhere in Boston. John knew for sure that she was next on his list of people to track down. He would start enquiries the very next day.

Someone was whispering in his ear and the Apothecary returned to reality. Coralie was looking at him sharply. 'You've been miles away.' It was a statement, not an accusation.

'Yes, I have. I'll tell you later,' he murmured as the congregation started on their final hymn.

TWENTY-THREE

I t was not the merriest of Christmases. Though Coralie had made a great effort to make it enjoyable, the shadow of the fact that she had released Rose into the arms of a stranger clearly weighed heavily upon her. And after midnight, when she and John lay together in her comfortable bed, she wept heartbreakingly.

'Don't, my sweetheart. Please don't cry. You thought the woman had been employed by me. You were not to know what would transpire.'

'But I should have questioned her more closely. It was my duty to do so.'

'How could you in the chaos all around you? Pupils shouting as their parents rejoined them, everyone running about excitedly. How could you have managed to do so? Believe me, Coralie, I am not blaming you. As for Rose, she is of unbeatable spirit. She says her gift helped her, that she knew I was coming to rescue her. The experience has left her undamaged.'

'She is a remarkable young woman.'

'I still think of her as a child.'

'She is rising fifteen now, is she not?'

'Yes,' John answered quietly. 'Yes. I suppose you are right to call her grown up. But where goes the time, can you answer me that? Why, I can vividly recall when I first saw her, presented to me on a cushion. It feels like yesterday. So what of the years between? What have I achieved? Precious little in the grand scheme of things.'

'We can all say that,' Coralie answered thoughtfully. 'We all come into this world with nothing and we all go out with nothing, save what poor pickings one has left behind for one's descendants. But in that period we must strive our very best to achieve what small amount we can within our given circumstances. And you have done that, John. You have indeed.'

In the darkness, he smiled wryly. 'And what of you, my dear?

You have been a great and beloved actress – and could be again if you so desired.'

'But I am afraid to go back to England and face my demons. My daughter's death – it was so terrible, John. Just hideous. The newspapers were full of the tale. I was glad to sail to the Colonies and start a new life.'

'Come, sweetheart, you must not blame yourself for everything.'

'I was her mother. It was my fault.'

'I won't have that. The girl had nothing of you within her. Now stop these feelings of guilt and sleep peacefully. You were not and never have been to blame.'

But Coralie just sighed, a sad sigh, even though John's arms were wound tightly round her.

As soon as the festivities were over, John Rawlings decided to scour Boston for the woman who had stolen his daughter from her school – the mysterious Miss Sopwith. The first thing he did was to go to the Old Corner Book Store which, as its name implied, stood on the north corner of School Street. Here he bought a street directory and departed with it to the nearby White Horse tavern. Sitting there quietly, he read the list from cover to cover, then again, this time more slowly. There was no family living in Boston with the name Sopwith, so it had been a pseudonym. Now he had no chance of tracing the woman. Ordering himself another glass of ale, John considered his next move.

It was at that moment that the door opened and in came Lieutenant Harry Dalrymple, frowning and muttering slightly under his breath. At first he did not look up, but finally his eye took in the fact that the Apothecary was sitting alone at a table and he hurried over.

'Ah, my dear Sir, it is very good to see you. Tell me, how go your enquiries? Have you come up with anything yet?'

'Quite a lot.' Motioning him to a seat, John poured out the entire story.

Harry listened in absolute silence, then said, 'You are pretty sure you know the identity of your daughter's kidnappers?'

'Pretty sure, Sir. There was a certain turn of phrase that gave me the clue.'

Dalrymple nodded. 'You're a sharp one, I'll say that for you.'

'Thank you. But there's one thing that eludes me.'

'And what might that be?'

'There are no Sopwiths living in Boston. So where is she?'

'You're certain of this?'

John slapped the street directory with his hand. 'None in here, at any rate. She obviously used a false name.'

'Or was a camp follower,' Dalrymple answered slowly.

John stared at him, aghast. That was one idea that simply hadn't occurred to him. As he had seen for himself in the mortuary, there were a great number of women, both old and young, to say nothing of children, who camped on the Common with the militia.

'You don't by any chance have a list of them?' he asked the lieutenant.

'A basic one, yes,' Harry answered, and his face broke into a boyish grin.

'Can I have a look at it?'

'When I have finished my drink the answer is yes.'

Shortly afterwards, they stepped out into the thick snow that seemed to be a speciality of the town and walked, with a certain amount of slipping and sliding, to where the Common stretched out before them, encrusted with white. Dalrymple made his way to a house behind Boston's granary, which had been taken over by the army as its headquarters, and where there sat a miserable officer behind a desk piled with papers, slapping his arms back and forth in an attempt to keep warm. The lieutenant came through the door and saluted stylishly.

'Good morning, Sir. May I introduce my friend, John Rawlings?'

The other soldier looked up and made an attempt at smiling. 'Yes, by all means.' He held out his hand. 'How do you do, Mr . . .?'

'Rawlings,' Dalrymple and John chorused.

'I take it you are here on army business, Sir.'

'He is actually working with me, Captain McLynn. He is making certain confidential enquiries on my behalf.'

'I see.'

The captain rose from his desk and, approaching the fire, held his hands out to it. 'My God, these winters are cold. Are you a settler here, Rawlings?'

'In a way, Captain. I really arrived by accident, if you follow my meaning.'

'Can't say I do, but no matter. Now, how may I help you?'

'I would like to have a look at the list of camp followers, if that would be convenient.'

'Can't say it is but I expect it's lurking around somewhere in this damned chilly establishment. Not that it's complete, mark you. Women come and go like straws in the wind. Some buxom bitch from Boston will move in with her fancy soldier for a week or two and then she's found by her father, given a cuff on the ear – or two or three – plus a stern talking to, then lugged home by the straps of her boots.'

'A vivid picture,' John remarked, shooting a look at the lieutenant, who was laughing behind his hand.

'Here it is,' said the captain. 'Can't let it into your possession, I'm afraid. Army regulations and so on. What did you say the name was?'

John told him and the army man thumbed through the register which was in sections, each with a capital letter denoting the part.

'Sopwith, Sopwith,' he muttered. 'No, there's no one of that name here.'

'Try the men,' suggested Dalrymple. 'Maybe she's a new arrival.'

Captain McLynn produced another book, this one from the top of his desk. A huge affair, he handed it to the lieutenant. 'Here, you can look for yourself. I have other duties.'

Dalrymple seized it and staggered beneath the weight. An hour later he and John drew in a joint breath. Private Sopwith had a bivouac on the Common.

'A very small space to accommodate a second party,' the Apothecary remarked drily.

'Shall we go and see?' answered the lieutenant with a twinkle about his eye.

Walking on the Common during daylight hours was a revelation. It was clearly a thriving community for women bustled about, all of them occupied with some task or other. Scrubbing clothes, with board and tub, seemed to be one of the lighter duties.

'Of course,' Dalrymple said as the two men made their way through the throng, 'the daughter of Lord Rockingham does none of this.'

John shot him a questioning look and the lieutenant explained, 'She is the colonel's light-of-love. She lives with him in Court

Street while his wife languishes at home with their eleven overweight children.'

'How do you know that? That they are fat?'

'Because he has a portrait of them in his house at which his mistress throws paper darts.'

John laughed aloud as both men stopped to buy a tot of brandy from a sutler who was standing with her little cask and tot measure, hoping for some custom. Having warmed themselves, the lieutenant approached a woman washing out a soldier's shirt and she dropped a curtsey as he drew near.

'Excuse me, Ma'am. Do you know of a woman staying with Private Sopwith?'

'Oh, you mean his latest? Gives herself some airs and graces. A stuck-up Yankee bitch in my opinion.'

To the two men listening it seemed that Private Sopwith was a man of many parts and obviously great reserves.

'Do you know where she might be at the moment?'

'Gone into town, I imagine. She works as a maid in some house or other.'

John spoke. 'You couldn't be more specific, could you?'

'What's that?'

'Where does she work?'

'For Colonel Mountford, I think. She's a kitchen slave, I believe.'

'Thank you very much for your help.' John slipped a coin into the woman's soapy hand.

'So what do we do now?' Dalrymple asked him.

'I imagine that I wait till the servants come off duty and tackle Miss Sopwith then. I'll take Rose with me so that the woman can be properly identified. Meanwhile, I think I'll go and call on Jake O'Farrell and find out why he did not drive Hancock's coach the other day.'

Dalrymple gave him a smart salute. 'Goodbye, my dear Mr Rawlings. Keep me posted with all the latest developments.'

'I will indeed.'

He never afterwards could tell why he did it but John sought entry to John Hancock's great pile through the hole in the palings and approached the house as quietly and as secretly as he had once before. From the minute he entered the coach house he was

gripped with a multitude of feelings. Firstly one of fear, remembering the man who had beaten him so savagely on the stairs.
Then he recalled a conversation which he had had with the porter
on the gate about a man with an English accent who had come
enquiring for the late Demelza. A big, dark fellow with an upper-
crust voice. So that had been it. There was definitely a fourth
man involved in all this. But where to start looking?

The door of Jake's apartment was closed but on turning the
handle it wheezed open and the Apothecary entered cautiously.

'Jake?' he called out. 'Are you there? I wondered how you
were getting on.'

There was no answer and, looking round, John could see
in the afternoon light that the living room was empty but there
were signs of a small struggle. A couple of chairs and a modest
table had been knocked to the floor, as if two people had engaged
in a physical fight. But of Jake there was no sign. Nor did the
bedroom reveal any clue as to his whereabouts. The whole place
was frighteningly, yawningly empty. And this is what the other
servants must have found when they had come looking for him
to go to work on Christmas Day.

John was just about to leave when his eye was drawn to a
wooden cupboard situated across the corner of the bedroom.
Peeping out from underneath was a tiny piece of torn clothing.
Staring at it, suddenly full of dread suspicion, John pulled the
handle and there was Jake O'Farrell, standing upright, his head
at a grotesque angle, his eyes wide and staring, the pupils quite
blown, his throat slit wide. John clutched a hand over his mouth,
utterly shaken. Then he ran downstairs, breathing in choking
gasps as he rushed to get help.

TWENTY-FOUR

'I reckon you're right, John,' said Irish Tom, putting a glass of brandy before his former employer and taking a great swallow from his tankard of ale. 'There's a filthy murderer somewhere whose identity is a complete mystery. First Lady Conway, then her lover. It must be someone who has a grudge against the two of them.'

'Her husband?' John asked.

'But how could he have sailed from England?'

'Perhaps he followed her but got here first because of the shipwreck.'

'I reckon you might be right at that.'

'But where is the bastard?'

'Who knows? He could be anywhere.'

It was six o'clock, pitch dark, and the two of them were sitting in The Bunch of Grapes where they could talk privately. The Apothecary, still shaken from his experience, had actually fetched John Hancock himself to look at the body. On seeing it, the intellectual had turned a greenish colour but had maintained his wits. He had called for two slaves to carry the corpse into an outhouse and had then sent a rider for the coroner. Then he had shaken John Rawlings by the hand and sent him on his way, asking him only how he had known Jake and questioning him no further. Instead he had courteously offered the Apothecary a ride home in a small chaise, which John had accepted with gratitude. And now he sat with his oldest friend as they earnestly discussed the situation.

'How can I find him?' John asked, emptying his glass.

'I don't know, John, and that's a fact.'

'I was informed that a tall, dark man with an upper-class accent made enquiries about Demelza. But who's to say that he was the guilty party? It could have been anyone.'

'As you state. But weren't you going to look for Miss Sopwith tonight?'

'Yes, I was. But I don't know that I feel like it.'

'Well, I would advise that you do. It will take your mind off any other nasty business.'

'I was going to take Rose with me to help with the identification.'

'Miss Rose is at this very minute seated in your shop and sharing a cup of tea with Master Tristram.'

'Good God, are you sure?'

'Positive. It was served to them by Suzanne herself. So I'll come with you, Sir. I feel in an adventurous mood.'

John had yet another restorative brandy and then they left the tavern and walked the short distance to Court Street where, so John had been told, resided Colonel Mountford and the beautiful daughter of Lord Rockingham. But even as he stood gazing at the elegant lines of the large and imposing Woodchester House, a figure appeared from the kitchen quarters, removing a soggy apron and wrapping herself in a black cloak.

Irish Tom stepped forward. 'Good evening, Ma'am. Has anyone ever told you that you've a face as fresh as sunlight over the lakes of my homeland?'

She turned to him crossly. 'You've got the wrong woman, Mister. You'll be looking for Nell Kinsley.'

'Why do you say that?' Tom answered, astonished.

'Because she's the only one who might be described as free to come and go.'

John stepped forward. 'Do you happen to know if she has a friend in the militia?'

The woman looked blank. 'What do you mean?'

'Does she sleep with soldiers?' translated Tom.

'I'll say she does. Though lately she's quietened down. Got a regular chap, so she says.'

'Do you happen to know his name?'

'Peter, I think.'

'I meant his surname.'

'Oh, Milksop – or something like that anyway.'

'Where is she, do you know?'

'She slipped off early to join him. They'll be on the Common by now.'

John and Tom looked at one another and, with one accord, headed off in the same direction.

The camp at night was a different place entirely. Off-duty soldiers huddled round the many braziers which had been lit round the perimeter, muffled up in greatcoats, their hats pulled well down. John, observing from a distance, thought it looked like something from a dream, the snow creating a kind of mist through which the figures of the men were distorted into shadows, unreal and vaporous. Sounds were muffled and he heard them as distant cries of long-lost beings. For who were they in the main but pressed men, taken from their hovels by force and made to fight to maintain the right of Britain to rule all that it could lay its empire-building hands on? Suddenly, in a clear-headed moment, John vividly sympathized with the plight of the Colonists and the terrible predicament in which they found themselves – ruled by distant laws from a country that most of them had never even seen. He could clearly understand why men like Dr Joseph Warren and his followers were staging a violent protest against such unfairness.

'Which bivouac is Sopwith's?' asked Tom, running his eyes over the several hundred which appeared in the eerie gloom.

'We'll have to ask directions.'

'And find a pair of poor souls going about their private business with a certain enthusiasm, I don't doubt.'

'Come now, Thomas. You've never appeared cowardly before.'

'I hope you are joking, Sir, for that's something of which I've never been accused.'

'Of course, of course. But you do realize that as many men as can be have been housed elsewhere for the winter. Only a few hardy souls remain.'

'But given the straight choice of trying to smuggle a girl into my room in a house in which I've been billeted – complete with beady-eyed landlady who hates the guts of the British – or taking her to a chilly but private bivouac, I know which I'd choose. As would you, John, and don't deny it.'

The Apothecary had no intention of doing so, thinking that his former coachman had put his finger on the spot, then realizing that this was a rather rude double entendre. Smiling to himself, he and Tom proceeded cautiously into the misty scene.

Whether Private Peter Sopwith had a billet elsewhere or whether he was braving out the wintry conditions was never revealed to them, because as they approached a small tent that had been deliberately pitched at some distance away from the others, they heard the loud cries of mutual enjoyment. Miss Kinsley certainly did not restrain herself and neither did the good soldier boy, if their ears were telling them the truth.

Turning to Tom, John said, 'Perhaps we ought to give them a few moments.'

'I think you're right.' And sitting down on a tree stump, Tom pulled a pipe from the depths of his pocket and began to puff away. After a second's hesitation, John joined him and the two men sat together, as contented as the biting cold would allow, and conversed in low voices. Ten minutes passed and then a head covered with longish hair poked itself out of the tent flap and said nervously, 'Is there anybody there?'

John strolled over. 'Private Sopwith?'

The man emerged from the bivouac in a state of some disarray. 'Yes, Sir.' He narrowed his eyes. 'Who asks?'

'Rawlings is the name. Investigator assisting Lieutenant Harry Dalrymple, enquiring into the recent deaths of two people.'

In the whitish light thrown by the snow the soldier's face turned a shade of lilac. 'I don't know who you mean?' he gulped.

'You refer to Lieutenant Dalrymple? Don't you know your commanding officer, man? What kind of solider do you call yourself, eh?'

Behind him the Apothecary could hear the Irishman give a low chortle as John played up his act.

'I've a damn good mind to put you on a charge, soldier. Stand to attention, blast you. Tom, fetch the lieutenant, this second.'

The Irishman played his part. 'I surely will, Sir, immediately, now and at once. But a thought occurs, Milord.'

'And what might that be, my good man?'

'That it is not this young fellow that we ought to be questioning, begging your pardon, your Grace.'

John thought that he was being promoted through the aristocracy at the speed of flight. 'Then who is it, fellow?'

'Why, his light-o'-love, Sir. The woman with whom he has relations.'

'D'you mean me?' asked a voice from within the bivouac.

'Yes, Madam, I do,' replied John grandly. 'Step forth and show yourself.'

So there she was, the woman who had so cleverly kidnapped his daughter. John's blood quickened as he saw her, so smug-faced and pale beneath the winter moon. She had black hair, loose about her shoulders, and rather small dark eyes. She was also thin as a broom handle and just as attractive.

'Miss Kinsley, I believe,' he said in a voice that would have cut ice.

She must have felt a touch of alarm because she bobbed a curtsey and said, 'Yes, Sir.'

The Apothecary decided to throw caution to the wind and said, 'I am making a citizen's arrest for the part you played recently in the kidnapping of Rose Rawlings. You will come with me now.'

At that Tom loomed out of the shadows and stood, large as an Irish giant, beside John, his very presence oozing menace. Private Sopwith gazed at him, wondered about hitting either of them, then thought better of it. He then proceeded to act in a highly ungentlemanly manner and said to Miss Kinsley, 'Sorry, Nellie, but I can't help you. You'd better do as the man says.'

She turned and ran, lithe as a fox, pelting in the direction of the bushes. John immediately sprang into action, followed by Tom, who with his great long legs quickly passed the Apothecary and disappeared into the darkness. There was a crash, followed by the sound of a body hitting the ground, then silence. John, seriously thinking that he ought to get back into condition, sprinted in the general direction of the ruckus.

Tom was lying on the ground, gasping for air, all the breath knocked out of him. John glanced round for the Irishman's quarry but she had disappeared into the night. Instead of chasing after the girl he sat down beside his oldest friend and waited for his panting to stop which, eventually, it did.

'The evil little shrew escaped,' Tom said, half sitting up. 'By God, I'll have her tongue for toast before I die. How dare she.'

'She probably did the most sensible thing in the circumstances,' John answered, giving a wry irregular smile. 'But she won't get away for long. Tomorrow I shall call on the colonel's lady and put the case to her.'

'Now that,' Tom answered, 'would be something that I'd very much like to witness.'

TWENTY-FIVE

E nchanting, thought John. The only way to win friends and
get information is to be utterly enchanting to everyone.
But he was having a great problem living up to this.
The colonel's mistress, the Lady Anne Temple, was nowhere to
be seen. Instead he had to contend with the colonel's sister, a
large, tall and somewhat fearsome female who closely resembled
a man in women's clothing.

'And why do you wish to see one of our sahvants, Sir?'

John bowed deeply and tried to give her an awestruck glance
as if she were someone of enormously high rank. 'The truth is,
Ma'am, that I need to question her about the recent kidnap of
my daughter.'

Miss Mountford raised a quizzing glass which hung round
her long neck on a faded black cord and peered at him intently.
'What's that you say?'

John smiled winsomely, feeling an absolute fathead as he did
so. 'I was asking, dear lady, where your servant Nell Kinsley . . .?'

But he got no further. The woman suddenly rounded on him,
resembling nothing so much as a militant horse. Her full and
fluid lips curled. 'I do not pass the time of day discussing the
sahvants with total strangers. Out with you, Sah. Out, I say.'

It was at this moment that Lady Anne Temple walked into the
room and gazed round.

'Whatever is the matter, Augusta? I heard you shouting from
my bedroom.'

'This madman has entered our house without invitation and
wants to know details of the housekeeping arrangements.'

John bowed again and tried to adopt his most sincere expression, ending up with a somewhat constipated look. He opened
his mouth to speak but Lady Anne cut across him.

'Tell me, Sir, what is your business here? Are you trying to
sell something?'

To hell with enchantment, he thought, and answered her very

dircctly. 'Madam, I am here about one of your servants who was involved in the kidnap of my young daughter t'other night. Would you be so kind as to tell me whether Nell Kinsley is below in your kitchens?'

Lady Anne raised her delicate brows and gave the Apothecary a penetrating glance. Instantly he was able to see why the colonel had singled out just such a woman to live with him while he served out his allotted time in Boston. She was, without doubt, incredibly pretty.

'I think not,' she answered, then turning to the colonel's sister, said, 'My dearest Augusta, there is no need to fear. This man has not come to attack us but you are obviously deeply distressed. Why do you not retire and I will get Carstairs to bring you a little restorative cordial.'

'I thank you, my dear, but I wish to stay. I do not trust the fellow and you might need my protection.'

Anne laughed. 'Then sit over there and watch developments while Mr . . .?'

'Rawlings, Ma'am.'

'Rawlings and I discuss his problem.'

She sat down and looked elegant. After a moment the horse folded herself on to a small chaise longue which let out a tiny squeak of protest. John waited till they were seated and then perched on the edge of a hard chair.

'Tell me what happened,' said Lady Anne, and gave him a charming smile.

The Apothecary found himself recounting everything – indeed, confiding much more than he had intended. She listened attentively while the horrible horse made scoffing sounds deep within her chest – a most disturbing interruption.

'And so that, Milady, is exactly what transpired. I think it is quite urgent that I speak to Nell and find out who she was working for.'

'Yes, indeed. I quite agree. I shall personally go and quiz the staff as to her whereabouts.'

'Might I come with you?' John asked, feeling somewhat nervous at the thought of being left alone with the colonel's sister, who was clearly deranged.

Milady caught his eye and read it correctly. 'By all means. Augusta, you watch the door while I am gone.'

But there was not much news to be gathered below stairs. All the information they could give the mistress of the house was that Nell had not come in for work and nobody knew anything. However, an address was given – Cow Lane, one of the places situated in the area lying to the south of Boston. John's heart sank as he heard it, wondering how he would find his way amongst the many houses that had been erected in that area. However, having made his polite farewells to Lady Anne, who smiled helpfully, and to Augusta, who looked ready to chew him, the Apothecary hurried down the street, intent on making his confrontation with Rose's kidnapper happen sooner rather than later. But he slowed his pace as a large printed notice came into his line of vision.

It read as follows: 'Monsieur Piemont, French Peruke Maker to the Gentry and general Barber, has pleasure in announcing that Mr Charles Shirley of England has joined him as an Assistant Friseur and Facotum. His services are available now.'

John hesitated, his rapid stride decreasing as he spied Lady Eawiss through the front window. Knowing that she lived in the vicinity of south Boston, he wondered if she could tell him how to find the place he was seeking. Looking for an excuse to enter the barber's, he fingered his chin, realizing that he had forgotten to shave that morning. Small wonder that Augusta had regarded him with such a suspicious eye – she had probably put him down as a vagrant. Without further ado, John marched into Monsieur Piemont's.

It was overflowing, quite literally, with Lady Eawiss, who had come in in preparation for her wedding. A vast array of false yellow curls stood cascading down a stand, clearly designed by Monsieur Piemont, who stood fussing around his client, who was busy criticizing everything.

'I don't know if they will quite become me, Monsieur. Would they look too artificial?'

'*Mais non*. If I may pay you the little compliment, Madam, you are beautiful enough to carry any style. These tumbling fair locks will make you look twenty again – or even younger.'

'What is your opinion, Monsieur Charles?'

The other man, a tall, dark, languid fellow with a pitted face and a pair of eyes the colour of ebony, drawled, 'Perhaps Lady Eawiss would prefer a hat atop.'

'With the curls below, surely?' answered Monsieur Piemont testily.

'Oh, yes, indeed. But then if Milady wishes to emulate the latest fashions of London . . .'

'Oh, I do, Sir. That is where my heart is. And as soon as my future husband – he is a major, don't you know – retires from the bustle of army life, we will return to my late husband's estates. They were at Sutton Valence and he was Sir Bevis Eawiss, of course.'

The other man, presumably Mr Charles Shirley, raised his eyebrows, which were moon-shaped and looked well attended, but made no reply.

'I would be so obliged to you, Sah, if you could trick me out with the very latest thing from *Londres*.' She laughed gaily.

'Then I would suggest that we put on your head a cushion, on which we will place Monsieur Piemont's waterfall of curls and then, according to my lady's mood, we can decide to dress the hair *a la Zodiaque, a la Frivolite* or even design it into the shape of a ship or, perhaps, a birdcage.' He gave a sudden irrational laugh. 'Which we could even fill with a canary for your wedding day.'

John, who absolutely nobody had noticed, watched the expressions of delight flit one after the other over Lady Eawiss's podgy cheeks. She clasped her hands together in supplication.

'Oh, please, Monsieur Charles, I can think of nothing better than a birdcage with a songbird within to express my sheer delight to my bridegroom. Will you do it for me, I beg of you.'

Charles flashed his sardonic eyes at his employer, gave a mock bow and answered, 'If my master will allow it.'

The Frenchman, who was clearly none too pleased that his creation was to be toyed with, gave a brief nod and answered, 'Of course, my dear fellow. That was what I employed you for.'

John said into the sudden silence that followed, 'Please may I have a shave?'

An hour later he emerged sweet smelling and smooth skinned, leaving Lady Eawiss uttering little shouts of pleasure as Mr Shirley, assisted by a boy, wrestled manfully with a large cushion, a bunch of assorted ribbons, a handful of jewels, a nest of pearls, four huge ostrich feathers and a terrified canary.

Making his way towards the southern part of town, John picked his way amongst the small houses – if they could indeed be named that – for they stood packed closely together, as bad as the hovels of the North End where the sanitation flowed freely from one privy into the next. Lady Anne had not been given a number, so all the Apothecary could do was follow directions and look for a dwelling that seemed inhabited and knock. A woman stood outside one, manfully doing her best to chop a few logs. She was wrapped in a miserable shawl and was shivering in the bitter weather that threatened yet more snow.

John called out, 'Can I help you?'

She gave him a gaze of pure terror and answered, 'And what will be your price?'

He stood askance. 'I was only offering you some assistance. I don't want rewarding.'

She softened, very slightly. 'I thought strange men always wanted a reward.'

'If you mean do I want some favour from you, the answer is no. I was merely offering to help you with your task. But as you do not wish it I will be on my way.' He strode off with dignity.

A few seconds later she called after him. 'Please, Sir, I didn't mean any offence. But you can't be too careful in these times.'

John turned, bowed a little and said, 'None taken, Madam. Now, if I may chop your logs for you?'

She eyed him warily but nonetheless handed him the axe and John set about hewing a few pieces from the rather recalcitrant bit of timber that the poor woman had been hacking at.

Eventually she said, 'Would you like a glass of ale?'

John wiped his brow with his sleeve. 'If it's no trouble.'

'None at all.'

She disappeared into the house and the Apothecary, watching her retreating form, thought how thin she was and how drab, a pathetic specimen of womanhood. She returned a few minutes later and handed him a rough glass with some pale yellow liquid inside it. John eyed it curiously, thinking that it looked horribly like urine but despite that taking a tentative sip.

It was surprisingly good, redolent with apples and a touch of cloves. He finished the glass and handed it back to the girl.

'Tell me,' he said, 'do you know Nell Kinsley at all?'

'Do you mean the cobbler's daughter?'

'Yes, that's her,' John improvised. 'I was hoping to call on her.'

The woman surprisingly winked a knowing eye. 'I knew you were up to no good. You had that look about you. Well, you're a bit late, Sir. She's hooked up with a soldier boy.'

'Oh, yes, I am aware of all that,' the Apothecary answered, winking back madly. 'It was just that I hoped to talk to her but the cunning little vixen would not tell me which number she lived at.'

The woman extended a grubby brown hand. 'She lives next door, my friend. And I wish you luck of her.'

'Why? Don't you like her?'

'I am being honest when I say I can't stick the sight of her.'

'Why is that?'

''Cos she's stuck up, that's why.'

'Gives herself airs, does she?'

'And some.'

'Which side did you say she lived, because I will tell her to mind her manners.'

The woman gave a grin which displayed a few rotting brown stumps and gesticulated with her thumb. 'That way.'

John gave her another bow, thanked her for the ale and turned to his right, knocking loudly on the neighbouring door. A woman answered and he knew at once that he had found his quarry. Rapidly quelling an overwhelming urge to hit her, John said, 'So we meet again, Nell Kinsley.'

'What do you want of me?'

John put his foot in the entrance. 'I would like to have a word, please. In private.'

'About what?'

'Business.' And he bared his teeth at her in a smile that did not bode well.

She went to slam the door on him but the Apothecary was too quick and hurled himself forward and into her meagre parlour. Then he forgot his good manners and seized her arm roughly.

'You bitch,' he hissed. 'You could have cost my daughter her

life. Why did you do it, eh, Miss Kinsley, or should I call you
Sopwith? How much were you paid?'

She looked defiant but her skin had blanched skeletal white.
'I don't know what you mean.'

John's attractive face had contorted so that now he presented
an almost demonic look. 'Unless you tell me the name of the
man behind the plot I shall have no hesitation in strangling you
to death.'

'You wouldn't,' she answered, insolent to the end.

'Oh, would I not.' And he put his hands to her throat.

She fought him and just for a moment the Apothecary considered the idea of actually killing her. But then all that he had
ever been taught by his beloved father, Sir Gabriel Kent, came
surging back and he knew that to take the life of this wretched
creature, smaller than he was and weaker, would have been
stepping into another realm of being. He loosened his grip though
still holding her captive.

'Tell me. And don't pretend you don't know what I am talking
about. The luring of my daughter Rose away from her school
and out to the Mill Cove where you abandoned her to her fate.
How could you have done that, you cold-hearted whore?'

'Because that was what I was paid for. I didn't know what
was to happen next, did I?'

'And who paid you?'

She met his eyes. 'I don't know, and that's God's honest truth.
I'd never seen him before in my life. He came up to me on the
Common and asked me if I would play my part in a little trick
he was going to spring on his friend.'

'And you believed him?'

'Yes, I did, Sir. Heaven help me but I thought he was playing
straight.'

John relaxed his grip a little. 'Who was he?'

'That's the point. I'd never seen him before, nor since. He
was a complete stranger.'

'Then why did you do it? Why enact your part in some
masquerade for the benefit of a man you did not know?'

She lowered her gaze. 'Because I needed the money, that's
why. Haven't you ever felt that? Been so poor you didn't know
where the next penny was coming from?'

'But surely the colonel pays you a living wage?'

'I wanted extra for a new dress. I'm going to get married to Private Sopwith and I longed to be turned out smart for the occasion.'

She looked at him again and he saw that her eyes were awash with tears. In that instant most of the Apothecary's animosity dwindled away and he released his hold on her.

'Is what you are saying true?'

'I swear it on my mother's grave.'

He motioned her to a chair and sat down opposite, staring at her most seriously. 'You say the man was totally unknown.'

'Yes. He must be a new arrival. A ship came from England the other day. He was probably on board.'

'Somehow I doubt that. It's more than likely that he has been lying low somewhere.'

He stood up and leant over the girl who gazed up at him, nervous again.

'In future, however hard up you are, do not lower yourself to take part in any affair of which you do not know the whole circumstance. My child could have been killed and if she had been I would have laid half the blame at your door. Be warned, Miss Kinsley. You have played with fire and got away with only minor burns. Next time you might be consumed by the flames.'

And with that he walked from her front door and never saw her again.

TWENTY-SIX

Much had been made by George Glynde and Tracey Tremayne of their forthcoming ball to celebrate Twelfth Night. People were enjoined, by way of posters pasted liberally throughout the town, to wear their finest frippery and feathers, gems and gewgaws, frills and furbelows. Gentlemen were warned that evening dress would be required and that admittance could be refused at the entrance to those not properly attired.

Rose had been talking about it ever since Christmas, begging her father to buy her a ticket and protesting that she felt quite grown-up enough to attend. Irish Tom, determined to win the heart of Suzanne and settle down at last, had hired a suit of ill-fitting clothes from a man shorter than he was by several inches. John, on the other hand, had gone to his favourite tailor and had ordered a suit in shimmering purple brocade, richly shot with pink, its sumptuous jacket being cut with the tails somewhat drawn to the back. For Rose he had asked the dressmaker to create a simple but vibrant gown in emerald green. When she had tried it on he had been forcibly struck by how well the colour became his daughter's beautiful abundance of red hair.

By means of working hard and diligently and thereby building up a good clientele of patients, many of whom were recommended by Dr Warren, who frequently named John as the dispensing apothecary, he had at last paid off his debt to Lady Eawiss – she who had firmly held on to her redoubtable portmanteau and thus had been the only person with any money amongst the raggle-taggle group that had made their way to Boston. Now, John thought, two of that group had been murdered by a person or persons unknown. Irish Tom could obviously be cleared of all suspicion but as to the rest – who knew?

He thought about them all now. There was Julian Wychwood, apparently a dandified fop, but was that all there was to him?

There was Matthew, who had killed a deer without remorse –
could he have substituted a human for the animal? There was
ugly little Suzanne – what hidden side had she? Was pretty Jane
Hawthorne really as demure as she seemed? Apparently not. For
who but a wanton would take an Indian brave for her lover?
Lady Eawiss was really too large to consider. Yet despite her
size, was she capable of slashing the knife? And what of George
and Tracey, that most elegant pair of ripsters? John thought of
them and a smile played about his lips for a moment before he
compressed them into a thin, unrelenting line.

On the night of the grand ball John and Rose took a hackney
coach, the stand for which stood outside the Orange Tree Tavern,
and went to fetch Coralie from her home before making their
way to the concert hall which stood on the south corner of
Hanover and Court Streets. It had been built by Stephen Deblois,
a musician, for the purpose of concerts, dancing and various
other entertainments. It had been hired tonight by that duo of
charming dancing masters and had been decorated throughout
in grand and wondrous style. On arriving at the door, John
presented his tickets and was scrutinized thoroughly, as were
the two ladies, by a huge man clad in sombre black. They were
then admitted into the glittering ballroom.

George and Tracey, cooing like a pair of glorious doves, stepped
forward to greet the Apothecary personally.

'My dear John, how lovely to see you, and Madame Clive,
looking even more beautiful, if such a thing t'were possible. And
surely this cannot be Miss Rose?'

'Oh, but it is,' put in Tracey, who tonight wore the white enamel
make-up, his lips heavily carmined.

'My goodness me, but she is grown into a regular beauty. Quite
the tempting armful, 'pon my word.'

John smiled and said, 'Careful, my dear Sir. Someone might
throw a rub in your way.'

Was it his imagination or did George's eyes narrow a fraction before he bowed and moved away with his friend to greet
some new entrants? But the music was striking up and the
aged fop who the couple hired regularly to act as master of
ceremonies was calling out, 'Take your partners, please, for
the gavotte.'

Rose was immediately surrounded by young men, and though she admitted she did not know the steps was reassured that neither did they, but that they would be called out. Bowing politely to her father, her partner, who had beaten the others to Rose's side by a fraction of a second, whisked her away. The Apothecary, who had been most fond of dancing whilst living in London, led Coralie out with a flourish, all bows and claps, which she acknowledged with a smile from behind her fan.

The years had not jeopardized his performance at all. John still vigorously attacked the steps whilst making a decent leg of it, though he had to admit he was breathing somewhat faster by the time the last chord was sounded. That done, he hurried to the punch bowl in order to refresh his glass and that of Coralie and ran straight into Tracey, who was observing his patrons through an elegant quizzer which hung round his neck on a velvet ribbon. The dancing master, staring over the heads of the crowd, gave a little laugh and drawled, 'Damme, John, if your daughter ain't shining everyone else down. And her so young too.'

The Apothecary answered in a measured voice, 'Come, come, my dear friend. Surely you have no thoughts of that sort.'

The quizzer turned in John's direction and, close as he was, he could see an enormous yet startled pair of blue eyes regarding him.

'No offence, dear Sir. I was merely remarking.'

'D'you know my daughter would not be here now if a pair of wicked bastards had had their way.'

Was it John's imagination or was there a flicker in the depths of those eyes before the quizzing glass was abruptly dropped?

'You shock me, Sir. How so?'

'Firstly she was persuaded to leave school with a strange woman posing as someone sent by myself. Then she was delivered to the Mill Creek for the hands of a person I have yet to identify. But two other people were there and, knowing that I would be present – a note having been sent to my house to advise me to be so – they tied her up and left her in the Mill House, alone and frightened. She could have died.'

'I wouldn't have thought so. I don't think you pay your child enough credit, Sir. I think your little redhead is a hardy young sprite.'

The quizzer was raised once more and John looked into eyes that were growing less friendly.

'Is that why you chose to imprison her instead of setting her free?' he asked.

Before his gaze Tracey Tremayne transmogrified. The handsome, slightly effeminate exquisite vanished and in his place stood a man of steel, in total control of himself and ready to shoot to kill in an instant. The carmined lips curled as he whispered to John, 'That we may have done, but we never physically harmed her. You said yourself that the girl who brought her was looking for another. We merely took advantage of the situation.'

'Who are you?' the Apothecary asked, not quite believing what he had just heard.

A beautifully manicured hand shot out and held his arm with a grip like an iron clamp. 'George and I are just about to tell you that.'

And even as John watched he saw the elegantly clad body once more adopt the pose of a mincing dandy and heard the voice rise a few decibels. The acting ability was phenomenal. They had lived in one another's company for weeks, tramping across the most wild and beautiful terrain and never for a moment given the impression that they were anything but a pair of effeminate fops.

George simpered his way across the room. 'John, my dear fellow, how can I help you?' he asked, and gave a flourishing bow.

Tracey turned to him. 'He has guessed everything. I suggest we inform him of the truth immediately before he inflicts some real damage.'

George gave a long, drooping wink, his black-rimmed eye momentarily disappearing, then he turned to John with an expression hard as ice. 'What a good idea,' he said.

The next second the Apothecary felt his legs snatched from under him as he was carried – Tracey's hand resting, oh so casually, beside his mouth – into the corridor that led backstage. There he was shoved without ceremony on to a small wooden chair. Tracey and George simultaneously removed their exquisitely embroidered jackets and stood towering over him in their shirt sleeves. In an act of defiance, the Apothecary rose to his feet.

'Well?' he said.

'Well, nothing,' replied George. 'How did you guess that we were at the Mill Cove that night?'

In the teeth of great danger, John tried to act as calmly as was possible. 'Your turn of phrase, gentlemen. Together with your rather bad Bostonian accents.'

Tracey burst out laughing. 'And I thought we were so convincing.' He looked at John narrowly. 'How much do you know?'

'Only that you threatened to kill my daughter.'

George put in, something of his old drawl returning, 'T'was merely a bluff, dear boy. We would never have done it. Too fond of the child.'

'My guess is that you are political agents. Am I right?'

'Of course you're bloody right. As usual.'

'But which side are you on? The British or the Colonists?'

'British, damn you. We came to Boston – albeit by a long and hazardous journey – in pursuit of a ruthless daughter of liberty. But then you know all about her, I suppose.'

'I believe that you killed her,' John answered, hedging his bets.

There was an audible silence, during which George and Tracey shot one another a look of total surprise.

'If you are referring to Demelza, Lady Conway, née Moll Bowling, you are mistaken, Sir. Yes, she was the woman we were pursuing but we could not make a move against her until we were certain. Oh, the hours we spent on that journey with that tedious fat woman complaining and the rest of you all so damnably stoical. We had had our instructions in London from the Secret Office to track an agent provocateur who was shipping out to Boston to stir up trouble. Little did we think that we would be shipwrecked with the evil bitch.'

'But did you kill her?' John asked, perplexed.

'No. You know that we were standing close to you throughout the raiding of the tea ships. We heard her fall to her death, though we weren't aware of it at the time. Good God, John, you won't get any points for observation. Not always right this time.'

The Apothecary smiled wryly, his lips curling up in their usual winding way, suddenly feeling at a total loss. Though one puzzle was now clear to him, he looked at the two men standing before him, stripped of all their rakehell behaviour and at the height of their particular game, and knew that though they had answered one query, he was now presented with another. Who had killed Demelza Conway and her hapless lover?

John asked them a question he had asked before, though this time he expected a different answer. 'Tell me, was it you who punched me on Jake's wooden staircase or were you just observing?'

'No, we fight fair,' answered George, which was, John thought, a total pretension when they had practically frightened the wits out of him. But he said nothing. They were supporting a cause they believed in and being paid for their services as well.

Tracey took up the story. 'We were watching Jake's dwelling. Had bribed our way in – not difficult with underpaid servants – and were just about to go up the stairs when you appeared. At that moment someone burst out of his apartment and knocked you flying.'

'Who was it? Did you see?'

'No. Nor could we catch the bastard. We gave chase as best we could without raising an alarm but we lost him in the darkness.'

'So it was a man?'

'Clearly.'

'But I don't think he did come from Jake's apartment. I think he was lying in wait at the top of the stairs. I say that because Jake was still alive at that time. He came down and attended to me.'

They both grew tense and John thought that if the pair were not lovers then they were indeed close, trained to the hilt to respond at precisely the same moment. There were a few seconds of silence, then George said, 'What do you mean by "alive at the time"?'

'Well, he's dead. Didn't you know?'

Their very attitude told John that they were not the killers.

'No,' answered Tracey. 'When did this happen?'

'Sometime over Christmas. I saw the Hancock coach pulling out of the gates on Christmas Day and Jake was not driving. To

cut to the heart of the matter, I called on him shortly after and
when I searched I found him in a cupboard, standing upright,
his throat cut wide.'

Tracey and George exchanged a glance. Finally Tracey spoke.
'What did you do?'

'I called John Hancock, or rather, I should say that his servants
roused him. Anyway, he came to look at poor dead Jake and
made a great gulping sound when he saw the remains. Then he
contacted the coroner and I left.'

'And that was all?'

'Not quite. It is my belief that Lady Conway's husband is
after her. I presume you know the story?'

George and Tracey laughed cynically, a rather cruel sound.
'We knew more about that doll trapes than she knew herself.'

'But did you know this? A servant at the Hancock mansion
told me that a tall, dark man came enquiring for her. He had
an English accent and raised his whip to her when she tried to
ride away.'

'Either a husband or an ex-lover.'

'Of which there were a great many,' added Tracey.

'But do you think it possible that a former fancy man would
take a ship from England and hunt her down?'

'You're right,' answered George. 'I'd lay money the husband's
the one.'

'But who is he? And where is he? And was it him who killed
her? And, if so, how did he get access to raid the tea ships that
night?'

Tracey shook his head and said, 'Damned if I know.'

George answered, 'We'll track him down somehow. We are
not without our informants.'

John raised his brows. 'In this colonist city?'

The spy nodded slowly. 'I think you would be very surprised
at what and who we know,' he replied.

A few days later, Lady Eawiss took Major Roebuck for her
husband. The bride wore purple and gold and had the most
enormous hairstyle that John had ever clapped eyes on. It rose,
powdered and puffed, to a staggering height of three feet, the
golden curls designed by Monsieur Piemont peeping coyly over

one shoulder, the rest *a la mode*. Atop the lot was a birdcage, a miserable-looking canary within, clinging to a swaying bar for dear life. As the bride processed slowly up the aisle on the arm of a small man whom John did not recognize, she emitted shrill trills of greeting to her various friends, most of whom had accompanied her on the tremendous journey across country to Boston. Present beside the Apothecary and his daughter were the two British agents, Tracey and George, Irish Tom, Matthew and his various offspring – both step and actual – and sitting at the back with the twins was pretty Jane Hawthorne. Sir Julian Wychwood came in late, as usual.

The ceremony over, the bridegroom, still obviously affected by the gout, limped down the aisle, his enormous bride on his arm, and was helped over to the Marlborough Hotel – where a room had been hired for the nuptial party – by Colonel William Dalrymple, father of John's friend, Lieutenant Harry. Looking round the salon at the fellow guests, John saw that not one but two of her hairdressers were present. Monsieur Piedmont and Mr Shirley had clearly left the shop in the hands of a young apprentice and taken the day off.

Jane Hawthorne hovered in the entrance. 'I'll take the boys home now, Mr Rawlings.'

'You can leave them here with me, Jane. I'm sure they'll behave themselves.'

He looked at his sons, who gazed back at him silently, scrubbed clean beyond recognition and in matching sailor suits, representing innocence personified. John gave them a penetrating glance. 'You will, won't you?'

'Yes, Sir,' answered Jasper.

James added, 'Of course, Sir.'

Satisfied, John said to Jane, 'I don't suppose you would wish to stay?'

'You're right, Mr Rawlings. I am glad to have left her service and work for you.' Then she let out an uninhibited chuckle. 'Lord love me but she looks like a Covent Garden Lady with that monstrous fandango upon her head.'

John felt an overwhelming urge to join in and tittered aloud. Jasper looked up at him. 'Why are you laughing, Papa?'

'What's so funny?' asked James.

The Apothecary could not help it. He suddenly creased up with the giggles, behaving with no decorum and unable to help himself. Outside it was snowing but inside the room was warm and full of good cheer. Everyone, including the roly-poly bride and her poor, gout-ridden husband started to laugh, as did Sir Julian Wychwood, bellowing with mirth, his eyes streaming and foot stamping. Into this melee came the sound of somebody breaking wind and this set the whole company off into further hysterical raptures. But how wonderful, John thought in the middle of his guffawing, to have such merriment at a wedding. He found himself hoping that the affected Lady Eawiss and her gouty spouse would find mutual enjoyment and a kind of devotion in their life together.

When order was restored once more a toast was made to the bride and groom, and after this formality people began to think about leaving. Before they did so, however, John managed to get a conversation with Monsieur Piemont.

'A wonderful creation on the bride's head, Sir. Your style is very *au courant*, if I may say so.'

Monsieur Piemont bowed – an adorable little man whose very Frenchness made him irresistible to the more modern ladies of Boston.

'Thank you so much, my good Sir. You came the other day for a shave, I think. But these London fashions were brought to me by my new assistant, Mr Shirley. I cannot claim credit for them.'

John bowed before the Frenchman's companion, the tall, slightly brooding man who had rolled the latest fashionable hairstyles off the tip of his tongue in rollicking style.

'My dear Sir, it was a pleasure just to hear you talk the other day. Tell me, are the hair modes nowadays really as high and as mighty as you described?'

'Even more so,' Charles Shirley answered in a gravelly voice. 'Women can barely walk upright under the weight of their immense coiffures. D'ye know it was reported to me on the best possible authority that the Duchess of Billingham had a mouse's nest within hers that was not noticed until her friseur saw her style moving of its own volition.'

John pulled a face. 'What a ghastly thought. Have you been in Boston long, Sir? I do not recall seeing you around town.'

'I arrived some time ago but spent the months before coming here with an old aunt of mine who lives near Lower Falls. When she died I decided to up sticks and work in the city.'

'But you were a friseur in London?'

'In a way. I guided the ladies on what hairstyles would suit them. One could say that I worked in an advisory capacity.'

To ask Charles why he had left London would have been impolite, but just as the Apothecary was turning over the problem in his mind, he spoke.

'Of course, I do miss the city. But I had to leave it all behind when the letter from Aunt Mildred arrived. She was always in poor health, you know. In fact, I think it might be fair to say she enjoyed it. But her last plea was that I should come and see her before she died. The fact was that she had planned to leave me a fair amount of money so I got the next ship out, having nothing left to encumber me.'

'You were not married, Sir?'

Charles sighed heavily, his dark eyes pits of melancholy. 'Alas, no. I was, once. But she, poor soul, was called away. I was left alone to grieve.'

John muttered condolences but his attention was distracted by a loud shriek from the bride.

'Oh, my dear people, I just want to tell you how happy we were to find you all present. My husband and I . . .' she gave a girlish laugh, '. . . are so delighted to have had you with us. Major Roebuck will now say a few words.'

'Damned fine,' pronounced the major, staggering to his feet and looking blearily round the assembled company. 'I think it's a damned fine turn out. Yes, damme, I do.'

There was scattered laughter and then applause before the guests slowly began to make their way out into the bleakness of the snow-filled night. John took the twins under his cloak – they had behaved well and been a credit to him, other than repeatedly staring in amazement at the bride's extraordinary hairstyle. His daughter, like several others present, snuggled into a fur-lined cloak of her own. Thus they walked through the quiet, dark streets of Boston to their home, which was warm and welcoming, a smell of scones wafting through the air as the boys rushed in. But their father's mind was preoccupied. Somewhere, even in these very crowded streets, there resided a cruel murderer who could strike again at any moment.

TWENTY-SEVEN

T he trouble was that he no longer knew where to look. As far as he could tell he had explored every possibility, had followed every lead there was and had still come up empty-handed. Yet the thought of the poor drowned body of Lady Conway and that of her former groom and lover, Jake O'Farrell, pushed into a cupboard, his corpse ghastly, the throat cut raw, spurred him on to find whoever was responsible. But what further clues were there? With a load on his mind, John went to bed that night and, as was quite usual for him, had a vivid dream.

He dreamed that he was watching the sacking of the tea ships once more but that this time the rape of the tea chests was being done by his many and various friends. They, quite undisguised and quite clearly themselves, were romping over the decks of the three ships having the holiday of their lives. Rose was there and the boys and, sitting in a chair, quite at ease amidst the busy and bustling throng which careered all around him, was Sir Gabriel Kent. In the dream John bellowed the word 'Father' repeatedly, over and over again, but Sir Gabriel either could not or would not hear. Instead he took an elegant pinch of snuff from within a silver, monogrammed box and, as if he hadn't a care in the world, crossed one elegant white stockinged leg over another. Just as the Apothecary was about to give up in despair his father looked straight at him and said one phrase, 'Here lies the answer,' and the dream faded away and John returned to normal sleep. But he awoke the next morning convinced that he had received a message from something beyond his understanding.

Having washed, shaved and dressed, and having seen that his children were happy, John left the house and headed straight for Griffin's Wharf. It was hard to believe that just before Christmas the quayside had heaved with seven thousand onlookers, to say nothing of those Sons of Liberty together with the journeymen, apprentices and strangers who had come to help them as they set about the rape of the three British ships.

But, before the gaze of the huge crowd, that is precisely what they had done. They had boarded the vessels, broken open the tea chests and thrown the contents into the harbour below. And not only the tea. In the midst of all that pitching chaos, a body had fallen as well. But today all was calm and there were none at the wharf except those going about their lawful business. That is, with the exception of a group of nasty-nosed urchins who were throwing stones and other rubble at a helpless individual who danced about, crying piteously and begging them to stop. John, looking at the poor wretch intently, diagnosed from the jerkiness of the boy's movements that the poor creature was suffering with St Vitus Dance. Brandishing his walking cane, the Apothecary approached them with a rush and was delighted when they dispersed, one child clutching his behind where the cane had accidentally landed.

The boy turned to him. 'I love little old King George, I do.'

'Of course,' John answered calmly. 'But it might be best not to say it out loud.'

The boy went into a spasm of jerky movements. 'I'm not daft, you know.'

'I never said you were, my friend.'

'Them boys say I am. They call me Looney Luke, they do.'

'Where do you live, Luke?'

'In the workhouse on the Common. But I got a guv'nor, I have.'

John examined him closely, thinking to himself that if it wasn't for the awful twitching gait and crazy spasms the boy could have been called handsome. But as it was, the face beneath the straw-blond hair contorted, hiding the pair of vivid viridian eyes and the kindly mouth.

'So who might that be?'

'He loves King George, he does. He comes to see me every day and brings me something nice to eat. His name is Sergeant Frankland and he's in the army, he is. And he took an oath to King George to serve him well. So . . .' The wretched boy went into an enormous convulsion, his feet rising from the ground and his arms hanging by his side, jerking as if they were separate entities from his body. '. . . So that's why I love him.'

Whether he was talking about the monarch or the army man the Apothecary was not certain, but in either case the poor child obviously meant every word he said.

John asked, 'What are you doing down here at Griffin's Wharf? Shouldn't you be back home?'

'No. My guv'nor's on duty, he is, so I wanders about on my own till he can come and see me. I likes it down here, I do. There's plenty going on with the ships and all. But I hates them urchins – they torment me because I'm a bit simple. That's what they say up workhouse anyways.'

Staring into those frank eyes, presently looking so open and honest, John's heart bled for the accident of illness that had rendered this child incapable of living a normal life. And, whoever he was, he blessed the name of the kindly British soldier who had seen him, taken the poor boy and given him the thing he craved above all else: love.

Luke was seized with another minor spasm then sat down on the cobbles, gesturing to the Apothecary to do the same. 'I comes here every day and watches the goings-on. My guv'nor comes with me when he's got the time. But that ain't often so I sits by myself.'

John said, more out of politeness than anything else, 'Were you here on the night they raided the tea ships?'

'Yes, I'd known something was afoot all day, I did. So I creeps out and comes down here and watched them at it all night long. When I gets back to the workhouse I got six of the best for my pains.'

John laughed. 'Did you now?'

'Yes, but it was worth it. Watching them Injuns – though they wasn't really, you know – tear them tea chests apart.'

The Apothecary quickened, suddenly feeling intensely alive. 'I was there that night too. I didn't see you.'

'No, because I was a loony they let me sit in the front. I didn't like that, I didn't. People kept shoving me and every time I jerked they hit me, they did. But I saw it all.'

John's next question was written in the stars. 'Did you see a woman climb the rigging?'

'No,' Luke answered shortly. 'I didn't.'

'What?'

'I sees *two* women, both dressed in breeches, they was. One was climbing up and so was t'other. Chasing her, you see.'

John stared at him incredulously. 'You say there were two of them?'

Luke did a violent dance. 'Yes. There was. I saw them, I did.'

'How is it that nobody else did?'

'Perhaps they weren't looking,' Luke answered.

Which was very true. Most of the fevered citizens of Boston had been concentrating on the work on deck, the rending open of the tea chests, and if several of them had glanced up and seen two cabin boys climbing the rigging they would have thought little of it. But John persisted.

'Luke, you are certain that both the people you saw were female?'

The boy twitched. 'Yes, because I was sitting on the ground and had to look up.'

John was silent, trying to focus his mind on the fact that there had been another woman up on the sails at the same time as Moll Bowling. But as he tried to concentrate, Luke suddenly shook all over.

'I've got to go back to see my guv'nor now. I promised to buy him some sausage, I did. Goodbye.' And he was gone, shambling up the dockside without a backward look. John contemplated running after him but decided against it. If the boy had been speaking the truth it brought a whole different bearing on the case. Or was it the truth as Luke had seen it? With his mind seething over the new facts, the Apothecary turned and walked away from the wharf to somewhere quiet where he could sit and ponder.

His thoughtful progress took him to the Bull Tavern in Summer Street, an ancient building erected by the early settlers. Inside was a roaring fire and John went to sit by it, warming his hands and feet. The snow continued to fall on Boston, though in spasmodic drifts, and the Apothecary could not remember when he had been colder. The door opened and he was just about to ask the newcomer to shut it behind him when he stopped short. The man standing with his back to the white light was none other than Joe Jago, John's old friend and clerk to the court of Sir John Fielding. And then realization dawned: though very similar in looks and build it was a complete stranger who stood there. The Apothecary let out an audible sigh.

The man smiled. 'You look disappointed. Were you expecting someone else?'

John nodded. 'Yes. Excuse me, Sir, but you bear a striking resemblance to somebody who was a particular friend in London. I thought for a moment . . .'

'That I was he? I am sorry to disappoint you. My name is Alexander, but I do know the chap you are talking about – at least I think I do – because I have often been mistaken for him in town. People have commented that we could be twins. I take it you are referring to Sir John Fielding's assistant?' John nodded and the man continued, 'I have attended the Blind Beak's court once or twice and have remarked on the strange similarity between his clerk and myself. Quite uncanny. But perhaps we are distantly related. May I buy you a drink, Sir? I have just arrived from London and would like to share a little companionship.'

What could John do but agree despite the fact that he needed badly to think quietly? His new companion rambled on, telling him of the latest plays and gossip from the metropolis, laughing heartily as he spoke and generally giving the impression of being a thoroughly decent man. John watched him, thinking that his similarity to Joe was only skin deep. But his mind was changed as a ruffian in torn and ragged apparel came staggering through the door and demanded ale in a loud and bleary voice. The blowsy serving girl began to protest but the stranger, walking up to the ancient bar, seized her by the throat and began to shake her like a waterside rat. Suddenly, with no warning, Alexander was on his feet and with a monumental strength delivered a blow to the ruffian's chin that shook the very rafters of the aged building. As the tramp fell in a heap on the floor the newcomer picked him up by the scruff of his neck and deposited him outside the door into a heap of falling snow. Then he brushed one hand against the other and said, 'As I was saying . . .'

The Apothecary gazed at him in open admiration. 'By God, Sir, I have never seen anyone move so quickly.'

'It's the only way,' replied the other. 'Can't bear to see a pretty woman molested.'

The girl, who was rubbing her neck and recovering, gave him a smile that revealed she had two teeth missing and placed a large glass of brandy in front of Alexander.

'Thank you, good Sir. You acted with extreme courage.'

'I'll say you did. You were like a bolt of lightning.' The Apothecary looked at the other closely. 'Have you had any experience with this kind of thing?'

Alexander gave a half smile and at that moment John had the strange feeling that he was dealing with someone from an organization which probably ran the whole of the British Isles. Boston was like a powder keg waiting to explode and a representative of the Secret Office, sent especially to deliver messages back to London as quickly as was humanly possible, in view of the long voyage that even the fastest vessel could make, might well be considered essential by those in power. He looked into the other man's eyes, noting to himself that despite the kindly smile on his lips his eyes were sharp as a knife blade.

'How do you communicate with your masters?' he asked directly.

Alexander's gaze tautened. 'Now who might they be?' he asked in a lazy voice that belied his visible response.

John leant back in his chair. 'I am only surmising, of course, but I would hazard a guess at the Home Secretary.'

Alexander laughed and took a sip of his brandy, rolling it round his mouth before he swallowed. 'You're a very sharp fellow. Do you always greet strangers in this manner?'

'No. But I have recently had a close encounter with two representatives of the Secret Office and I can tell you frankly that their tactics left me breathless.'

Alexander smiled enigmatically. 'It has been felt in London for some time that there was an element in Boston that needed a careful eye kept on it.'

The Apothecary decided to go directly to the point. 'Did you ever hear of an actress called Moll Bowling, Sir?'

There was no immediate reply but the Apothecary felt himself being scrutinized by those cold sea eyes. Eventually the other man spoke. 'I think that is my business, don't you?'

John plunged on, throwing caution to the breeze. 'She's dead, you know. Perhaps the news has not reached you yet.'

Alexander laughed aloud. 'You're very sure of yourself, aren't you? Quite the little cock bantam.'

John smiled crookedly. 'I'll admit that I am acting on instinct alone but I have the feeling that you would like to know exactly how it happened. Do you wish me to proceed?'

'If it is your desire to do so then by all means continue.'

'Very well. It was the night of the sacking of the three tea ships.'

John could tell by the other man's lack of expression that this fact was news to him. He had presumably been on his way to the Colonies when the event had taken place. However, he was trying to mask what he was thinking with an unreadable face.

'Go on,' he said.

'I spoke to a boy on the quayside. He was looking upwards at the time and saw two figures climbing the rigging. Both were women.'

Now, at last, John saw the metal of the man. Alexander's eyes became as piercing as diamond cutters. His face grew hard and ruthless though he still spoke quietly.

'And did you know who the young man was talking about?'

'Yes. One of them was Lady Conway, née Miss Bowling. The other was her killer, whose identity remains a mystery.'

Alexander finished his brandy in one long swallow. Then he looked at John as if he were finally taking in the measure of the man sitting opposite him. 'Very well,' he said, 'let's to business. You have surmised correctly that I work for the Secret Office and that I have come to Boston to get to know the Sons of Liberty, as they call themselves. Furthermore, I was to stop the activities of Lady Conway – born to rebellion if ever a woman was – that is, if my two agents . . .'

John caught himself thinking that the man must be high up the ladder indeed to use that expression.

'. . . had not done so already. But it seems that they were beaten to the task by someone else. Let me ask you a question.'

'Yes?'

'Was she murdered that night? Was she pushed out of the rigging?'

'I am sure of it. I saw her body next day. She had drowned

and there were some faint signs of a struggle upon the corpse. The army doctor who examined her commented that it was all very strange.'

'Why were you given leave to see the corpse?'

'Because I am an apothecary and traded in London, in Shug Lane, Piccadilly, to be precise. Lieutenant Harry Dalrymple, a British officer and son of a colonel of the same name, asked me to investigate on his behalf. I think I was the only medically trained person available at the time,' he added.

'I see.' Alexander leaned forward. 'So now I will tell you something. You asked about Moll Bowling. She was born into a family of early settlers who decided that they wanted to be free of the yoke of Britain for good. Somehow the girl took ship for England and wandered into the theatrical profession accidentally. I believe that from an early age she was groomed to spy for the Colonists and probably sailed for London at about fourteen with this object in mind. Everything was going according to plan until she met Lord Conway, when her life went slightly adrift. But though love might have possessed her for a time she was undoubtedly returning to Boston to add her voice to the fight for freedom.'

'Didn't she have a child?' asked John.

'Yes, when she was about seventeen. Apparently it was put out to a baby farmer. I presume it died. Why do you ask?'

'I don't really know. Just a feeling I have. It was a daughter, wasn't it?'

'I think so. I'm not really certain.' Alexander stretched himself. 'I would like to question that boy of yours, the one you met at the wharf. He might have some further information. Where can I find him?'

'In the workhouse,' John answered bluntly. 'Are you going now?'

'Directly.'

'Then I will accompany you.'

They stepped outside into a world changed beyond recognition. Boston was by now under heavy snow and the flakes were falling, thick as a fist, blinding the eyes and making it hard to breathe. Before them stretched crystal streets, ice crunched beneath their slipping feet, and overall there was the immense stillness and silence that only a blizzard can bring about.

John turned to Alexander. 'It is going to be a dangerous walk, Sir. The ways are like ice pits.'

'You're right. I shall go back to my hotel and see you in the morning at nine o'clock outside the workhouse.'

'Very good. I'll make my journey home as best I can.'

So saying, they parted company and the Apothecary slid to his house along the icy streets, thinking of all the women he had met since he had arrived: Suzanne, Jane, the former Lady Eawiss. Eventually his mind turned to Coralie, who had once acted with her. Were any of them a possibility for chasing Moll Bowling into the ship's rigging and clawing at her heels, unsteadying her balance until she had plunged to her death in the midnight ocean below? The more he thought about it the more he thought it a distinct possibility, for those older ladies might well have hired a wench from the backstreets to do their bidding. And all of them had come from London at some time in the past and might well have made a connection with that secretive and most hidden of spies, Lady Conway herself.

TWENTY-EIGHT

The next day did not start well. Despite his enormous mental and physical fatigue the Apothecary hardly slept. By the time he had reached his home he had fallen down three times, the last being a painful experience, jarring his spine and hurting his neck. The evening had darkened and he had had no lantern. Thus for the last quarter of a mile he had risked life and limb just to get indoors to safety. Suzanne had been at the Orange Tree and there had been a note from Jane Hawthorne to say that she had retired early owing to a headache but had left Miss Rose reading by the light of the fire. John had walked into a quiet house with a feeling that all was not well in his realm of existence.

Rose had risen and rushed into his arms. 'Father, you're covered in snow. You have fallen over, I think. Did you hurt yourself?'

'Nothing broken, sweetheart, but I landed hard on my behind and jolted my old bones.'

Rose grinned up at him, looking quite cheeky. 'Come, come, Papa. You are maturing in your cask like a good sherry. You will be young when you are eighty.'

He smiled, his crooked grimace never more apparent. 'You are a true charmer, child. Now fetch your aged parent a glass of brandy before he faints at your feet.'

They had conversed for a merry hour before Rose had finally taken herself off to bed. Then John had sat in silence, gazing into the flames, wondering until his mind felt as if it were bleeding about the identity of the woman who had sent Moll Bowling to her death. But when he had at last retired, sleep would not come. He had finally fallen into a deep slumber as the ghostly grey of a snow-laden day had come creeping in at his bedroom window.

When he woke it was to see that it was almost nine in the morning. He dressed hurriedly and sped out of the house without breakfast. Fortunately sweepers had been out, but his progress to the workhouse for all that had been slow and difficult. He arrived there to find that Alexander had been and gone and a militant Corporal Romney was standing over a traumatized Luke, demanding an explanation for the questioning of his adopted brother. As best he could, John tried to calm him down.

'I do apologise to you, Sir. It was just that Luke saw something that night when the tea ships were sacked and Mr Alexander, being a representative of British High Command, wanted to find out if the boy could tell him any more.'

'And who might you be?' the corporal demanded in a militant fashion.

'I am working with Colonel Dalrymple,' John answered, exaggerating wildly. 'I cannot discuss with you the nature of my enquiries but, believe me, they are genuine.'

The corporal patted Luke's head and the boy did one of his shambling and somehow unbearably poignant little dances. He looked at the Apothecary and said, 'My guv'nor,' with a great deal of pride. John's heart bled.

'I think you are to be commended, Sir, for taking this child under your wing,' he said in a low voice.

The corporal looked stern. 'I had a brother who had the very same illness. He was teased and picked upon. Eventually he died. I think the poor soul was tired out with all the tormenting. Luke reminded me of him. What else could I do?'

John did not answer, silently shaking his head, wishing that the whole world possessed the generosity of spirit and kindness of heart that Corporal Romney exhibited.

'Well, even if that Alexander was the King himself I don't think he had the right to barge in here and frighten the young lad like that.'

'No, he hadn't, and I do apologise.'

'You're not going to ask Luke anything else, are you?'

'No,' John answered hastily, though that had been his very intention. 'I shall leave the boy in peace. Good morning to you.'

He left the workhouse hoping to catch up with the extraordinary Mr Alexander, but there was no sign of him. Gazing around the snow-bleached streets, the Apothecary saw that despite the awful conditions the hardened citizens of Boston had opened shops and were pursuing ordinary life as far as it was possible. Tavern doors were being flung wide as figures, stark and black against the

whitened background, made their way within for a nip of brandy
to warm them in such blistering conditions. John made his
way to the north corner of Hanover and Court Streets, where the
Orange Tree was situated. Kicking the snow to one side, he
proceeded to the premises at the back which had been turned
into an apothecary's shop. Inside he found a pale-faced Tristram
desperately trying to serve an overweight man whose face was
constructed entirely round a formidable mouth of protuberant
false teeth. If these were the handiwork of the compact Paul
Revere, who had skilfully fashioned two for Dr Warren, John
would have been very surprised.

'No, no,' the man was shouting, 'I have to take them out
when I eat. I only want something to hold them in place while
I am speaking.'

As if to give a demonstration, his teeth flew upwards and
outwards and were only saved by the man clapping his jaws tightly
shut and putting a hand over his mouth. John intervened.

'Good morning, Sir. I apologise for the lateness of my arrival.
Weather conditions, don't you know. May I suggest that you
use a glue made from ground down whalebones? That should
seal your dentures in place for several days.'

'Excuse me,' the man answered.

'I said several days.'

'No,' gasped the other through layers of material. 'I meant
excuse me.'

And with that he slipped the gargantuan set into the confines
of a red spotted handkerchief, looking a little pinched and
downcast as a result. It was at this moment that Suzanne walked
in, pausing in the doorway as she saw that John had custom.
He looked at her questioningly. Was it she who had climbed
the rigging that night, murdered Moll Bowling and then
raced back to join Irish Tom? The more he thought about it
the less likely it seemed, for hadn't Luke said that both the
women were dressed in boy's clothing? If that were the case,
if the poor, afflicted youth were right, then it could not possibly
have been Suzanne. But could she have hired someone else to
commit murder in her place? And the same could be said of
Lady Eawiss. Could all her smiles, simpering and elderly
coquettishness be a great act? Remembering her horrible

behaviour during the journey to Boston, the Apothecary thought it highly probable.

Suzanne dropped a small curtsey. 'Oh, begging your pardon, Mr Rawlings, I didn't know you had custom.'

'It's quite all right. I shall come and see you later.'

Suzanne smiled and went out, and John turned to his customer, who was standing looking much smaller without his teeth.

'You say you take your dentures out when you eat?' His customer nodded. 'Then, may I suggest that with this particular fixative that will no longer be necessary. And may I further suggest that you go to Paul Revere, the silversmith, and ask him to make you another set.'

The man nodded once more and the Apothecary realized that without his set in place the poor fellow was afraid to speak. Taking the handkerchief, John gave it to Tristram, complete with contents.

'Clean these up for me like a good apprentice and then spread this glue . . .' John handed him a bottle, '. . . fairly liberally, then give the teeth back for the customer to try.'

Five minutes later it was all over, the newcomer restored to his big, blustering self, gnashing his teeth with pleasure and pressing a tip – which John pretended not to see – into Tristram's palm.

'You have solved my problem, Sir,' he said, bowing in the doorway, hat in hand. 'I bid you good morning. Now, where did you say your friend Revere could be found?'

Knowing that Jane was looking after his house and children, John fortified himself with a little cognac before making his way homeward, for there was much good cheer in the Orange Tree Tavern as darkness fell. All his old friends were present, with the exception of those two men of steel, George and Tracey. John thought about them as he sipped his drink, considering that they were two of the finest actors he had ever met. He imagined them in conference with the mysterious Mr Alexander and deliberated to himself that the Sons of Liberty had a consid· erable force to be reckoned with. But, when the final analysis came, what were three men, however clever, pitted against the weight of hundreds?

His silent contemplation was interrupted by a voice at his

elbow. 'May I join you?' He looked up and saw Charles Shirley, creator of the immense hairstyles, standing there.

'Please do, my dear Sir.'

The dark, saturnine creature took a seat and remarked, 'By God, but it is a cold night.'

'It is indeed. Colder than it was back home.'

'Ah, you still refer to England as such. I was wondering if you intended to stay in Boston.'

'No, Mr Shirley . . .'

'Please call me Charles.'

'Charles. I miss London too much. The old haunts, the gossip, the stinks, the people, the whole bustling atmosphere of the place.'

'Yes, indeed. I spent a great deal of time there despite the fact that I had a place in the country. Do you know what I miss most, though – the theatres. My father used to take me when I was a mere youth. I was in love with all the actresses.'

John smiled a quizzical smile. 'Did you know that one of them is now living here in Boston?'

'No, I didn't. Pray who? Do tell.'

'Coralie Clive, sister of the wonderful Kitty.'

Charles clutched his hands together in ecstasy. 'Oh, the Clive sisters! How well I recall them. I adored them both.'

'As did I, 'answered John. 'As did I.'

'When I last left London I went hunting for them but I heard that Kitty had retired and that Coralie had married into the aristocracy.'

'With rather sad results,' John said.

A dark cloud passed momentarily over Charles Shirley's face and he let out a melancholic sigh. 'Speak to me not of it. Such things are better left unsaid.'

It was a peculiar remark to say the least, and the Apothecary's interest was piqued. 'You have had experience of such things?'

Charles smiled and peered into his empty glass. 'I would be saying too much if I betrayed a confidence. But let me get you a drink, my dear Mr Rawlings. More brandy for you?'

'I should get home.'

'Ah, let me persuade you.'

John weakened and was glad he did, for at that moment three people advanced on him: Suzanne followed by Irish Tom and

Sir Julian Wychwood. All of them seemed in high spirits and, John thought, it would only need Matthew to enter and the ship-wrecked party would be almost complete.

'We've something to tell you,' Suzanne giggled, all of a fluster.

John smiled at her but within his thoughts piled high on each other. Was this the woman who had contrived Moll Bowling's death? For he knew full well how murder could wear a grinning face. But her next blushing words rather threw him off balance.

'Irish Tom and I have some news.'

The mighty ex-coachman spoke up. 'Yes, we have. And I don't suppose it will be too great a surprise to you, John, to hear that I have found love at last. I have asked Suzanne to marry me and we were wondering if you would act as her father for the occasion, seeing as she has no living relatives in Boston.'

John was both delighted and devastated at the news. He knew that as soon as he had discovered the identity of the murderer he would be making enquiries about the next ship back to England, hoping that fortune would be kind and that Coralie would decide to go with him. But even if she did not – he could hardly bear the thought – he knew that the whole powder keg which was Boston was one day going to explode, and in future it would be a difficult place in which to make a home unless you were wholeheartedly behind the Colonists.

'What do you say, Sir?' Tom asked anxiously.

John rose to his feet. 'It will be my pleasure. Suzanne, I wish you great happiness. Now, do you know Charles Shirley who has created some outrageous hairstyles and is currently working with Monsieur Piemont?'

There was a yes from the happy couple but Sir Julian raised his quizzer and said, 'By Jove, I think we have glimpsed one another over the gaming tables at Almack's.'

John mentally raised an eyebrow, the gambling club being a haunt for the fashionable young bucks of town and not the sort of place where one would expect to find a friseur. However, he said nothing.

Charles behaved well, eyeing Sir Julian up and down before he answered, 'I think not, Sir.'

'Oh, surely. I never forget a face.'

'Then I must be the exception to your rule, Sir. I am but a humble working man.'

The conversation veered back to the forthcoming nuptials, about which the Apothecary had many mixed emotions. He wanted Irish Tom to be happy and settled even though he knew that he would be losing the greatest friend he ever had. But the bride-to-be was a great deal younger than her future husband. Yet, he thought, who was he to question anything? That the ill-matched couple loved one another was plain to see. That their future would be unbridled happiness was entirely in the lap of the gods.

Eventually, after much jollity and merriment, a slightly inebri-ated John Rawlings made his way back through the snow. Sir Julian and Tom were spending the night at the Orange Tree, and so it was just the Apothecary and the hairdresser who slipped and slid their way back to the North End, holding each other up. But for the last lap of the journey John travelled alone – Charles Shirley having branched off to go to Monsieur Piemont's dwelling, where he had a room. But as the Apothecary rounded the corner he saw to his horror that every lamp had been lit in his house, the reflection lighting the snow. His heart pounding, John went as fast as was humanly possible to his front door. It was opened by Rose, fully dressed, holding a twin in each hand. He stared at her.

'Sweetheart, what's wrong? Why are you all up and where is Jane?'

'Father, she has been kidnapped. We are here on our own and the boys are very frightened.'

'No, we're not,' said Jasper bravely. 'We are just a little bit scared.'

'Tell me exactly what happened,' John asked as he took them into the living room and put more wood on the fire.

Rose answered, 'It was at about nine o'clock. Jane said she had to go out to get a breath of air. I warned her of the cold but she put a cloak on and went up the road a little way. Then I heard a faint cry and looked out of the door and saw her being picked up by a man in a cloak and hat and carried off.'

'Was it Blue Wolf who took her?'

Rose nodded. 'I reckon so.' Then she added, 'I couldn't see

him distinctly, Papa. His clothes disguised him. But I thought it
was obvious that she had gone with him.'

'Did your gift tell you so?'

She shook her head, puzzled. 'No, it eluded me completely.
It was as if something had blocked it from my view.'

John pulled himself together. 'Then I must go after her. She
might possibly be in danger.'

'But Papa, it was over two hours ago.'

'I know, but I must try.'

'It would be a thoroughly foolhardy gesture,' said his daughter
with great reproof.

The Apothecary sobered up and knew she was right. 'As always,
you're quite correct. I must wait until morning before I search.'

'I don't think they will be far away. Even an Indian would
have difficulty getting through a night like this.'

'Where could they have holed up?'

Rose looked wise. 'Maybe with a friend. Where does Matthew
live?'

'Not far away. Sheafe Street, I believe.'

'Then set off early, Papa, and hopefully you'll catch them
before they leave.'

'But they may not be there.'

'I don't think they will have gone far,' Rose answered certainly.
Suddenly she looked very serious. 'But if it was Blue Wolf who
took her she will never come back – you know that, don't you.'

'Yes, I do and I wish them well. I think they have loved one
another for a long time.'

'I believe so too.'

It was the day's first blink when he found them. In the east a
rose-pink aureole had just peered over the horizon but in the
west night reigned triumphant, though its inky blackness was
bleached to a lovely shade of cerulean blue as the oncoming day
triumphed over darkness. Stars glimmering in the sky slowly
vanished one by one, as if some almighty conjurer was concealing
them beneath his hand. The spires of Christ's Church caught the
first rays as the sun rose in wintry grandeur and the Apothecary
watched his breath fly out like spun glass as he knocked with
his hand on Matthew's door.

The little widow woman whom he had married was up and at her baking. She answered and looked at John in great astonishment. Then she bobbed a little curtsey. 'Why, good morning to you, Sir. Is it Matthew you want to see?'

'If you please, yes.'

But the countryman was already coming down the stairs, his braces over his woollen vest, his shirt not yet on. John caught his eye and silently asked a question, and Matthew gave a small smile and nodded.

'I couldn't turn them away, my friend. A night on the streets would have meant death.'

'It is Rose Hawthorne and Blue Wolf?'

'Yes. And don't lecture me about them coming from difference races, I beg of you, John. They are a pair of star-crossed lovers if ever I saw one.'

The Apothecary wondered if Matthew had ever seen a Shakespeare play but kept the notion to himself.

'Don't worry, I mean them no harm. There is something I want to ask Jane, that is all.'

'They are in the eaves, the only shelter I had to offer them.'

Matthew's wife made a token click of disapproval but her husband merely smacked her on the behind very gently and she laughed at herself.

John ascended the stairs then climbed the ladder to the loft. He was very quiet, his footsteps soft and cat-like, his breathing hushed, and thus he caught them asleep, their bodies entwined, wrapped round each other like a pair of love-starved children. He saw how brown Blue Wolf's skin was, his dark, beautiful hand encircling one of Jane's round and marbled breasts. How black his hair, one lock of which fell over her rose-drenched cheek. The Apothecary stopped and drew breath, seeing the two of them together, wishing that he could paint and capture their beauty for ever on a canvas that would always be there. Then he felt like an intruder on their privacy, their loveliness cheapened by the eyes of an onlooker, and began to descend the ladder. But at that moment Blue Wolf opened his ebony-lashed eyes and said, 'Is that you, Matthew?' in his unusual French-accented voice.

The Apothecary hesitated, then called out, 'No, it is John Rawlings. Forgive me for trespassing. I just wanted to have a word with Jane.'

Her voice answered, 'I rather thought you might, Sir. Go downstairs and I will come to you as soon as I can.'

It was a dismissal and, feeling terrible for intruding on the lovers' privacy, John crept down the ladder and into Matthew's kitchen. There he sat, drinking his first cup of coffee, while various children came down and washed in the sink before being inspected by Sarah, Matthew's wife, and then sent upstairs to dress, the big ones helping the smaller, as was the custom.

Eventually the runaway couple came down, Blue Wolf dressed in the clothes John had given him when employing him as a servant, Jane in the plain skirt and apron she had worn when she had run away last night.

Matthew called out, saying, 'If you would like a little privacy then you are welcome to go into the parlour. We don't use it during the day.'

The room was small but with the door shut it offered a quiet place in which they could speak frankly. The three sat down in an ominous silence, John suddenly too embarrassed to say a word. Eventually, after clearing her throat, Jane said, 'You have come to ask me whether I killed Lady Conway, have you not?'

'Why do you say that?'

'Because no doubt you have been informed by some observant person that she was seen climbing the rigging on the night of the tea raid, and that she was being pursued by a girl dressed in a young man's clothing.'

'That is correct.'

'Well, the answer is that it was indeed myself who was following her. But as for killing her . . .' Her voice suddenly broke, a strange, heart-rending sound. 'The answer is no. How could I? She was my mother.'

John gazed at the girl, not quite sure exactly what she was telling him. 'You mean that you were the child she put out to a baby farmer?'

Jane started to weep silently, the tears running down her fresh-faced cheeks. Blue Wolf put a protective arm round her, meanwhile, treating the Apothecary to an unblinking stare.

'My dear, I feel completely at a loss. Can you tell me the story from the beginning?'

'There is no story. Not really. One day, when Mrs Boucher had been on the gin, she told me that my mother was an actress called Moll Bowling. Then two years later she informed me that my mother was being kept by a rich man and had changed her name to Demelza. I was twelve years old and I made my way to London on foot and went to find her. But she had moved on. The last thing I heard of her was that she had married a Lord Conway. The rest you know.'

'No. I'm sorry, I don't.'

Jane looked at Blue Wolf who suddenly kissed her – a lovely kiss which told her how much he loved her.

'Tell him, my Silver Fox. He needs to know everything.'

'I decided to leave for the Colonies. I took work as a kitchen drudge and in ten years I had saved ten pounds for my passage. It was an act of fate and fate alone that I was booked on the same ship as you and Lady Conway and Jake, and that we were shipwrecked. At first I thought it must be a coincidence, that it must be another woman with the same name. But gradually I picked up enough information to realize that it *was* my mother, that she had said farewell to her husband and had eloped with Jake. The trouble was that I liked him, and quite liked my mama too. I wanted to hate her, to kill her, but instead I found myself becoming fond of her. Oh, dear God, it was a terrible position to be in.'

She clung to Blue Wolf and wept bitterly, and John wished that he had never started on this line of enquiry. Yet the ruthless side of his character persisted. 'Go on,' he said.

'I wanted to talk to her privately, to tell her who I was, to forgive her and ask her to love me. But we were never alone. Jake was always at her side. Sometimes I just wanted to shout it at her. But between Jacob and Lady Eawiss I never got the chance.'

'Could you not have seen her in Boston? Surely you must have had some spare time.'

'By then I had fallen in love with Blue Wolf and I did not feel the need for affection as despairingly as I once had.'

'So what happened on that fateful night?'

'As you know, Blue Wolf went aboard.'

The French-accented voice took up the story. 'It was quite easy. There were journeymen, apprentices and strangers taking part. I simply joined in.'

Jane gave a little laugh which turned into a sob. 'I had gone dressed as a boy. It seemed to me that I would stand a better chance of seeing something that way. If I had gone in women's garb I don't know what might have happened. There were some rough elements loose that night. Anyway, when Blue Wolf went aboard I couldn't resist it. I joined in. We were silently divided into three groups on the quayside and when I looked round I saw that my mother had gone aboard the *Beaver* so I went too. We were face-to-face and I simply said to her, 'Lady Conway, I am the daughter who you gave away all those years ago.'

She fell silent, weeping once more, and Blue Wolf finished the story for her. 'Demelza looked at her and thought she was a mad boy. She felt so frightened that she was about to be attacked that she climbed the rigging to get away. Jane went after her, pleading with her not to be afraid. She put out her hand to stop Milady's flight and with that Demelza must have lost her balance and plunged into the sea below. Jane let out a terrible cry and I, seeing what had happened, dived in to rescue her but the sea was full of tea, chestload upon chestload of it. I could not find Lady Conway. I swam to one of the jetties and willing hands pulled me out.'

'And this is the truth?' asked John, but it was a superfluous question. The very sight of the broken girl and the veracity with which her Indian lover had spoken confirmed every word they had said. He sat in a stunned silence, knowing that they had told him the facts as they had happened.

Eventually John said, 'But what about Jake? Did you murder him, Blue Wolf?'

The Indian looked at him with an expression that spoke more than words could ever say. 'It is not the habit of my people to kill one's friends.'

John felt the size of a pygmy. He had been lowered by asking the very question. And one look at the weeping Jane Hawthorne spoke louder than any words. Now the question remained. If neither of the young couple had killed Jacob O'Farrell, then who had?

TWENTY-NINE

I t was a question which John turned over in his mind constantly but could never come up with an answer. Of one thing he was certain. The husband of Demelza Conway, née Moll Bowling, was responsible – but who was he? In the end he whittled the suspects down to the mysterious Mr Alexander, who had claimed to be from the Secret Office and who had known so much about her past. Nor could John omit his friends. Irish Tom could be ruled out because of their long and great association, but George Glynde and Tracey Tremayne were both in the running. Matthew he considered but mentally discarded. He was too honest a citizen to be capable of such a cruel crime. Sir Julian Wychwood, however, gambler extraordinaire and man about town, might well have been involved in some shady dealings. But of them all Alexander, about whom he knew so little, seemed to be the man most likely.

The snow had cleared sufficiently to allow the citizens of Boston to move around more freely and so, having escorted his children to school, the term having begun once more, John took a hackney carriage from outside the Orange Tree and in it piled all of Rose's luggage as he took her back to Coralie's emporium. He turned to her as they clattered along.

'Tell me, sweetheart, are you happy studying at that school?'

'Oh, yes. But I would not like to do so indefinitely.'

'But how could you? You will grow too old for education.'

'And then what? Marriage and children? No, Papa, I want to be an actress, like Coralie and her sister. And as theatre is not allowed by the pious people of town it is my ultimate aim to go back to London.'

'And mine too,' he said before he had had time to think.

'Is it? I thought you were settled here.'

'No, I long for all the sights and smells of London. Don't mistake me – I love the Colonies, with all their bravura and fighting spirit. I shall never forget the beauty of the countryside we came through after the shipwreck. But I was born to enjoy the splendour of the capital with all its vice and filth thrown in. I am just hoping that when I go your headmistress might come with me.'

She turned a glowing face on him. 'You want Miss Clive to accompany us?'

'Yes, I do. Do you think she will?'

Rose looked very serious. 'I don't know. It is a chance you will have to take.'

Having deposited his daughter into the hands of one of Coralie's minions and after enquiring about Miss Clive's whereabouts, only to be told that she was unavailable and probably would be for the next few days, John returned to the hackney and ordered it to proceed to the Marlborough Hotel. But the staff within told him that Mr Alexander had gone out and nobody knew at what hour he would be returning. Somewhat disconsolately, the Apothecary paid the hackney off and decided to walk, thinking.

John trudged, hands deep in pockets, hat pulled well down, and almost ran into Sir Julian Wychwood who was walking along looking well pleased with himself.

'John, my dear chap, what a gloomy face! What weighty matters are you considering that you should look so serious?'

'I was thinking about the murder of poor Jake O'Farrell and who can be the guilty party.'

Julian changed his expression. 'Yes, a very sad business that. I always liked Jake. Got on well with him. He liked a game of cards, you know.'

'Talking of cards, do you know a man called Alexander?'

'Alexander what?'

'No, it's his surname. I don't know the rest of it.'

'Can't say I've met him. It's not the fellow you introduced the other night, is it?'

'No, that's Charles Shirley.'

'I could swear that I've seen him in London. If it wasn't at Almack's gaming club it was somewhere like that.'

'Perhaps he has a double,' John answered, but his mind was going down wild avenues.

'Perhaps,' Julian said doubtfully. He brightened. 'Look, two of my favourite people are coming. My compliments, friends.'

He swept an elaborate bow and waved a greeting as George and Tracey appeared sauntering nonchalantly down the street. To look at them, the Apothecary thought, it would have been totally impossible to imagine that beneath the veneer of the posturing dandy lay a ruthless killer streak. They stopped, beaming broadly, only their eyes, John noticed, calculating and taking in everything that was going on around them. After the treatment he had suffered at their hands he found it difficult to smile. But then, he thought, they had apologised after a fashion, so there was no point in being childish.

Tracey spoke. 'Good morning, gentlemen. Will you be attending our Welcome 1774 dance on Saturday? We hope very much to see you there.'

'Of course I shall be present. I always am,' answered Julian. 'I wonder which young lady I should invite. Perhaps Miss Dolly Quincy.'

'I thought she was the intended of John Hancock,' said John.

'Nonsense. He can't make his mind up and meanwhile she is free as air.'

'I don't believe you,' put in George good-humouredly. 'I don't think she would be seen at a public ball with the likes of you.'

Julian was all smiles. 'Is this a wager? Because if so I will see you.'

'I'll take it on,' from Tracey. 'Twenty dollars you can't get her to come.'

Julian frowned but John could see the gleam of mischief in his eye. 'I'll go one better.'

'How?'

'I'll wager fifty dollars to everyone present that I will get you all invited to take tea with Miss Quincy this very day.'

John could not resist it. 'I'll take that if you mean what you say.'

'Of course I mean it. Gentlemen . . .' He turned to the spying dancing masters. 'What say you?'

'You're on,' said Tracey.

'Agreed,' added George.

'Right. Let us congregate at the Orange Tree at thirty minutes after two and I will take you all out to tea.'

With much laughter and merry quips the four went their

separate ways, John bidding farewell to Sir Julian Wychwood, his last glimpse of whom saw the young man rubbing his hands together with an air of triumph, a gesture which set the Apothecary thinking deeply.

The Orange Tree was unusually full that midday. There were several ladies taking tea and cakes but there was a goodly gathering of gentlemen present, so much so that Irish Tom was called in to serve ale and wine as well. John, looking round, saw that the former Lady Eawiss had graced them with her company and was doing her simpering best to interest a stern-faced lady of considerable stature and girth who the Apothecary recognized as Lydia Hancock, aunt of John. With her was a sharp, small, pretty little creature, overdressed in ruffles and flounces, with bows in her hair and a permanent smile on her knowing lips. This surely must be Miss Dolly Quincy herself, the ward of Mrs Hancock who had moved into the Hancock house in the hope of gaining the attention of John, who was so mad for love of Sally Jackson that he could see no one else.

Sir Julian Wychwood had obviously hurried straight from his earlier meeting and had arrived looking handsome and terribly English. He stood at the bar letting his beautiful eyes wander in the direction of Miss Dolly, who caught his roving gaze and lowered her own in apparent modesty, the illusion somewhat shattered when she looked up again and gave him the faintest of smiles.

Julian bowed low and said to Mrs Hancock, 'Madam, we meet again. I came to your delightful mansion some time ago to play cards with your nephew.'

Lydia Hancock looked at him with a steely gaze. 'I can't say that I can recall you.'

Miss Dolly spoke up. 'Why, Mrs Hancock, I do remember the gentleman playing cards with John, I truly do. Sir, I know we were introduced. Sir Julian Wychwood, is it not?'

Julian slid into a bow that would not have disgraced a nobleman. 'Indeed it is, Miss Dolly. Would it be forward of me to remark how beautiful you look today?'

The old silk worm, thought John, but could not resist a grin.

Miss Dolly obviously revelled in sweet talk and also had a

weakness for British titles. She smiled charmingly. 'How very kind of you, Sir.'

'May I assure you that I really mean it. As for Mrs Hancock, may I say that you carry yourself like a queen, Madam.'

Lydia gazed down her nose in an uncompromising manner. 'You may say what you wish, Sir, but I'll have you know that I personally do not care for idle talk.'

The old harridan, John considered, but there his ideas were abruptly terminated as in walked George and Tracey, still playing the role of effeminate dancing masters, with Mr Alexander, all smiles and warmth and general affability. It was hardly believable that the man who claimed to be from the Secret Office and who had come to the Colonies deliberately to spy could look so genuinely pleasant, an atmosphere, almost cosy, surrounding him like a comforting cloak. Even hard-nosed Mrs Hancock looked at him with approval. Lady Eawiss's voice rose above the general hubbub.

'Of course, m'husband is a high-ranking officer, don't you know. We had our nuptials quite recently. The reception was at the Marlborough Hotel, a very fine place.'

But she was drowned out by a squeal from Miss Dolly as Monsieur Charles, alias Charles Shirley, arrived, pulling off a pair of very fine kid gloves and blowing on his fingers.

'Why, if it isn't that most wonderful friseur. You dressed my hair quite recently, good Sir. All my friends were most taken with it. I wondered if you could do it once more. Perhaps *a la Zodiaque* this time.'

Charles regarded her solemnly, his dark eyes very serious. 'No, Miss Dolly. For you it must be *a la Zephire*, because with your delightful personality you are like a gentle summer breeze laughing and cavorting amongst the leaves.'

To say that she adored the compliment would have been an understatement. Her sharp little chin rose in the air, she clapped her gloved hands together and her laugh was a peal of silver bells.

'Why, do you hear that, Mrs Hancock? I declare that I wish to invite this coiffeur to take tea. He is a perfect English gentleman.'

Lydia looked him up and down with a face like a gargoyle,

totally unsmiling and severe. Eventually she said, 'Who are you, Sir?'

Charles bowed low and John thought him a fine figure with his sombre looks and brooding features.

'The name is Shirley, Ma'am. Charles Shirley. I used to advise on styles in London but came to Boston on business which has subsequently been transacted. Monsieur Piemont was looking for an assistant so I offered my services, having nothing better to gain me useful employment. May I say how much I admire your house, Madam. It is one of the finest – if not *the* finest – that it has been my pleasure to look at.'

Something resembling a smile crossed the weather-beaten features. 'Kind of you to say so.'

'I only speak the truth,' Charles answered, putting his hand on his heart and inclining his head.

Lydia stared at him long and hard, then said, 'In that case you may come and view the interior. Dolly, you may invite this gentleman to sup tea.'

Her ward rose from her seat and whirled to where her hairdresser stood. 'Do you hear that? How delightful. I am so pleased.'

The fact that she had a bit of a fancy for Mr Shirley was obvious to one and all. Charles took one of her minute little hands into one of his own.

'May I buy you a cordial, Miss Dolly? And one for your esteemed aunt also.'

She giggled, her small face growing flushed with excitement. 'Oh, Mrs Hancock is not my aunt, Sir. We are related but, more importantly, she has adopted me as her ward, which was just so very kind of her.'

Alexander spoke up, his voice sounding very high-class London. 'I say that kindness is one of the most important things in the world. Would you not agree, Rawlings?'

John, who had been observing things with some amusement, wondered why he had been asked. 'Oh, yes, absolutely.'

Alexander shot him an amused smile. Lydia Hancock, meanwhile, had been glancing round the room, obviously approving of all the highfalutin Londoners speaking English with cut-glass accents while Dolly, on fire with frisky flirtation, whirled from man to man, gazing at all of them with the kind of confidence that her pretty face allowed. Charles, bowing before the older woman, handed her a glass of canary which she sipped with great enjoyment, meanwhile slipping an arm round and giving a quick squeeze to Dolly's whaleboned waist. The Apothecary, observing, thought that this was indeed all human life.

Exactly one hour later – John having slipped back to his shop to see that Tristram was coping with everything – the party was gaining momentum. Irish Tom and Suzanne were standing hip on hip as they served tea and alcohol simultaneously; Mrs Hancock was in serious conversation with Mr Alexander, though what about John could not overhear; George and Tracey were dancing together, showing any of the assembled company that cared to watch the latest steps from London; Sir Julian had engaged Charles Shirley in a game of cards while Dolly fluttered like an enraptured moth. It was a pretty picture indeed and yet, John knew, somewhere in its depths it sheltered the person who had murdered Jake O'Farrell and stood him up in his cupboard with his throat cut wide. But Mrs Hancock was speaking, her words ever-so-slightly blurred.

'Gentlemen – and I think you can all be granted the honour of that title – I invite you all back to Hancock House, now, this very afternoon, to take a small libation with myself, Miss Dolly and, of course, my nephew, John Hancock himself.'

She's an old snob, thought the Apothecary and, catching Julian Wychwood's eye, knew that he was like-minded but triumphant.

Leaving Tom and Suzanne to serve the few customers left, the four men made their way outside to where the hackney cab stand was situated. This had been set up in 1708 by Jonathan Wardwell, who had been the proprietor of the Orange Tree at the time. Mr Alexander and Sir Julian had been invited by the ladies to join them in the lumbering Hancock coach – presumably because they were the most gentlemanly of all the gentlemen present. George, Tracey, Charles and John took the two carriages that stood waiting for hire. In a somewhat disorderly fashion they joined the small procession making its way to the Hancock mansion.

Yet again, the town of Boston buzzed with activity. The snow having been cleared and the footpaths being accessible once more, the place bustled with life. Street-sellers were out and shouting their wares loud and long, drowning the sounds of carts rattling and the high, bright clipping of horse hooves. Small, sad black chimney sweeping boys dragged their brushes along the cobbled streets hoping for a bit of custom even at this time of year when fires had been lit in all the hearths. The air was filled with the smell of wood smoke and the sharp redolent tang of Newcastle coals. Yet it was the sounds that thrilled John Rawlings most. The city was alive with industry, people hammering, looms thudding, fishermen hauling in their silvery, slippery catches. It was a time of vast and enormous energy. It was a time of revolution.

The cavalcade of coaches reached the Common and the occupants looked out to where a canopy of canvas indicated the place where the men of the British Army, in all their redcoated glory, had encamped. Beyond the small white cluster stretched green pastures on which sheep and cows grazed contentedly. Riders were out in the sunshine, their horse's feet lifting high above the turf where recent snow had made the ground soggy. Above all towered Beacon Hill, on whose majestic heights John and Julian had once found the remains of a poor dead dog. But it was to Hancock House that every eye was now drawn.

It stood, quite brazenly grand, proclaiming that its owners had a position in life. Yet for all its pretension, John liked the place. Surrounded by its magnificent gardens, paled off by its white fencing, it looked part of the landscape yet so utterly removed from the squalor of some of the alleys in the North End that the Apothecary felt it must cause jealousy in some stout Bostonian hearts. Yet his thoughts were a million miles away as his conveyance pulled through the gates, which were opened by a black slave. John leant forward and remembered talking to the man, then watched the slave's face as he looked inside first the coach, then the two hackneys following it. It was quite clear he had identified one of the occupants as someone he had met before and his expression changed from that of smiling welcome to an appearance of total shock. The Apothecary knew at that moment that one of the travellers visiting the Hancock home was a murderer. But which of the other five was it?

*   *   *

'It was a damnably difficult situation. I knew one of them had killed poor Jake but I had no means of finding out who it was,' said John, swigging down a large glass of brandy.

'But why not?' asked Coralie Clive. 'Surely it wouldn't have been an impossibility to have found the gatekeeper and asked him.'

'My dear, you have been entertained by the Hancocks. Surely you must appreciate the difficulties of leaving the room and going in search of one of their slaves.'

Coralie looked at him questioningly. 'Well, in that case, how are you going to solve it?'

'I am going back there tonight to ask the gatekeeper directly. If anybody wants to know what I am doing I shall say I came back to retrieve my gloves.'

'Which you cleverly left behind.'

'Quite so. I did.'

There was a brief silence. John stared out of the window on the darkening afternoon. He had refused to ride back to Boston with the other men, saying that he preferred to walk. But actually he had called in at Coralie's house fully aware that there was something of prime importance he had to ask her. But now that the time had come, he was hesitant. Though there had been a lifetime of experiences between them he was afraid, as the years ticked by, of losing her for ever. And that was something he dreaded. He was past the age for cheap affairs. All he wanted now was stability and mutual consideration. But then, he thought, he was only forty-four and very far from his worst. Nonetheless, he loved Coralie very dearly and now was the time to speak.

'You know that I am seriously considering returning to England.'

She gave him an inscrutable glance. 'So I've gathered.'

'How? How did you know?'

'Because of your manner. You've had an edge about you in the last month or two. A kind of impatience that you are wrestling with.'

'It's not that so much. I just have the feeling that the American Colonies are straining at the leash. I am sure that at any moment the powder keg will blow. Then I will be forced to take sides, and this I cannot do. I think the Bostonians have right on their side, but I was born in Britain. I am British. It is to the mother country that I owe my allegiance. So what chance will I have when the war breaks out?'

'You could keep your head down and say nothing.'

'But Coralie, how could I? I am me and bound to do something or other. I could not just lie passive while all about me are fighting like dogs. I would be shot, sure as fate, and then what chance for my children?'

She smiled – a sad, wistful smile. 'Oh, my dear, I know exactly what you are saying.'

'Do you? Do you realize that in my roundabout sort of way I am asking you to give up everything and sail with me? Come back to London with me, Coralie. We can be married and live happily ever after. But if that is not to your taste then we can take dwellings close to one another. I can return home to Nassau Street. And so can you, if you wish it.'

He rather childishly went down on one knee and clutched her hands in his. The actress that was the true woman came out. She fluttered her eyelashes. 'La, Sir, is this a decent proposal?'

'You know perfectly well it is.'

'Then I must have time to ponder. Seriously, though, it would mean giving up my school and my life here. I have become a respected member of the community.'

'And what price your school, your position, if a revolution should break out, as inevitably it must?'

Coralie sighed. 'And what if it does not?'

'It will, you can rest assured. You did not witness the savagery that was everywhere on the night of the tea raids. I tell you as an old friend that the British are not going to be popular unless they side with the Colonists. Are you prepared to do that?'

'I might. I don't know.'

John rose to his feet. 'Then it will be up to you to decide which path you take. You know that I love you, that the circumstances of life have chosen we are now both free to marry. I leave you with my offer. Remember it well, Coralie.'

She rose also. 'I thank you with all my heart. And I promise to consider it with all of mine.'

'Then I cannot ask more.'

And so saying, he put his hat on his head and made his way out.

It was but a short walk back to the Hancock House, and here John had a stroke of good fortune: the black slave was still on duty at the gates. As soon as he saw the Apothecary approaching on foot the servant opened the bars sufficiently enough for John to squeeze through.

'Good evening, Master. I think you kept very strange company today.'

'Did I, by Jove. Who was it, pray?'

The slave pulled him close and whispered in the Apothecary's ear.

John looked extremely surprised. 'You are sure it was him?'

'As sure as my name is Robin, Sah, which was the first thing my moma saw after giving birth to me.'

'Well, thank you most kindly, Robin. I shall hasten back to town and charge him with it.'

'Then you will have taken a weight off my mind, Sah. Poor old Jake. He wus a good fella and no mistake.'

'Indeed he was,' John answered. 'And now I'll collect my gloves and hurry back before the man has had a chance to shift.'

'Good luck to you, Sah. Oh, thank you, Sah,' the man said as the Apothecary pressed a coin into his hand and hurried away into the darkening evening.

There were very few customers in the Orange Tree – perhaps because the night was getting bitingly cold and the wind had snow on its breath, or perhaps because the Sons of Liberty were meeting in another tavern to discuss the next moves in their inevitable game. John could not blame them.

The atmosphere in the place had always been one of friendly discussion and not conducive to the hatching of serious plots. But two of his former companions were sitting in a corner, laughing over a glass of cognac. They had their heads quite close together and it struck the Apothecary at once that they had known one another for quite a considerable time. He approached them, bowing politely. 'May I join you, gentlemen?'

'Of course, of course,' answered Mr Alexander, gesturing

towards an empty chair that stood at the table, while Charles Shirley smiled and nodded.

John quietly took a seat. 'I'll come straight to the point,' he said.

Mr Alexander did not move a muscle but Charles's eyebrows shot up. Neither of them said a word, however.

'Tell me, Lord Conway, how well did you know Jake O'Farrell?'

There was total silence and for one terrible second John Rawlings wondered if he had made a most almighty gaffe – if Robin the gatekeeper had been wrong all along. Then there was a scraping sound as a chair was pushed back and Mr Alexander shot to his feet.

'So we meet again,' he said in a voice that was little above a whisper.

'Yes,' drawled Charles Shirley, 'so we do.'

At that point John felt totally uncertain, then a second later he was knocked sideways. As he hit the floor he saw Charles's booted foot flick out and fasten round Alexander's ankle. There was an enormous crash as the man joined the dazed Apothecary on the deck. Irish Tom appeared from behind the bar and attempted to leap over it in order to enter the fracas. Unfortunately he had forgotten the passing of the years and landed on the obstruction, knocking the wind out of himself entirely. It was little Suzanne who came rushing to the rescue, brandishing a wooden club which she crashed down over Charles's head, sending him to his knees. At that Alexander rose to his feet and, taking a pistol out of his pocket, fired a deliberate shot into his opponent's leg, then retook his seat and finished his brandy.

John gazed at him, awestruck. Then his training rushed back to him and he crouched down beside the groaning Charles, who was grabbing his leg where the blood spouted forth in a great red fountain. 'Lord Conway?' he asked uncertainly, at which Charles smiled his most cynical of smiles and nodded before turning his eyes to Alexander, who had refilled his glass and was knocking back the alcohol as if he hadn't a care in the world.

'You bastard,' Charles said.

'My dear chap, 'tis but a flesh wound. You'll probably walk with a limp which no doubt will amuse the judge when you stand trial for murder.'

'Damn your blasted eyes, Alexander. I had every right to kill O'Farrell. The man seduced my wife under my very nose.'

'Whilst you were whoring your way round London. Don't try it on with me, Conway. I've known you since we were both at Oxford and have followed your career with interest ever since.'

'Listen to me, Jack,' snarled the wounded man. 'You think you are so vastly superior just because you became cronies with the Earl of Holdernesse. Well, let me tell you that makes you nothing more than a jumped-up lackey.'

'I would suggest that you hold your tongue, Sir, or you will tempt me to shoot you in the other leg as well.'

During this acrimonious exchange John had been gallantly tying an old but clean sheet into strips to staunch the flow of blood, but felt incredibly thankful when Dr Warren – called by Suzanne, no doubt – arrived to relieve him. He thought as he stood up that he had never seen the doctor look better. Without powder on his gleaming hair Warren resembled a Nordic god, his light blue eyes alert and expressive as he took in the fact that there was a seriously wounded man lying on the floor.

Alexander rose and made a bow. 'So,' he said, 'you are the famous doctor, are you?'

Warren gave a small salute. 'Yes, Sir. I did not realize that my fame was so widely known.' Then he knelt down and examined Charles Shirley, his hands, symbolically, getting covered in blood.

'Allow me to introduce myself. I am Jack Alexander, recently arrived from London.'

'Joseph Warren, Sir,' murmured the doctor, and John thought that if the name had meant anything to him at all, Warren had not betrayed it by so much as a flicker of an eyelid.

'The man you are attending killed the husband of one of your associates. I think you might know her. She was Lady Conway. Does the name mean anything to you?'

Dr Warren stood up and at that moment John admired him more than he could ever have imagined possible. 'She was a very charming woman. Everyone knew her and her husband Jake. They were employees of John Hancock, I believe,' he answered evenly.

The doctor was going to reveal nothing and Jack Alexander

of the Secret Office knew it. 'Well, in that case I'll be on my way,' he said.

'I think not, Sir,' Dr Warren stated. 'You maliciously wounded a man in a public place. I think the sheriff would like to question you further about that.'

Jack Alexander smiled urbanely. 'Then he will know where to find me. I am staying at the Marlborough Hotel. Good evening to you.'

And with that he sauntered out, cool as a cube of ice.

Warren looked at John. 'Is there any point in going after him?'

'I think not. He will be up and away before you even begin the chase.'

'He's a British spy, isn't he?'

'Somewhat higher than that, I think. Doctor Warren, I believe it would be best to leave that particular hound to his own devices. He is probably boarding ship even while we speak. But the surname of the man you are attending is Shirley, which is also, I believe, the surname of the Earls of Conway.'

Warren's eyes narrowed to diamond points. 'You believe that he pushed his wife to her death?'

John looked away. 'No, I don't think anyone is responsible for that. I consider it to have been an accident. But according to the servants at the house of John Hancock, Shirley slit Jake O'Farrell's throat for him and thrust the body into a cupboard.'

Warren flashed one of his rare and beautiful smiles. 'Well, he won't be going anywhere for some time. I shall deliver him to the sheriff's office and let the law takes its course.'

'It could all be a coincidence, of course.'

'Whatever the truth, he will have the fairest of trials, I can assure you of that.'

From the floor Charles Shirley, Earl of Conway, let out a groan then said to John, 'Pour me a brandy, for the love of God.'

'If I do will you tell me one thing?'

'What?'

'How did you come to be such a good hairdresser?'

'Because it was my hobby, that's why. I used to dress the hair of the ladies of the *ton*. Just for a joke, you understand. Now give me a drink before I die of the pain.'

'But your creations,' John persisted. 'They would not have disgraced a lady of the highest quality.'

'No,' Charles answered bitterly, 'if there is such a creature living.'

'What do you mean?'

'I mean, Sir, that I do not believe there is so fine a being as a lady of true distinction.'

And with that he relapsed into silence and refused to speak another word.

THIRTY

E xactly three weeks later John Rawlings left the seething city of Boston and sailed once more for his beloved home-land, having said farewell to his companions who had walked with him through the great wild and beautiful country of America. He had sold his business to a recently qualified young apothecary whose papa was a prosperous merchant who had paid to set his boy up, and had passed to him his apprentice, young Tristram, who had held the fort so often for his master when he had been off on his detecting trips. There had been some mois-tening of the eye when the youth had been told that the beautiful Rose would be leaving with her father, but he had sighed a great sigh and accepted the ill fortune of fate.

John had been to see Matthew during the time left, reminiscing over the incredible journey they had undertaken together. Inevitably the conversation had turned to Blue Wolf and Jane Hawthorne.

'Have you heard from them at all, my friend?'

'I received this through the post a few days ago.'

'Where was it sent from?'

'From Plymouth. They are nearing Haut Island. But take a look at it.'

It was a miracle that it had ever arrived for it was a present – a pair of moccasin shoes large enough to fit a small child. John had looked up questioningly and Matthew had grinned. John had smiled back.

'And how many does this make, with your combined children?'

'This will be the sixth, Sir. A hale and hearty family.'

'Did you tell the runaways there was another on the way?'

'No, John, I didn't. It was too early. But you know how Blue Wolf was. He sort of knew things.'

'Yes. I think he and she will have a wonderful life together. Blue Wolf and Silver Fox – very vulpine, don't you think?'

But it was clear that Matthew had not understood him and John had smiled in the firelight and talked of something else.

The dancing duo had bidden him farewell with overwhelming smiles and eyes like rapiers. That Jack Alexander – of whom there had been no visible sign since the night he had walked out of the Orange Tree – was still giving them instructions was abundantly clear from their manner. They would kill you while sharing a joke and a laugh. Trying to think the best of them, John had remembered that they had spared the lives of both himself and his daughter. It was in an unsettled frame of mind that he had left their company for good but they chattered gaily, acting the role of cream puffs to the end, knowing that this was how he would always recall them.

The former Lady Eawiss, more affected than ever if such a thing were possible, had forced out a tear or two and had half smothered Rose in an all-consuming embrace as she had said a tremulous *au revoir*.

'Of course, my husband and I will be returning to British soil just as soon as his tour of duty is over. We will be going to live on my late husband's estate – he was Sir Bevis Eawiss, of course. But then I have probably told you that he left me rather well orff, don't you know.'

'Yes, you have, dear lady. I was quite aware that you were wealthy. Remember your portmanteau? Without it I don't think many of us would have survived.'

She trilled a laugh which she hoped resembled silver bells. 'Yes, I was your banker, was I not?'

'You most certainly were,' John answered with feeling. 'Do I owe you anything?'

Lady Eawiss made a mouth. 'No, Sir Apothecary, you do not. Which is more than I can say for most, particularly the Conways.'

'You mean Jake and Demelza? Surely you could claim off their estate.'

A sound emerged which could have been a long-winded fart disguised by a loud 'huh'. 'No hope of that. I have had to wish my money goodbye.'

'Never mind, Lady Eawiss. I am sure that you have earned a place in Heaven.'

She made a moue to end them all, tossing her head with its

heavily feathered hat which stood atop her enormous hairstyle, over her shoulder.

'La, Sir, you say the nicest things. I truly do admire you. Faith but I do.'

She unfurled her fan and peeped at him mischievously over the top, at which John retreated hastily, bowing fulsomely as he left.

It was saying farewell to Irish Tom that cut John Rawlings to the quick. The years they had spent together, the adventures they had had, were as precious to the Apothecary as a hoard of emeralds, the colour of the Irishman's eyes reminding him not only of the gemstones but also of that beautiful island from which his great comrade hailed. And, looking at him now, he saw that those sincere eyes, that beautiful rich green, were misted with unshed tears.

'I will be lost without you, John.'

'Nonsense. It is just that life will be different, Tom. You'll have a wife and children to come. You'll have part of a successful business to run. You'll be in clover, man.'

'There can never be clover without the pasture to grow it in. You were my garnering field, John.'

'Everything has to change, Tom. That is the law of the universe. You either accept that or go raving mad.'

'I would come with you but Suzanne does not want to leave the Orange Tree.'

'And I don't blame her for that. She enjoys life in Boston and provided you don't take sides when the trouble starts you should sail through it with ease. But I forgot, you're an Irishman and have no particular love for the British.'

'Except for one of them who has given me such great humanity, the answer is no. Don't trust 'em much.'

John had thrown a party at the Orange Tree for a handful of old friends but there had been many absentees. He had invited George Glynde and Tracey Tremayne but the high-stepping strutters had not replied – out spying on someone, John supposed. Sir Julian Wychwood came with Miss Daisy Quincy, all tossing curls and merry giggles. Sir Julian, no doubt quite prepared to swap a title for a fortune, dribbled impeccable manners and high *ton* speech which had her in raptures. But notably absent was

Coralie, and when John went to her house on the following
evening he was told that Madame Clive had gone out of town
for a few days to arrange some important business. He imagined
that she had gone off in a huff but could not for a moment work
out why.

Now things moved swiftly. He had booked four places on the
vessel *Ondine* but first had his duty to do for Irish Tom's wedding.
This was a quiet affair during which Suzanne looked like a doll
by the side of the massive Brian Bóruma, King of the Irish figure
that Tom seemed to be that day. Afterwards there was a small
but merry party at the Orange Tree at which, once again, Coralie
was absent.

Sir Julian, for once not smiling but frowning deeply, approached
John and said, 'I've a mind to join you on board the *Ondine*,
you know.'

'Good heavens. I thought you were going to marry some
prosperous colonist's daughter and settle in America.'

'That's just the point. Dolly Quincy is being fiercely guarded
by that hideous old gorgon, Lydia Hancock, who apparently
has her lined up for her nephew, John, and as for all the rest
. . . John, they lack *bon ton* and I cannot see myself putting up
with them for any length of time.'

John shook his head, laughing aloud. 'Julian, you are a case
indeed. I can't imagine you ever taking a wife. I think you will
be charming and seducing like mad until your dying day.'

'I sincerely hope so. But you've left something out.'

'What's that?'

'That I can gamble my way to a fortune which those ladies
of quality will not get their adorable white fingers on.'

'Nor any other part of your anatomy,' John answered, and
winked his eye.

It took him two days, with Rose, excited, indeed thrilled, to
be returning to the country she loved, helping him pack up the
few possessions they had acquired during their stay in Boston.
Then they hired a carter and solemnly made their way to the
Long Wharf which was humming with activity. On the right as
they approached they could see the mighty transatlantic ship,
which had approached the wharf inch by inch at low tide on the
previous evening. It lay surrounded by smaller vessels but with

the name *Ondine* proudly appearing on its high wooden prow. On the wharf itself heaved a mass of humanity: a slatternly girl come to service the sailors, black slaves running round the feet of the wigged and wonderful merchants, ledger-laden clerks hurrying forward with their accounts. The air was full of splintering noise: ship's capstans turning, inching their vessels in, the men grunting, the captain shouting orders. The shrill whistle of the bosun's pipe, the irritating bark of dogs, the cry of the great sweating, stinking, fiercely independent multitude.

Rose was excited, loving it all. The twins were a little scared, hand in hand with John, their fingers betraying their slight panic by a simultaneous tightening of grip. A leather-aproned porter wheeling their luggage behind them made his way as best he could. John felt close to tears as he lifted the twins on to the gangplank. He had loved Boston, despite all the difficulty in getting there, and had had some rare raw experiences there. The place would be for ever carved in his heart.

'John,' he heard a distant voice call and, turning, saw Sir Julian Wychwood, a large portmanteau being carried high above his head, thrusting his way through the massive crowd. John waved. He wished it had been another voice that had called out, the voice that at that moment he longed to hear, even if it were only to bid him goodbye.

'Come on, Papa,' ordered Rose, and gave the gentlest push at his behind.

They made their way on board and stood at the rail, watching the Bostonians go about their business. Julian panted his way up and stood beside them as slowly the tide came in and the mighty vessel slipped anchor and made its majestic way out to the sea beyond.

'Goodbye, Boston,' John said, just under his breath.

And then he felt somebody unknown, standing right behind him, put their arms around his waist.

'Hello,' said a voice.

John did not turn round and stood perfectly still while his heart danced amongst the stars and he felt a great warmth course through his entire being.

'I thought you weren't coming with me,' he answered in a whisper.

'It's just for a visit, you understand. I have sold my school but will always be welcomed back there any time.'

'Then let it be hoped that your visit might just last for a month or two.'

'Perhaps it will, Apothecary. Perhaps it will.'

And with that Coralie pulled John round and into her arms as the port of Boston slowly slid away and into memory.